PURGATORY

PURGATORY:

A Chronicle
of a
Distant World

Mike Resnick

A TOM DOHERTY ASSOCIATES BOOK
NEW YORK

This is a work of fiction. All the characters and events
portrayed in this book are fictitious, and any resemblance to
real people or events is purely coincidental.

PURGATORY: A CHRONICLE OF A DISTANT WORLD

This book is printed on acid-free paper.

A Tor Book
Published by Tom Doherty Associates, Inc.
175 Fifth Avenue
New York, N.Y. 10010

Tor® is a registered trademark of Tom Doherty Associates, Inc.

Library of Congress Cataloging-in-Publication Data

Resnick, Michael D.
     Purgatory / Michael Resnick.
          p.   cm.
     "A Tom Doherty Associates book."
     ISBN 0-312-85275-4
     I. Title.
PS3568.E698P87   1993
813'.54—dc20   92-43881
                                                        CIP

First edition: March 1993

Printed in the United States of America

0 9 8 7 6 5 4 3 2 1

To Carol, as always,

And to Barbara Delaplace,
fine friend, fine writer

Contents

Foreword

There is a parable that Zimbabweans, white and black alike, sometimes tell when they sit around a campfire at the end of the day:

It seems that there was a scorpion who wished to cross a river. He saw a crocodile floating a few feet away and asked to be carried across the river on its back.

"Oh, no," said the crocodile firmly. "I know what you are. As soon as we're halfway across the river you'll sting me and I'll die."

"Why would I do that?" scoffed the scorpion. "If I sting you and you die, I'll drown."

The crocodile considered the scorpion's answer for a moment and then agreed to ferry him across the river. When they were halfway across, the scorpion stung the crocodile.

Fatally poisoned, barely able to breathe, the crocodile croaked, "Why did you do that?"

The scorpion thought for a moment, and then, just before he drowned, he answered, "Because it's Africa."

I have exercised my author's prerogative and related this anecdote to you only because it is an amusing story. It obviously has nothing at all to do with this novel, which is about the mythical world of Karimon rather than the very real nation of Zimbabwe.

M.R.

I

JALANOPI'S TREE

One

J alanopi's tree was almost five hundred years old.

It reached to a height of nearly half a mile and was a full one hundred feet in circumference at its base. Once it had been surrounded by many trees like itself, tall and stately, but now it was the last, and it could be seen for more than five miles in every direction. Its trunk and limbs were a deep purple, smooth and glistening in the sunlight. Its circular leaves had been falling for almost a month, and its silver flowers were a distant memory.

The tree had been there for three centuries before the coming of Jalanopi's people. Huge animals had rubbed against it and eaten of its bark; small animals had burrowed into it and lived in its base. Later, prisoners had been tied to its bole and hanged from its branches. Dwellings had been made of its bark, medicines from its leaves, and poisons from its blossoms. Its twigs and branches had supplied the firewood that lit the village Mastaboni at nights, its fruit had been eaten by untold generations of villagers and animals, and its sweet sap was prized by the local children.

Over the years all of its branches, to a height of more than seventy-five feet, had been removed for various purposes, but it was home to more than one hundred avians, nesting far above the ground. Untold generations of Tailswingers had been born, lived, and died in its branches without ever descending to the ground. Dozens of green-and-gold lizards sunned themselves on the branches. A huge serpent had made its home in the tree when Jalanopi's people first arrived; no one had seen it for almost half a century, but since no Tailswinger or lizard corpse was ever found on the ground, the villagers were convinced that it was still up there, a thousand feet or more above their heads.

Every section of Jalanopi's tree was a page in the living history of his people. The first human explorer, Robert Elroy, had carved three long notches on its bole to mark his path almost two centuries ago, only to fall prey to a pack of Devildogs two miles farther on. The first human missionary, Father Patrick Dugan, had made his first convert beside the tree, then died of fever a month later. Jalanopi's grandfather had been killed beneath this tree, chopped to pieces by his enemies. Years later Jalanopi's father had retaken the area, pinning his rival chief to the trunk of the tree with a spear and leaving the body there until the raptors and insects had picked the bones clean.

Jalanopi himself had been born less than a quarter mile from the tree. As a child he had broken a leg trying to scale it, which left him with a slight but permanent limp. He had used the tree for target practice when he first learned to hurl a spear, and had happily lost his virginity one spring evening in the shadows cast by the tree's enormous purple branches. It was beneath this tree that he himself had been proclaimed king when his father died, and beside this tree his father had been buried. As king, Jalanopi had held court and passed sentences, made treaties and declared wars beneath his tree.

And so it remained a very special tree, viewed with an almost religious awe by the members of the Tulabete, who were Jalanopi's people. It was said that as long as the tree lived they would survive and prosper, and that if the tree should ever die, then so too would the Tulabete.

Jalanopi himself was an imposing sight, and commanded even more awe than his tree. He stood fully seven feet tall, and wore a tunic of spun spider-silk and a cloak made from the skin of a Wildfang that he had taken while armed with only his spear—an act that had cost him one of the long pliable fingers from his three-digited hand. He had just completed the annual shedding of his old skin, and the tiny new scales on his green-tinted body glistened in the sunlight, emphasizing the rippling of his enormous muscles. Atop his bullet-shaped head sat the copper crown that signified he was the rightful king of the Tulabete, a crown he had defended twice in war and three times in personal combat, and for which he had not been challenged in more than a decade now.

He viewed his world through striking orange cat's-eyes, and all that he could see, to the horizon and beyond, was his domain. It stretched from the ocean in the east all the way to the broad river hundreds of miles out to the west, from the northern desert to the southern mountains. Jalanopi was certain that there was more to his world, but he had sent out scouts and none had ever found any land worth conquering. There were deserts out there, and mountains, and salt water, and jungles where the rain never ceased and the sun never shone, but he had no interest in them. There was no tillable land that he did not rule, no game animals that did not graze on the Tulabete's vast savannahs, no fresh water that did not flow through his domain.

There were rivals for his land, of course—once-powerful clans that now scratched out a living on its outskirts, and, it was rumored, a huge, powerful tribe beyond the mountains to the south—but he had beaten back challenges before, and he knew that as long as his tree stood the Tulabete were invulnerable in battle.

He leaned back against his tree now, lazily surveying his domain, as a flock of avians took off from the upper terraces. It was a warm day, dry and clear, as almost all the days were. In a few minutes he would have to sit on his wooden throne and hold court, but for the moment he was content just to stare out across the lush green fields, dotted here and there with the domiciles of his people, each dwelling constructed in the mystic shape of a coiled serpent.

Finally a man clad totally in black approached him.

"Good morning, Jalanopi," he said in the language of the Tulabete.

Jalanopi stared at him but said nothing.

"I trust you slept well," continued the man.

"I always sleep well," said Jalanopi, his long, lean tongue flicking out to capture an insect that flew too near his face. He reeled in his tongue and brought his teeth down on the insect's carapace with a loud crunching noise.

The man looked away, trying to hide his distaste for the Tulabete's dietary habits. "I would not sleep well if I were you," he said. "Not with that party of Canphorites camped just a couple of miles away."

Jalanopi continued staring at the man. "You are a very unusual servant of your god," he said, dwelling sibilantly on the *s* sound in each word. "He preaches love, and you preach suspicion."

"My god did not create the Canphorites," replied Reverend Andrew McFarley. "They are a vicious and duplicitous race."

"They came from the stars," answered Jalanopi. "*You* came from the stars."

"And there all similarity ends."

"Do not fear for us, Man Andrew," said Jalanopi easily. "The Canphorites are in Jalanopi's kingdom; they will obey Jalanopi's laws."

"I doubt it."

Jalanopi flicked away an insect that had landed on his face, leading McFarley to wonder once more why certain insects were considered delicacies by the Tulabete while others were viewed merely as pests.

"Then they will suffer the consequences."

McFarley's expression reflected his doubts on the matter.

"But in the meantime, they have brought me many gifts," continued Jalanopi.

"They seek to buy your friendship with trinkets," said McFarley.

"As you yourself gave me a hat?" suggested Jalanopi.

"I wish only to live among your people and educate them in the ways of Jesus Christ."

Jalanopi stared at him with expressionless cat's-eyes, his features more alien and inscrutable than usual.

"You are wasting your time, Man Andrew," he said at last.

"It is mine to waste."

"How long have you been here?"

"On Karimon? About four months."

"And have any of my people accepted this Christ of yours?"

"Not yet," said McFarley. "But they will."

"You seem both friendly and harmless, Man Andrew, and you are welcome to remain—but they will not accept your Christ," said Jalanopi. "Why should a race of warriors worship a being of a different race who was unable to defend himself and let himself be killed by his enemies?"

"It is not that simple," said McFarley.

"It is that simple," said Jalanopi with a cold reptilian smile. He pointed to the cross that hung around McFarley's neck. "You even wear the instrument of his destruction. How can a man who worships death preach to beings who worship life?"

"I do not worship death," answered McFarley, "but rather what he died for."

"You have learned our language, and you have brought us medicines, and you have helped us care for our old and our infirm, and for that we are grateful," said Jalanopi. "But you had best keep those books you brought with you; there is no wisdom in them for the Tulabete."

"There is wisdom in the bible for *all* sentient beings," said McFarley, stepping aside as a pair of Tallgrazers, the local meat animals, wandered by, almost brushing against him. He noticed recently healed scars at their joints and wondered how they survived when the Tulabete inserted narrow tubes and drained them of their marrow—a substance that, along with the insects, formed the Tulabete's staple diet—on a monthly basis.

Jalanopi looked at him, his face still an unreadable green mask. "Do you truly believe that?"

"Absolutely."

"In a few minutes I must hold court and sit in judgment," said Jalanopi. "One of the cases that will be brought will be from an outlying area. Two females both claim to be the mother of the same infant. His father has been away fighting a tribe called the Rakko and cannot say which of them is the true mother. The father is very wealthy, and the day will come that all he possesses is passed on to his progeny. It can reasonably be expected that the son will favor his mother more than the other woman, which is doubtless why they both claim to have given birth to him." He paused. "What is there in your book to deal with *that*?"

McFarley smiled. "As I said, there is wisdom enough in the bible for *all* races." He wiped some sweat from his forehead, flicked away a flying insect and barely got his hand out of the way of Jalanopi's amazingly swift tongue, then continued. "Once, a very long time ago, there was a king named Solomon, who was praised far and wide for his wisdom. And into his court came two women, each of whom claimed to be the mother of the same baby."

"Truly?" asked Jalanopi, his eyes narrowing, his earholes pulsating, both signs of sudden interest.

"Truly. He questioned both of the women, but they each kept to their story."

"As these will do today."

"Finally, he announced that he could not tell which of them was the true mother, and that the only fair decision was to cut the baby in half and give one half to each woman."

Jalanopi exhaled a long, high-pitched hiss, which McFarley had come to recognize as a display of contempt.

"This king was *not* wise," said Jalanopi at last.

"Hear me out," said McFarley. "When he announced his decision, one of the women came forward and said that she could not allow him to kill an innocent child, and that she would forsake her claim to motherhood. And Solomon immediately knew that she was the mother, for no mother would allow her baby to be slaughtered."

"Your Solomon was a fool, Man Andrew."

"Why?"

"Do you know what would happen if *I* made that same judgment?"

"Suppose you tell me," said McFarley.

"Neither female would say a word, and then, because a king does not retract a threat made before his tribe, the infant would have to be cut in half."

"Surely the real mother would protest."

"The penalty for disputing my judgment is death," said Jalanopi. "Do you really think they will protest?"

"Try it," urged McFarley. "You'll see that you're wrong."

"And if I am *not* wrong?" said Jalanopi. "Will *you* kill the infant?"

"No."

Jalanopi hissed again. "You see, Man Andrew? You wish

to offer your god's advice, but if it proves wrong you do not wish to bear the consequences."

"How will *you* solve the problem?" asked McFarley.

"It would be foolish to reach a decision before hearing both females, would it not?"

"Yes," said McFarley. "Yes, it would."

"You are both fair and honest, Man Andrew. Very few beings of any race are willing to admit when they are wrong."

"*I* may be wrong," said McFarley. "I have never claimed to be infallible. But my religion is *not* wrong."

"It is well that you should feel that way," continued Jalanopi. "It is a matter of belief. I should no more be able to talk you out of worshiping your gods than you can talk me out of worshiping mine."

"God," McFarley corrected him. "One god."

"He must feel very overburdened at times."

"But He persists."

"An admirable trait. And now it is time for me to put on my ceremonial headdress and hold court."

"Do you mind if I watch?" asked McFarley.

"You wish to compare my judgment to that of King Solomon?"

"I'm just curious to see how you handle the problem."

"Then come," said Jalanopi, walking off across the short brown grass to his intricately winding dwelling, which seemed to curve back on itself time and again. Twice he sidestepped small rodents that were in his path; a third time, for no reason McFarley could fathom, he went out of his way to step on and mortally wound an identical rodent, which he ignored as it lay there writhing in its death throes.

Upon reaching his dwelling, Jalanopi crawled into it with a slithering motion, retrieved a huge feathered headdress, wrapped a cloak made from the skin of a Nightkiller around his shoulders, and returned to his tree. The members of the village followed him to the carved wooden throne, also in the shape of a coiled reptile, where he sat down and waited for them to fall silent. Finally he nodded to one of his counselors, who stepped forward.

"What have we today?" asked Jalanopi.

"First, there is a petition from the human, Fuentes, to continue hunting on your land for three more months." The counselor nodded to an assistant, who placed three bags at Jalanopi's feet. "He offers this salt as a gift."

"He may hunt for ten days," said Jalanopi. "No longer."

"It is a large amount of salt, my king," noted the counselor.

"True," agreed Jalanopi. "And it is very valuable to us." He paused and allowed himself the luxury of a cold, totally reptilian smile. "But it is obviously not very valuable to *him*, for he has given us salt the last three times, and he has not left our world for almost a year, which means he came with a great supply of it in his ship. Salt must be very easy for him to obtain on his homeworld, and we must take that into account when bargaining with him."

"What if he says no?"

Jalanopi scooped up a handful of dirt. "If I offer you this in exchange for something I want, and you tell me you must have two handfuls, am I likely to walk away simply because I know dirt is valuable to you?" He smiled and let the dirt fall to the ground. "Fuentes will be back with more salt in ten days' time."

"Yes, my king."

"Next?"

"Three members of the Fani tribe claim that a party of Tulabete warriors attacked one of their merchant caravans."

"Good. Our warriors are to be commended," said Jalanopi. "Where did this take place?"

"Along the Karimona River, just south of the Pundi Pools."

"Offer the Fani my apology, and tell them such incidents

will continue if they persist in penetrating so deeply into my territory."

"They want compensation, my king."

Jalanopi shook his head. "They had no business being where they were," he said in his sibilant manner. "There will be no compensation."

"They claim that to avoid the river would force them to traverse the Tenya Mountains, which would double the length of their trip and seriously cut into their profit."

"They should have considered that before they went to war with me seven years ago."

"May I make a suggestion?" asked McFarley.

Jalanopi turned to him. "Would your Solomon have paid them recompense?" he asked caustically.

"No."

"Well then?"

"Your land is sparsely populated, and the Fani don't seem to be in a position to do you any harm. If it is really in their best interests to use this route, why not charge them a tribute for each crossing?"

"No," said Jalanopi. "Give them no thought, Man Andrew," he continued, hissing his contempt. "The Fani are burrow-dwellers who lack the courage to stay above the ground at night. They are not worth your consideration." His long tongue suddenly shot out, though no insects were near him. "Further, the day would come when they choose not to pay the tribute, and then I will have to go to war again to punish them. It is far better not to let them cross my land in the first place." He stared at McFarley. "You disapprove, Man Andrew?"

"It seems a bit harsh."

A frown crossed Jalanopi's lean reptilian face, and the constriction of its muscles forced beads of thick, glistening oil to the surface of his forehead and cheekbones. "It was harsh when they tortured my grandfather, or when they mutilated our livestock, or when they poisoned our wells.

This is not harsh." He turned back to his counselor. "Next?"

"We have two females, Tagoma and Sagara, who each claim to be the mother of the same infant. They are both wives of Kabulaki, who owns much land and many animals, all of which the infant will inherit when Kabulaki dies. You must decide which is the true mother."

McFarley watched and listened as each female, amidst much wailing and cursing, adamantly held that the infant was her own. One of them, Tagoma, was in the process of shedding her skin, and looked as if she had been brutally mauled by predators; the other, Sagara, had just acquired a new skin, and looked as sleek and shining as Jalanopi.

There had been no witnesses to the birth, and Kabulaki was still patrolling one of the frontiers. Jalanopi questioned each female perfunctorily, grunted at their answers, and finally reached out for the infant, which one of his minor counselors was holding.

"He is a good, strong, healthy child," said Jalanopi, staring at the infant. "See how he refuses to lower his gaze before my own?" He turned to McFarley. "And your King Solomon would have cut him in half?"

"He would have *threatened* to," answered McFarley. "There's a difference."

"What is your judgment, my king?" asked the senior counselor, who sensed that Jalanopi had no further questions to ask.

"A strong grip, too," said Jalanopi, holding out a finger for the infant to grab. "Someday this child shall become a mighty warrior, whose fame will terrorize his enemies and whose word will bear great weight with his king. See the fearlessness in his eyes!"

"Your judgment, my king?" persisted the senior counselor, who seemed to feel a need to keep Jalanopi's schedule moving.

Jalanopi stared at the two females.

"One of you is lying," he said. "And you are lying because you know that this child will someday be a wealthy and powerful warrior, and that as his mother some of his wealth and power will accrue to you. This cannot be permitted."

"Then which is the rightful mother, my king?"

"I cannot say," answered Jalanopi. "Therefore, from this day forward, the child will become *my* son. He will live in my house and be cared for by my wives, and since I am the wealthiest member of the Tulabete, the infant will inherit more land and more cattle than he would inherit from Kabulaki." He paused. "His true mother will realize that her child will fare better in my house than in her own, and her mother's heart will be content. His false mother will have gained nothing by her lies. That is my judgment."

Both females backed away, neither displaying any emotion, and Jalanopi proceeded to the next case, which had to do with the joint ownership of some domestic animals. When that was done, he waved his hand imperiously, indicating that he was through making judgments for the day and, as the villagers dispersed, he walked over to McFarley.

"What would King Solomon say to *that?*" he asked.

"He would say that you have robbed the true parents of their child," answered McFarley without hesitation.

Jalanopi's lips parted in what passed for a smile among his race. "The child will be back with his true parents before the long rains."

"How can you say that? You've already admitted that you don't know which one is the mother."

"We cherish children in our society, Man Andrew," answered Jalanopi. "When Kabulaki returns home and realizes that one of the females cost him his son, he will determine which is the true mother, and when he does, the child will be returned."

"You mean he will beat the truth out of her?" said McFarley distastefully.

"Does not such a lie deserve a beating?"

"Then why didn't you save him the trouble and do it yourself?"

"A king does not soil his hands thus," answered Jalanopi. "Besides," he added, "I am not the aggrieved party."

Jalanopi was about to remove his headdress when, from across the short brown grass, his senior counselor approached him.

"Yes?"

"The Canphorites wish an audience, my king."

"Again?"

"Yes, my king."

"I am hungry now. Tell them I will meet with them after I have eaten."

"Yes, my king."

Jalanopi turned to McFarley. "Will you join me, Man Andrew?"

"I'd be honored."

They walked over to Jalanopi's dwelling, where one of his wives had prepared a meal of still-moving little *things* covered with a sauce made from the pulp of some of the local fruits and flowers. McFarley took one look as Jalanopi inserted his tongue into the mixture and allowed some of the insectlike creatures to slither onto it, then averted his eyes just before Jalanopi drew his tongue back into his mouth.

"Perhaps you are not hungry," suggested Jalanopi.

McFarley listened for the hiss of contempt and watched for the quivering nostril that signified amusement; he thought he heard and saw both signs, but he wasn't quite sure.

"Perhaps later," he said.

Jalanopi nodded his head. "Or perhaps not," he said, and now McFarley was certain that he was an object of distaste and ridicule to the king.

"Tell me," he said, hoping to change the subject, "what do the Canphorites want?"

"The same as usual."

"And that is?"

"They will offer me many gifts in exchange for permission to dig in my hills."

"What's *in* your hills?" asked McFarley.

"Various metals that we use for decoration," answered Jalanopi; he secreted a clear liquid that caused more of his lunch to climb eagerly onto his tongue, then brought them back into his mouth. "They must have many people to decorate, because they have offered much more than the metals are worth."

"How much have they offered you?"

Jalanopi pointed to a pair of his domestic meat animals. "They have offered two thousand Tallgrazers, plus fifty bags of salt." He shook his head in disbelief, as if only a race of madmen would make such a munificent offer for the stuff of armbands and necklaces.

"Have they told you how much metal they plan to remove from your hills?" asked McFarley.

Jalanopi shrugged. "What difference does it make? They are fools."

"Then why have you not reached an agreement with them?"

"Because every day I wait, they increase their offer." He looked expressionlessly at McFarley. "They have also warned me not to treat with members of your race."

"I can believe *that*," said McFarley.

"They say that you eat infants of your own race, and conquer innocent races, and torture your enemies."

"Do you believe them?"

"I do not believe that you eat infants, for if you did, where would all your people come from?" said Jalanopi thoughtfully. "As for their other statements, it is only fitting that you should conquer races that are weaker than your own, and if your enemies try to kill you, why should you not torture some of them as an example to the others?"

"We torture no one," said McFarley. "And we do not conquer races that are weaker than ourselves. We protect them from races like the Canphorites, races that *do* believe in conquest."

"And Men never conquer or exploit other races?"

"If anyone—Canphorites or Men or anyone else— should try to exploit your people, I will do everything in my power to prevent it."

"You have been here only a short time, Man Andrew," noted Jalanopi. "What have we done to bring forth such love of our people and our planet?"

McFarley considered his reply for a moment. "Meaning no offense, it is not that I love you but that I hate the exploitation of innocent races—by Canphorites *or* Men."

"Do you truly believe that the Canphorites wish to conquer the Tulabete?"

"At the very least they wish to rob you."

"In what way?" asked Jalanopi.

"You remember the example you used earlier today, in which you picked up a handful of dirt?"

"Yes."

"Well, the metals in your hills may be worth very little more than dirt to you, but on other worlds—both mine and the Canphorites'—those metals are among the most valuable things one can own. And on their world, like mine, salt is almost as easy to obtain as dirt."

"But you have no Tallgrazers on your world," said Jalanopi, "and they have offered a number equal to that which I already possess."

"They have weapons that would seem like magic to you," said McFarley. "It would take almost no effort for them to go to a distant village, kill everyone in it, and return with all the Tallgrazers that village possessed."

"Truly?" Again Jalanopi's eyes narrowed and his ear-holes began pulsating.

"Truly."

"Tell me more about these weapons."

"They are terrible weapons of destruction, each of them superior to a hundred warriors with spears."

"If such weapons exist, why have not the Canphorites simply taken what they want from the Tulabete?"

"If there were no humans on your world, or in this sector of the galaxy, they would do just that, for they have done so on many other worlds," answered McFarley. "But they know that if they did, we humans would tell our government, and they would have a war on their hands—a war they could not possibly win."

"And your race also possesses these magical weapons?" asked Jalanopi.

"We do. But we use them only when there is no alternative."

"I can conceive of many situations in which no alternative presents itself," said Jalanopi with a dismissive wave of his three-digited hand. "Now explain, Man Andrew: why do Fuentes and the other human hunters not use such weapons? It would seem that with them they could slay thousands of animals in a single day."

"They hunt for sport, and it is not sporting to employ these weapons."

"But Fuentes sells the skins of the animals he kills, and the horns of the Horndevils, does he not? So it is not entirely sporting."

"These weapons would obliterate horns and skins."

Jalanopi was silent for a moment, lost in thought. "They are *that* powerful?" he said at last.

"They are."

"Then I now know what price to extract from the Canphorites," said Jalanopi.

"They will not give you such weapons," said McFarley.

"Then they will not be permitted to take metal from our hills."

"Or if they *do* give them to you, they will give you defective weapons, or weapons that work only for a brief period of time and will be useless once they have taken what they want and left your world."

"Perhaps," said Jalanopi. "But if I am to possess such weaponry, I have no alternative but to deal with the Canphorites." He stared, almost mockingly, into McFarley's eyes. "*Have* I, Man Andrew?"

Two

"This is a dangerous path you are treading," said Paratoka, Jalanopi's chief advisor.

The king was sitting beneath his tree, in conference with his closest associates.

"The humans seek to exploit us, do they not?" answered Jalanopi, his long tongue darting out to capture a small flying insect that got too near his face.

"Yes."

"And the Canphorites would do the same?" continued Jalanopi, his strong jaws crushing the insect.

"Yes, my king, but—"

"They think of us as their inferiors, as being but a step above the beasts of the forests and savannahs," said Jalanopi. "This will be our advantage, for they will not believe that we have the foresight to realize what they are attempting to accomplish, and they will never credit us with the wisdom to capitalize on our mutual animosity."

A hot breeze swept through the village, carrying a cloud of dust past Jalanopi's tree. None of the Tulabete moved or attempted to speak until it had swirled past, and then Paratoka leaned forward and spoke again.

"I have studied the situation, my king. It is the Men we must be wary of, not the Canphorites."

"They both wish to exploit us," said another advisor.

"True," answered Paratoka. "But the Canphorites control only their home planets, Canphor VI and VII, and a handful of worlds—no more than twenty—that oppose Man's Republic. The Republic itself has conquered or otherwise assimilated some *forty thousand* worlds. They are much the stronger race, and they have had far more practice at conquering worlds than we have at withstanding such empires."

"They have made no attempt to subdue or subjugate us," said a third advisor.

"*Yet,*" said Paratoka.

"But if they are as strong as you say, then it would be better for us to be associated with them than with the Canphorites."

"We will not be the satellite of *any* race," said Jalanopi firmly. "I do not intend to sit idly by while Men *or* Canphorites plunder my world."

"You have heard of their weapons," said Paratoka. "And surely what they have told us must be true, or else how could they have conquered so many worlds? How can we oppose them?"

Jalanopi looked coldly at his circle of advisors.

"Since we cannot be stronger than they are, we must be wiser." His tongue darted out again, capturing a crawling insect from the bole of his tree, and he carefully plucked it off his tongue and held it up. "I have already told you: our advantage is that they view *us* the way we view *this*—as mindless insects to be plundered and used."

"Man Andrew seems a friendly and respectful being," said yet another advisor. "I see no signs of aggression in him. Possibly we are being hasty."

"If I were to send one member of the Tulabete to a world I eventually wished to dominate, I would not send Kabulaki or one of our other great warriors, for their first instinct would be to fight." He paused. "No, I would send our gentlest member, a friendly and respectful being, as you say, to ease their fears. I would have him befriend their king, and offer help in their hour of need, and I would never allow him to suggest that we might someday wish to extract payment for that help." His lips parted in his version of a smile. "They have sent us just such a man, and never once has he suggested that payment might someday fall due for Man's help."

"Even knowing all this, how are we to protect ourselves against it?" asked the advisor.

"We must create a situation whereby it is in Man's best interest to help us," answered Jalanopi. "We will make them literally beg to arm our people with their weapons, and we will make a treaty that explicitly states that they do this of their own free will, and that no payment will be demanded, now or forever."

"*Can* this be done?"

Jalanopi nodded an affirmative. "I shall take the first steps this afternoon."

"Even if we obtain their weapons, will they not retain even more powerful ones—weapons that can destroy our entire world?" persisted the advisor.

"Almost certainly," said Jalanopi. "*I* would."

"Then I repeat: how are we to protect ourselves?"

"By being wiser than they are," answered Jalanopi. "We know that they have an empire of forty thousand worlds. We know they wish to add to it. From this, we can conclude that they do not want a dead, lifeless rock, but a living, breathing world that can be exploited." He paused. "So let them *have* their weapons that can kill the planet. We know that they will not use them."

"We *hope* that they will not use them," amended the advisor.

"We *know* it," repeated Jalanopi firmly. "For if they believed in the destruction of their enemies, why are the Canphorites, who have lost three wars with them, still alive?"

Paratoka got to his feet and emitted a low whistling cry of triumph.

"We shall triumph, for we have the greatest and wisest king of all!" he hissed. "Long live Jalanopi, warrior king of the Tulabete!"

The other advisors took up the chant, and after a moment Jalanopi stilled them by raising his hand.

"Now we must prepare," he said. "Pass the word to Kabulaki and my other generals that I wish to see them tonight. Send runners to those who are patrolling the borders that I want them to be on the alert, and that they will soon receive new orders."

"What do you plan to tell our people, my king?" asked Paratoka.

"That we are going to war."

"Against whom?"

Jalanopi leaned back against his tree, his face an expressionless mask even to his closest advisors. "I will know by nightfall."

"But—"

"I have issued an order," said Jalanopi. "See that it is carried out. And have Man Andrew brought to me."

Paratoka bowed. "Yes, my king."

"The meeting is over," announced Jalanopi. "Go about your business, tend to your land and your animals, and speak of this to no one."

One by one his advisors left, and a few moments later Andrew McFarley approached him.

"You wished to see me?" asked the man.

"Indeed, it is time that we had a serious discussion," said Jalanopi, getting to his feet. "Come, walk with me as we talk, Man Andrew."

"Is something wrong?" asked McFarley, as Jalanopi led

him through the nearby pastures, passing within a few yards of the huge brown, placid Tallgrazers.

"I am afraid that I must ask you to leave Karimon, Man Andrew."

"*Leave?*" repeated McFarley, startled. "Have I done something to offend you, Jalanopi?"

"No," replied Jalanopi. "You have been an exemplary guest."

"Then why . . . ?"

"Tonight I shall issue a declaration of war against both the Fani and the Rakko, our two most formidable enemies. Against either one, I know we would emerge victorious . . . but we will be fighting a war on two fronts and we will be severely outnumbered, and I cannot guarantee your safety."

"Why don't you let *me* worry about that?" said McFarley, brushing some flying insects away from his face and trying to ignore the odor of the Tallgrazers' pungent droppings.

"I do not want any incident to destroy the friendship between our races," said Jalanopi. "Especially the death of an honored friend. You will have to leave."

"What of Fuentes and the other hunters?"

"If we can find them, we will send them home. Their whereabouts are currently unknown."

"And the Canphorites?"

"The Canphorites have offered us weaponry with which to defend ourselves."

"*We* could give you far better weapons."

"But they have already agreed to do so, and for no cost: the weapons are a gift to cement the friendship between us."

"I told you not to trust them, Jalanopi," said McFarley. "They will want something in return. Mark my words."

"So would your Republic," replied Jalanopi, carefully watching McFarley out of the corner of his eye.

"How many weapons have the Canphorites offered you?"

Jalanopi paused, trying to think of a plausible number. "Three thousand now, five thousand later if we still need them. And experts to show us how to use them and keep them functioning."

"You are letting them buy your world for three thousand weapons," said McFarley. "And I can assure you that after the battle, the weapons will cease to function and the parts needed to repair them will not arrive."

"You have always been honest with me, Man Andrew," said Jalanopi. "But they *are* the enemy of your blood, as the Fani and Rakko are the enemies of *mine*. On this one matter I am not certain that you are to be trusted."

"Will you at least let me contact my people and see if they can match the Canphorites' offer?"

"So that *your* weapons will fail to function after the war, and *your* race can purchase Karimon for a trifling price?" replied Jalanopi with an expression that McFarley assumed was sardonic among the Tulabete.

"If *we* support you in this war," said McFarley, "we will give you not only weapons and advisors, but written guarantees, backed by the full power and prestige of the Republic."

"The *Republic* is just a word," said Jalanopi. "If it exists at all, it exists many trillions of miles from here. What recourse have we if you do not keep your pledges?"

"What recourse have you if the Canphorites break *their* word?" shot back McFarley. "*We* have not asked for mineral rights. We have not asked you to join our Republic. If you let us help you, there will be no strings attached."

"I do not understand."

"It's a human expression," said McFarley. "It does not translate very well. What I mean to say is that we will help you for only two reasons: first, because we wish to be friends to *all* races, and second, because we do not wish to see any world subjugated by the Canphorites. We will ask for no recompense of any kind."

They reached the end of a pasture. Jalanopi made a strange trilling sound, and a small avian that had been perched atop the broad back of a Tallgrazer, picking insects from its hide, flew over and landed on the broad palm of the Tulabete's outstretched hand.

"Do you see this avian, Man Andrew?" said Jalanopi.

"Yes."

"He came to me because he trusts me, just as your Republic wishes us to come to you because we trust *you*. Is this not so?"

"Yes," said McFarley, wondering what point the Tulabete was making.

"Five hundred times this avian has come to me, and never have I betrayed its trust. We have a special bond between us, this avian and I. It knows I am far bigger and stronger, and that it has no defense against me, but it willingly places itself in my hand." Suddenly Jalanopi closed his hand; the startled avian let out a single, panicked shriek and died, and Jalanopi carelessly tossed its corpse onto the ground before the eyes of the shocked human. "The 501st time was not so lucky for it, was it, Man Andrew?"

"What was the point of that little demonstration?" demanded McFarley.

"How many times must we put ourselves in your hand before you decide to squeeze?" asked Jalanopi. "What recourse have we if you break your pledge to us? We are as helpless before you as the avian was before me. . . . But we are wiser than the avian: we know better than to willingly perch upon the Republic's hand."

"All I can do is repeat what I said."

"But what are your assurances worth?" continued Jalanopi. "If a million Men should land here tomorrow to enslave my people, to whom can I go to say: 'This is not part of our agreement. Talk to Man Andrew, and he will tell you what he promised on your behalf'? Who will believe me?"

"Doesn't the same situation exist with the Canphorites?" asked McFarley, stalling for time while he tried to think of an acceptable answer.

"Canphor controls how many worlds, Man Andrew?"

"Twenty-seven."

"And how many worlds are in your Republic?"

"The worlds in the Republic are willing partners in a great galactic enterprise," said McFarley firmly.

"I am sure they must be," said Jalanopi. "How many willing partners do you have?"

"Forty thousand."

"There you have it."

"In numbers there is strength, and in strength there is security," said McFarley.

"I do not need strength to fight against the Republic's enemies, for they are not *my* enemies," said Jalanopi. "I need only the strength to fight against the Fani and the Rakko."

"You are making a serious mistake, Jalanopi," said McFarley.

"Then I shall have to live with it. I want you off the planet before sunrise, for beyond that I cannot promise to protect you."

"Will you at least let me contact the Republic?" persisted McFarley. "We may be able to make an offer that meets with your approval."

"It seems a waste of time," said Jalanopi. "I have already reached an agreement with the Canphorites."

"Let me *try*," said McFarley. "What harm can it do?"

Jalanopi pretended to weigh the offer in his mind for a long moment, then shrugged his entire body expressively.

"You may try," he said at last. "But I warn you that it is a waste of time. We are satisfied with the Canphorites' proposition."

They turned and began walking back to Mastaboni, where McFarley left Jalanopi and went over to the small church that housed not only his bibles and his religious artifacts, but also his subspace radio. Jalanopi stopped at Paratoka's dwelling long enough to tell his advisor to keep the Canphorites out of the village until otherwise instructed, for he didn't want an angry McFarley accusing them of making offers of which they were ignorant; then he wandered over to a nearby stream, where he waded into the water, sat down, and amused himself by catching the darting red-and-gold fish with his hands.

He did not throw them ashore, for the Tulabete did not eat fish, but it was an exercise that kept his mind alert and his reflexes sharpened, and none among his people could catch as many fish as he. They carried sharp teeth, these fish; one had cost him the middle digit of his hand before the last monsoon, and it was just now growing back, a phenomenon that the Tulabete took for granted but which seemed to astound both McFarley and the Canphorites, neither of which could regenerate any portion of their anatomy.

McFarley came by almost an hour later and squatted at the edge of the stream.

"I've been looking all over for you," he said.

"I have been here all along," answered Jalanopi. "Do you eat fish, Man Andrew?"

"From time to time."

Jalanopi's hands shot out beneath the rippling surface of the water, and an instant later he pulled a large red-and-gold fish out of the water and flipped it onto the bank near the human, where it flopped four or five times and then lay still, gasping in the bright sunlight.

"It is my farewell present to you," said Jalanopi. "Beware its teeth until you are certain it is dead."

"I've spoken to my people," said McFarley.

"And how many regiments of so-called advisors do they wish us to accept?"

"None."

"Very wise, Man Andrew," said Jalanopi. "That way we will never learn to use your weapons."

"Hear me out, please," continued McFarley. "We will give you eight thousand hand-weapons; we will ship as many or as few advisors as you request; and we will present you with a document, signed by the naval commander of this sector and witnessed by members of six other races, that at no time, now or in the future, will we attempt to extract payment in any form for the weapons or for our services. We want only to be your allies, and to prevent you, in your innocence, from falling under the influence of the Canphorites."

"That *is* a handsome offer, Man Andrew," said Jalanopi. "And you require absolutely nothing in return?"

"One thing."

"Oh? And what is that?" asked Jalanopi, repressing the urge to part his lips in his equivalent of a grin.

"The Canphorites must be told to leave."

"To be replaced by you?"

McFarley shook his head. "We will not come until we are invited."

"And if we should never invite you?"

"Then, except for the Men who unload your weapons and those you request to act as advisors, myself and the few hunters and explorers already on your planet are the only Men you will ever see."

"And I assume you have no objection to remaining hostage to our agreement, Man Andrew?" said Jalanopi.

"I don't believe I understand," replied McFarley.

"You will remain with the Tulabete until long after the war is over. If the agreement is broken, your life shall be forfeit."

McFarley swallowed hard, then nodded his head. "My people do not lie, Jalanopi. I will consent to remain hostage to your agreement."

"Then tell them I accept their offer," said Jalanopi. "How soon can the weapons be here?"

"By noon tomorrow."

"Have the ship land near my village."

"What about advisors?"

"We will accept five hundred advisors," said Jalanopi. "They will be under my direct command, and they must leave the moment the war is over. Does your Republic agree to that?"

"I am certain they will," replied McFarley.

"It would appear, Man Andrew, that you and I are to become allies against the Fani and the Rakko." His hands darted beneath the water once more, then emerged and tossed their squirming prey onto the bank. "Have another fish."

Three

T he war—*slaughter* would be a better word—took exactly nine days, after which the decimated Fani and Rakko sued for peace.

Jalanopi brought their leaders to his tree one by one. Each was given the opportunity to swear fealty to him and to pay tribute to the Tulabete. Those who did were allowed to leave in peace; those few who refused were chopped to bits where they stood. None of the enemy's warriors were killed or incarcerated; each was given free passage back to his homeland.

On the tenth day, Jalanopi informed McFarley, who had come to act as a liaison between the king and the human advisors, that it was time for the advisors to leave. McFarley suggested that the Tulabete, though they had wrought enormous havoc among their enemies with the weapons, hadn't properly learned to maintain them, and that the advisors would be delighted to remain for as much as a year until such time as Jalanopi's army had mastered the art of weapon maintenance.

"That would not be a good idea," replied Jalanopi. "I do not wish alien wars to be fought on my soil."

"I do not understand," said McFarley.

"I have told the Canphorites that they may return in three days' time," explained Jalanopi. "It would be best if your soldiers were gone before the Canphorites arrive."

"I thought you signed an agreement—" began McFarley.

"I agreed to deport the Canphorites before accepting your gifts, and I kept my word," said Jalanopi. "There is nothing in the agreement that said they must be barred from Karimon for all eternity."

"Thirteen days is *not* comparable to all eternity."

"Your race has been a good friend to the Tulabete, as you have been a good friend to me, Man Andrew," said Jalanopi. "I have no quarrel with them. This is a simple disagreement between myself and your king, and you need not concern yourself about it." He paused. "I will send Paratoka, my chief advisor, away with your advisors. He will represent me and speak to your king and the matter will be resolved." He parted his lips. "Who knows? Perhaps he will come back and advise me to join your Republic."

"I will convey your message to my people immediately," said McFarley, walking off to his church and his subspace radio.

Jalanopi next sent for Paratoka.

"How may I serve you, my king?" asked the chief advisor upon arriving at Jalanopi's tree.

"I want you to accompany the Men back to see their king."

"What shall I say to him?" asked Paratoka.

"He will do most of the talking," answered Jalanopi. "I have informed him that I intend to allow the Canphorites to return immediately; he will surely find this unacceptable. You will argue that he has no right to tell us whom we can befriend, and gradually you will allow him to make his points and win the argument."

"Is that all, my king?"

"Of course not," said Jalanopi. "We have not seen the last of Men yet. While you are there, you will find out what the metals in our hills are worth to them."

"They have said they will not return until you invite them," noted Paratoka.

"They will return," said Jalanopi with certainty. "What I must know is how much to charge them for the privilege."

Four

S even weeks passed before Paratoka returned with the information Jalanopi required. The hills, he explained, were filled with many kinds of metals, some highly prized by Men, some virtually worthless to them. There was no way they could know how much of each existed until they allowed some Men to land on Karimon and run a thorough survey.

"Go back," said Jalanopi, "and tell them that we will allow them to come and make their tests—but that they are not allowed to bring any weapons with them."

"I think they will insist, my king," answered Paratoka. "The Men who conduct the tests are in a branch of the military."

"It is *they* who want the metal, not *I*," said Jalanopi confidently. "We shall see who possesses more patience, their king or yours."

"They have no king," noted Paratoka.

"His name is Solomon," replied Jalanopi. "How could they function without a king? Probably he does not consider the Tulabete important enough to be granted an audience; he will soon realize that he is in error."

Paratoka went back to the Republic with Jalanopi's answer, and nothing more was heard from Men for five months. A few more hunters applied for permission to go after trophy animals, and a handful of missionaries were allowed to set up shop, but every day Jalanopi waited for the Republic to give in to his conditions, and each new day brought forth nothing but silence.

"They need encouragement," he announced to his advisors one night. "Invite the Canphorites back."

"We agreed not to," noted Paratoka.

"When the Men return, we will deport the Canphorites again," said Jalanopi.

"That is not fair to them," offered another advisor.

"What are they to us?" asked Jalanopi. "Since Man is the strongest race we have encountered, and since Man covets our metals, then we must use everything at our disposal to bend the race of Man to our will."

"Surely others have tried," said the advisor. "And yet they have forty thousand worlds in their empire."

"*I* am not others," said Jalanopi. "We will invite the Canphorites back again."

Five

The reappearance of the Canphorites had the desired effect upon the Republic. No sooner had the news reached them than a party of human diplomats and ranking military officers requested permission to land on Karimon and meet with Jalanopi.

Jalanopi set the time for the audience, which, of course, was held beneath his tree. As the moment approached, he donned his ceremonial headdress, sat upon his serpentine throne, and assembled his warriors—all armed with the Republic's weapons—in such a way that they appeared to be even more numerous than they were. Finally, satisfied, he allowed his guests to be brought before him.

A party of seven men and women, five in military uniforms, walked across the dry, grassy plains toward Jalanopi's village of Mastaboni. A member of Jalanopi's own race led them, beating the tall grass with his spear to frighten away any poisonous snakes. By the time they were within sight of Jalanopi the entire party was covered with sweat and dust. They stopped some twenty feet from Jalanopi's tree as the Tulabete formed a ring around them, and finally one of the two men who wore civilian clothing stepped forward.

"Greetings, King Jalanopi," he said. "My name is Arthur Gruening, and—"

Jalanopi held up a hand, and the man immediately fell silent.

"These fools have not even bothered to learn our language," he said to Paratoka. "You will translate."

"My Terran is not very good, my king," replied his chief advisor. "I suggest we summon Man Andrew."

Jalanopi nodded his acquiescence. "But you will remain and listen, for when all is said and done, he is one of them."

"Yes, my king."

McFarley arrived a few minutes later, was apprised of the situation, and began translating for both sides.

"My name is Arthur Gruening," recommenced the man in civilian clothing, "and I represent the Republic's Department of Alien Affairs, which is based far from here on Deluros VIII." He paused and wiped the sweat from his forehead with a handkerchief, and silently wished that he had brought a hat. "I have been instructed by my government to remind you of certain promises that were made in your name, and to urge you to reconsider your decision to allow our mutual enemies from the Canphor system access to your world."

"I made no such promises," said Jalanopi.

"I happen to know that you did," said McFarley.

"Just translate what I have said, Man Andrew," said Jalanopi coldly. "Great things are at stake here, and I will not have you jeopardize them."

McFarley shrugged and translated Jalanopi's statement.

"Your own representative gave us your assurances that the Canphorites would be permanently barred from Karimon," said Gruening.

"He had no authority to do so," said Jalanopi.

"Nevertheless, he spoke on your behalf."

Jalanopi held up his hand once more.

"Bring Paratoka before me."

Three of his warriors immediately walked over to a serpent-shaped dwelling.

"But he is sitting right before you!" said McFarley.

"Man Andrew, if you wish for these seven members of your race to survive the day, you will limit yourself to translating," said Jalanopi. "And do not forget that the real Paratoka will tell me if you have properly translated what I say."

A blindfolded Fani warrior, his hands bound behind him, was dragged out of the dwelling and over to Jalanopi's tree.

"Here is Paratoka," announced Jalanopi.

He waited for McFarley to translate, then withdrew a long sharp blade and, before anyone could react, lopped the Fani's head off.

"As you can see," continued Jalanopi calmly, as he sheathed his blade, "Paratoka is incapable of speaking for himself, let alone for me." He stared at McFarley, his orange cat's-eyes wide and unblinking. "Thus do I treat *anyone* who misrepresents me."

Gruening and the diplomats averted their eyes, while the military men watched with no show of emotion.

"Have we anything further to discuss?" asked Jalanopi after a momentary silence.

"Yes," said Gruening, forcing himself to look away from the corpse. "We have given you our weapons and our friendship. We have kept our promises to you. We have proven ourselves to be your friends. Why are you once again opening your planet to the Canphorites, whom you know to be our enemies?"

"I offered your race the chance to survey our hills and make your various tests for our metals," answered Jalanopi. "When you failed to reply, I naturally assumed that these things held no interest for you. We are a poor people, and if we cannot sell our metals to you, then we must sell them where we can."

"The Canphorites are surveying your hills right now?" asked Gruening, startled.

"The Canphorites are in our hills," said Jalanopi. "I have no idea what they are doing there."

"We would like to survey them also."

"Then why did you not reply to me when the offer was made?"

"Because of the conditions you imposed," answered Gruening. "You have many wild animals on your world, and you have not yet conquered all of your enemies. It would be foolhardy to send a party of Men out, totally unarmed, to survey your hills."

"All problems are capable of solution when peace-loving beings meet together and talk," said Jalanopi, and only McFarley recognized the open lips and the tightness around his eyes as a contemptuous smile. "Had you simply voiced your concerns, we could have solved this particular problem months ago. I will send an armed party of my warriors into the hills with you to act as your guards."

"We would prefer that our men carry their own weaponry," answered Gruening.

"You sound distrustful," said Jalanopi. "This is not the statement of a friend."

"One moment, please, King Jalanopi," said Gruening. He turned and conversed with his companions in low tones for a minute, then faced Jalanopi again. "We accede to your conditions, King Jalanopi. A team of forty surveyors will land here the day after tomorrow, and we will place their security in your hands."

"I accept this burden," said Jalanopi formally.

"And the Canphorites?"

"Soon they will leave."

"How soon?" asked Gruening.

"When it pleases me to send them away."

"They are a duplicitous race, King Jalanopi. If I were you, I would keep them under constant surveillance."

"I thank you for your advice."

There was a brief silence.

"Perhaps," continued Jalanopi, "your surveyors had better bring another thousand weapons with them, that we may better protect them from the Canphorites."

"We have total faith in your ability to protect us with the weapons you have," said Gruening.

"But *I* do not," answered Jalanopi. "I will require one thousand more weapons to guarantee your team's safety."

"McFarley!" snapped Gruening, turning to the translator. "This is blackmail! You tell him so!"

"That might not be wise, sir," responded McFarley.

"We won't be held up by this savage!" continued Gruening. "We've played by the rules, we've fulfilled our end of the bargain, and now he's trying to hold us up again! If we go home empty-handed, I guarantee we'll be back in force!"

"You won't go home empty-handed," said McFarley.

"What are you talking about?"

"You're facing more than a thousand of his warriors, armed with Republic weapons. If you don't agree to his demands, you'll never make it to the ship."

Gruening suddenly became aware of his surroundings. A single avian screeched in the upper terraces of Jalanopi's tree as the diplomat looked from one savage reptilian face to another.

"Surely he doesn't think he can get away with killing us!" he said at last.

"I've come to know him very well during the year I've been here," answered McFarley. "I think he is convinced he *can* kill you. He'll kill me as well, and blame the whole thing on the Canphorites. All that will happen is that the Republic will give him more weapons to protect himself against the Canphorites who are on the planet, and perhaps go to war with Canphor itself."

"By God, they'd *do* it, too!" muttered Gruening slowly.

"He's a clever bastard for an animated snake that walks around half-naked."

"Do not make the mistake of underestimating him, sir," said McFarley.

"That wasn't Paratoka he killed, either, was it?"

"I am not at liberty to say, sir," replied McFarley.

"So he speaks Terran?"

"No, sir, but *somebody* does."

Gruening looked around at the assembled Tulabete, trying fruitlessly to spot the Terran-speaker.

"Just whose side are you on, McFarley?"

"I'm on the side of peace," answered McFarley. "But if I have to tilt to one side or the other, I usually favor the underdog."

"All right," said Gruening. "The old bastard's got us over a barrel. Tell him we agree to all his conditions."

McFarley did as he was instructed.

"You had quite a conversation with him, Man Andrew," said Jalanopi, his lips slightly parted. "I assume you were explaining his options to him."

"His lack of options," McFarley corrected him.

"What more shall I demand of him, I wonder?" mused Jalanopi.

"If you push him hard enough, he'll leave."

"That would not be wise."

"Oh, he'll promise to give you everything you ask for, but he'll send in the Navy instead. If I were you, I'd quit while I was ahead."

"But you are not me," answered Jalanopi. His tongue flicked out and captured an insect. He chewed it thoughtfully for a moment, then looked up. "Ask him how he intends to pay us if we allow him to take our metal from our hills."

"We can pay in the Republic credit, or any of the 1,279 currencies currently accepted by the worlds of the Republic," answered Gruening promptly.

"What is a credit?" asked Jalanopi.

"A unit of barter," answered Gruening.

"Like our Tallgrazers?" asked Jalanopi, indicating a herd of the animals in a nearby pasture.

Gruening smiled. "The credit comes in paper form, like this." He pulled some bills out of his wallet and held them up for Jalanopi to see.

"That is not acceptable," answered Jalanopi. "It would take millions of them to make one Tallgrazer."

"Actually, you could buy a Tallgrazer for about two hundred of them, I should think," said Gruening.

Jalanopi shook his head. "Not from the Tulabete. And once you have obtained these credits, what do you do with them? Can you extract the marrow from their bones?"

Gruening tried to give Jalanopi a rudimentary education in economics, but the king would have none of it.

"It will not work, Man Gruening," he announced at last. "If I were to go among the Rakko and the Fani, or even my own people, and offer them your pieces of paper in exchange for their Tallgrazers, they would think me crazy."

"Then what *do* you want in payment?" asked Gruening.

"I will decide when the time comes," answered Jalanopi. He got to his feet, towering over them. "Now you will join me for the midday meal, and then you will return to your Republic and send me both your surveyors and your arms."

The meal was a disaster, as both McFarley and Jalanopi had known it would be, but the Tulabete king was enjoying his visitors' discomfort too much to cut it short. When they had finally reboarded their ship and were racing out of orbit, McFarley again approached Jalanopi.

"I would have thought Paratoka would have learned *something* about a cash economy during his time in the Republic," he said.

"He did."

"Perhaps he and I can clarify it for you now."

"Why bother?" replied Jalanopi. "I already understand it."

"Then—"

"If they give me credits, Man Andrew," said Jalanopi, as if speaking to a schoolchild, "they will never allow me to spend those credits on weapons; they will remain here until the paper rots. Therefore, I will play the fool until they decide that the only fee I will accept for our metal is more weaponry."

"Just who do you intend to use all this firepower against?" asked McFarley.

"Initially, the Rakko and the Fani. Then the other tribes. And eventually, if they prove to be too bothersome, I will use them against the Men who come to my world."

"That would be a mistake."

"I have no quarrel with your race, Man Andrew," said Jalanopi. "In fact, we are very much alike. I know how their minds work, I know what motivates them. But between us, there is a difference."

"And what is that?" asked McFarley.

"They crave money and power. I, who have no use for money, crave only power. If I can use them to secure my power on Karimon, they may use me to secure their money."

"And what of *their* craving for power?"

Jalanopi's lips parted with a slight hissing sound. "Let them exercise it over worlds that do not understand them as well as I do. We will be partners, Men and my people . . . but *I* will be the senior partner."

McFarley smiled grimly. "I wish you luck, Jalanopi."

"You think they will take advantage of me, do you not?"

"Yes, I do."

"It is good of you to warn me."

"I have not warned you, Jalanopi," said McFarley, "for I have no idea how they will do so. I have merely answered your question."

"Is this not disloyal to your own race?" asked Jalanopi, always trying to learn more about his enemy.

"To my race, perhaps. To my God, no. He teaches us to love our neighbors."

"At the cost of betraying your own people?"

"I have betrayed no one, Jalanopi," answered McFarley. "Nothing I can say to either side will make any difference in the long run. This scene has been played out many thousands of times on many thousands of worlds. Many of them had monarchs who thought they knew how to manipulate the race of Man, but almost all of them are now members of the Republic."

"*Almost* all," said Jalanopi. "Some were different. So shall I be."

"I wouldn't count on it, my friend," said McFarley. "Today you won. If I were you, I would savor it, for your victories over Man will be few and far between."

Jalanopi paused thoughtfully. "What will they do next?" he asked.

"Next? They'll bring in their surveyors and make sure your world is worth their effort."

"And if it is?" said Jalanopi. "Then what?"

"I don't know," answered McFarley. "Men are very creative."

Six

I t took four months for Man's creativity to manifest itself; once they found out that the Tulabete's hills were
rich in gold, platinum, silver, copper, and fissionable materials, they pulled all their surveyors out.

Then disquieting news began to arrive. A village of Tulabete had been massacred by the Rakko on the southern
frontier of their territory. A party of warriors sent out to
examine the carnage had never reported back. The males
from a trio of large northeastern villages were killed by the
Fani, and more than three hundred females were stolen.
Tiny tribes that had never caused any trouble were suddenly attacking the Tulabete, and successfully.

Finally the word reached Jalanopi, as he sat brooding
beneath his tree: the Fani and the Rakko and the others
were all in possession of Republic weapons, in far greater
quantity than the Tulabete possessed.

Jalanopi accepted the challenge, marched his men out
to war, and engaged the enemy. It was only due to his
superior generalship that he came away with a draw—a
very expensive draw, both in terms of warriors and weapons
lost. Two weeks later he committed to another battle, only

to discover that his enemy had been resupplied. He re-treated back to the heart of his kingdom, there to consider his options.

For two days and two nights he sat alone beneath his tree, lost in thought. Finally he summoned McFarley.

"You were right, Man Andrew," he said bitterly. "Men are more creative than I had anticipated."

"I am sorry, Jalanopi," said McFarley sincerely.

"It is both too late and too early for regrets," replied Jalanopi. "I must contact your Republic and make the best deal I can."

"My radio is at your disposal."

"Tell them I must have more weapons, and that I am willing to cede them the rights to take the metal from my hills if they will agree to stop arming my enemies."

"I will do so immediately," replied McFarley, hurrying off to his church.

He returned some twenty minutes later.

"Well?" asked Jalanopi.

"Let us say that your request was not unanticipated," said McFarley wryly.

"What was their response?"

"They have leased all mineral rights on Karimon to the Spiral Arm Development Company, which is run by Violet Gardener. Have you ever heard of her?"

"No. She is a *female?*" The tone of his voice was clearly contemptuous.

"So I gather."

"What use is a female to me?"

"Money knows no gender," answered McFarley. "I gather she is prepared to sign a treaty with you, by which you will give her the mineral rights she craves and she will assure your primacy over the tribes of Karimon."

"What good is the promise of a female?" said Jalanopi. "Females are little better than Tallgrazers. If a warrior wants one, he buys one. They have no brains. They are good only for preparing meals and producing babies."

"They have no *rights*," said McFarley, "which is quite a different thing than having no brains. You waste half of your race's potential by keeping them in such servitude." He paused. "Among my own race, females are treated as equals, and frequently prove themselves to be superior to males."

"This may be true of Men, Man Andrew," said Jalanopi firmly, "but not of the Tulabete. Our females are capable of nothing more complicated than cooking and weaving cloth."

"That is because the males rarely speak to them, and there is none among them capable of teaching them more. I assure you, Jalanopi, that there is no difference in ability between a newborn Tulabete male and a newborn Tulabete female, only in opportunity."

"With my own spear I have killed many Wildfangs and Nightkillers," said Jalanopi. "What Tulabete female could do that?"

"I do not know," answered McFarley. "Nor will *you* ever know what they are capable of doing, as long as you treat them no better than you treat your Tallgrazers." He paused for a moment. "Besides . . ."

"I know . . . I have no choice," said Jalanopi. His facial muscles contracted spasmodically, forcing a greasy fluid to the surface.

Long after McFarley had left, Jalanopi remained motionless, wondering if he would be the last king of the Tulabete to sit beneath his tree. Eventually his natural confidence reasserted itself, and he began thinking of ways to manipulate this female that the Republic had seen fit to reward with *his* hills.

II

GARDENER'S DREAM

Seven

H er name was Violet Gardener, and though she was hardly the seventh son of a seventh son, she was something quite special the day she was born: the only child of a father who'd made half a dozen fortunes mining the Frontier Worlds before he'd settled down in the heart of the Republic, and a mother who had tried her hand at acting, playwriting, and poetry, and been successful at all three. Great things were expected of the child of Lawrence Gardener and Belore Ivor, and she did her best not to disappoint.

She grew up on Lundquist IV, a gentle green world that was almost a bedroom suburb of Deluros VIII, the huge planet which was already on the brink of becoming the capital world of the race of Man. Her grades were such that not even her exceptional parents could object, and she excelled in most sports, though none truly interested her. She possessed bright red hair and a temper to match, and spent a goodly portion of her time trying to keep it under control or coping with the consequences of it.

When she was seventeen, she went to the university planet of Aristotle, from which she emerged seven years later armed with degrees in literature, metallurgy (her father had insisted), and political science, but still with no serious notion of what to *do* with her life.

She made the social scene on Deluros VIII and Earth and the other fashionable worlds of the race of Man for the next two years. It was said that she had taken a string of lovers, but if so, she was discreet enough that none of them were ever identified. It was also said that she twice enlisted herself in detoxification programs, but there no records to prove *that*, either. It is known that she briefly underwent analysis to learn to control her emotional outbursts; it is assumed the sessions were successful, because she never returned.

Then, as she drifted through the worlds of the Republic, trying her hand at this and that, never quite satisfied with her life, something happened. Her many biographers still disagree about the event, but something convinced her to return to Aristotle for another two years, after which she emerged with one more degree—cartography—and a driving sense of purpose.

Man's expansion through the galaxy had always been inward, toward the Core. Born on the Spiral Arm, where the stars are not closely clustered, he had moved farther and farther from his home planet, finally choosing Deluros VIII as his new headquarters world. He had meticulously assembled his empire in a number of lines of political, economic, and military conquest, each stretching out from the Deluros system. He had pushed toward the Core of the galaxy, the worlds of the so-called Inner Frontier, and toward the galactic Rim—the worlds of the Outer Frontier—but for some reason, probably simply the unthinkably vast scope of his operation, he had never made much headway in the Spiral Arm from which he had come.

At age twenty-nine, Violet Gardener set out to change that.

She had a vision—a dream, if you will—of expanding

Man's empire throughout the Spiral Arm. Her knowledge of cartography had shown her the most practical way of achieving her goal, for cartography had become an almost political science, dealing not only with maps but with alien races and lines of transport and power. Her studies of politics, especially interstellar and alien politics, imbued her with the requisite knowledge for dealing with human and alien governments alike. Her knowledge of mining, plus the occasional advice she sought from her aging, planetbound, but still mentally alert father, showed her a way to make her dream pay its own way. And her own intelligence and all-consuming drive—some biographers have implied that it was merely her wild temper, properly directed and channeled—made her initial successes almost inevitable.

While most of Man's expansion up to this point in his galactic history had been undertaken by and for the military, it was Violet Gardener who convinced the Republic to lease her the economic rights to seventeen star systems in the Spiral Arm, and she acted as almost a private arm of Mankind's empire-building machine. She was not concerned with lines of military force, but rather with lines of economic dependence and communication. By the age of thirty-two, her dream was no longer an ephemeral vision, but a logical, rational, well-reasoned 672-page tract that was almost a bible to her subordinates, explaining as it did precisely why seventeen specific star systems would spread Man's influence throughout the Arm, how and in what order each of the systems must be approached, the cost of each conquest, and the profit potential therein.

Violet began with Pirelli and Doxus II, a pair of seemingly insignificant, totally uninhabited oxygen planets whose sole function was to serve as fuel and munitions suppliers. Then she moved on to Castlestone, a planet rich in gemstones and fissionable materials. It took her three years to introduce a monied economy among the intelligent marsupials she found there, and though the exports from her mines on Castlestone were more than enough to capitalize her next few ventures, she had contracted both cancer (which was curable) and a very rare blood disease (which probably wasn't) in the interim. Always a realist, she decided that Time was her one irreplaceable commodity, and that she couldn't afford to spend as much as three years on any one world.

She refined and brutalized her approach on Narabella and again on Sugarmoon—an oxygen satellite of the huge, gaseous Borgo XI—and by the time she set her sights on Goldstone, the true cornerstone upon which she meant to build her little trading empire, she was prepared for any eventuality.

What she found when she landed was a primitive humanoid race, its various nations constantly at war, totally devoid of a monied economy. After two meetings with leaders of the most powerful nations had proven fruitless, she began working in concert with the Navy, bringing about various improvements in the inhabitants' lifestyles. They built bridges and roads, imported fertilizer and hybrid crops, even brought in a team of exobiologists to provide the inhabitants with sophisticated medical care.

It didn't take long for the natives of Goldstone to adapt to the innovations that had made their harsh lives more bearable, and during the interim she opened up two more worlds. Then one day, without any warning, all humans left Goldstone, all aid stopped, and most of the improvements upon which the inhabitants now depended began to crumble.

The leaders of the various nations sought her out—she had always made herself available to them—and begged her to restore what had been taken away from them. She explained that such benefits cost money, and that the Republic had cut off all funds to the Spiral Arm. Since they did not possess a monied economy, they obviously could not give her the money required to buy their way out of their current predicament. She sympathized with them, of course, but what could she do?

There followed a month of negotiations. Goldstone was willing to move to a currency-based economy, but the governments had no tax base since the civilian population had no way of earning money. Violet listened thoughtfully to their problem, then announced that she might have a solution: if they would cede to her all mining rights to Goldstone's mineral wealth, she would pay them a stipend of ten million credits per year or ten percent of her profits, whichever was greater. Furthermore, if they would guarantee her a work force of two million native miners to begin with, gradually increasing to an eventual five million, she would pay their salaries, in the amount of thirty credits per worker a week, with more for supervisors, thus creating a tax base for the government. With these two sources of revenue, the government could, in one enormous leap, move to a monied economy and would be able to afford to bring back the conveniences and necessities that had heretofore been supplied gratis by the Republic.

Within a year, Goldstone's mines were operating around the clock, more were being opened up daily, and Violet Gardener was wealthy beyond her wildest dreams. But her dreams were not of wealth, but of a human empire stretching from one end of the Spiral Arm to the other, and she realized that she still had work to do.

And so, standing on the roof of her recently erected office building, she turned her eyes skyward and saw, flickering faintly in the distance, two yellow stars around which circled two planets that she planned to assimilate into her financial empire. Though she had never set foot on either of them, she knew them as well as she knew the reflection of her own face, grown tanned from the sun and lean from disease, in the mirror.

Before long, *they* would know *her* even better.

Eight

"Throw Jalanopi's image up on the holoscreen," ordered Violet Gardener, sitting at the head of the table in her spaceship's conference room.

"Working . . . done," announced the computer.

As the image appeared, the overhead lights automatically dimmed and the portholes that looked out at the galaxy became opaque. Violet sat at one end of a long chrome table that was magnetically linked to the metallic floor of the conference room; six men and three women were clustered at the other end. "He looks like a snake with limbs," she remarked.

"Well, he *thinks* a lot like a Man," said Arthur Gruening bitterly. "He's a cagey old bastard."

"Yes," said Violet dryly, making no attempt to hide her contempt for Gruening; he was not in her employ but the Republic's and was therefore instantly classified as both an incompetent and a spy. "I understand he more than held his own with you."

Although barely five feet tall, her bright red hair turned an unstylish gray, and a sallow tint to her skin that reflected the early stages of her blood disease, her displeasure still inspired a sense of terror in her subordinates.

"What could I do?" said Gruening defensively. "The Republic had tied my hands. I wasn't authorized to act until the Spiral Arm Development Company signed its lease with the Republic and took control of Karimon." He smiled. "The poor devil doesn't know what he's in for."

"Linus?" said Violet, turning to Linus Rawls, a tall, lean mustached man who sat slumped in a chair, his formal outfit already wrinkled, a smokeless cigarette dangling from his lips. He'd been with her for almost ten years, and was the only one in the room who was unafraid of her, or at least able to keep his fears to himself.

"Yes?"

"Tell me about the inhabitants."

"*I* can do that, Madam Gardener," said Gruening.

"I'd rather hear about them from someone who has lived with them for a few months than from a man who was outmaneuvered in his only meeting with them."

"I've already explained that to you—" began Gruening petulantly.

"Yes, you have," said Violet. "Therefore, you've no need to do it again. Linus?"

"Well," said Rawls, "I spent three months hunting the northern part of Jalanopi's kingdom with Fuentes, as per your instructions. The game is phenomenal: they've something called a Redmountain that—"

"I'm not interested in the animals, Linus," she interrupted.

"Sorry," said Rawls. He swallowed and began again. "We used a batch of snakes as gun bearers, cooks, skinners, trackers, camp boys, everything, so I got to know some of 'em pretty well. By and large, they're a pretty malleable lot."

"You call them snakes?"

"Fuentes does, so I picked it up. They don't live in huts or houses, you know; they slither into these twisted, serpentine mounds when they go to sleep, and they've got tongues you wouldn't believe. They can pick an insect out of the air at twenty inches. Strange voices, too: they hiss a lot."

"They look humanoid," noted Violet.

"Well, *I* wouldn't call them human. They spend a lot of time in the water, and in those crazy mounds, and no human ever ate what the Tulabete eat."

"Minor differences," she said with a shrug. "How strong are they?"

"Well, Jalanopi can probably mount an army of twenty thousand on a week's notice. As for the others . . ."

Violet shook her head. "No, I meant how strong is an *individual* snake?"

"They can lift a pretty heavy load."

"Their shoulders seem very narrow and somewhat sloped."

Rawls nodded his head. "Yeah, I guess they are."

"Good. We'll give them .975-caliber projectile rifles."

"Madam Gardener, they can't shoot straight with the hand weapons we *gave* them," said Rawls. "They'll never learn to shoot those. For one thing, even Fuentes' bearers haven't figured out, after all the years they've been with him, that jerking the trigger as hard as they can doesn't make the bullet go any faster." He paused. "All that's going to happen is that they're going to take one shot, blow a huge hole in something they weren't aiming at, and have the recoil break a shoulder."

Violet stared at him expressionlessly. "What is your point, Linus?"

He stared back at her, and suddenly he grinned. "No point, Madam Gardener. Just an observation."

"Jalanopi will doubtless want weapons from us," she said. "I see no reason why we shouldn't give him the most powerful rifles available." She turned to another assistant. "Mr. Lohmeyer, I believe you have the surveyor's reports?"

A gray-haired, nattily dressed man got to his feet. "Yes, Madam Gardener. Gold in profusion, some platinum, huge copper deposits, some rare stones; we haven't come across any diamonds yet, but we know they're there."

"Fissionable materials?"

"There may be some uranium beyond the mountain range on the Tulabetes' southern border. We didn't get a chance to thoroughly explore it, but the geologic conditions seem right for it."

"How long before we can make the planet start paying for itself?"

Lohmeyer furrowed his brow as he considered the various factors. "I can't see it showing a profit for at least five years, Madam Gardener. We're starting from scratch here: no industry, no commerce, no spaceport, no dwellings or conveniences for the human supervisors. Everything will have to be built or imported. There's not much water in those mountains, either; we're going to have to find a source and divert it. And all that is assuming we don't have problems organizing a local work force." He shook his head. "No, I can't see us showing a serious profit any sooner, and my estimate may well be optimistic."

"That's not soon enough, Mr. Lohmeyer," replied Violet.

"Actually, I don't know how we can do it any faster, given the conditions we are presented with," answered Lohmeyer.

"You have your timetable, and I have mine," answered Violet, who had not shared the information that her blood disease, while not an immediate threat to her life, was incurable, and would leave her weaker and less able to stand the frenetic pace of her life with each passing year. "I have made it my business and my destiny to bring the Spiral Arm under Man's control, and I cannot allow each world to take five years to pay for itself."

"I would be happy to entertain any suggestions concerning how you think we might put Karimon on a paying basis in less time," said Lohmeyer.

"Simple," said Violet. "We open it for colonization—not only to farmers, but to miners. We will bring in our equipment and put our own people to work, but we will also allow any Man to put in a claim in exchange for a certain percentage of his profits."

"*What* percentage?" asked Rawls curiously.

"A fifty-fifty split, I think."

"Fifty-fifty?"

"That's right."

"How many miners will buy *that*, I wonder?" said Rawls with a chuckle.

"Anyone who wants to mine the world will," answered Violet. "Otherwise we will mine the entire planet ourselves; it will take longer, but we'll be richer for the waiting." She paused. "I think you can count on any number of miners signing up. Doubtless some farmers, too, since the miners will need food."

"We thought we'd open up Belamaine for farming," put in Gruening. "It *looks* like a sister planet to Karimon, but the only mineral deposits it has in any quantity are copper and iron. There's enough of a galactic market for copper that we can turn the concession over to the planetary government in exchange for farming rights on their northern continent. It's all but uninhabited, and the climate and soil samples indicate an excellent farming world."

Violet shook her head. "You don't understand these native races, Mr. Gruening. They have no monied economies, and precious little use for metals . . . but they understand the value of *land*. We will begin mining the copper on Belamaine, and we will open shops for our miners. As always, with planets controlled by the Spiral Arm Development Company, barter will not be acceptable in any of our stores. Once the natives understand that there is money to be made in mining, and things to spend it on, they will demand their mines back. We will give them some, in exchange for agricultural concessions, and we will create jobs for them in the mines that we still control." She grimaced contemptuously. "No wonder the Republic has had to go to war so often. You must understand the people you plan to subjugate, Mr. Gruening."

"You've had your share of little battles, too, Madam Gardener," he replied defensively.

"True," she replied. "But never at the outset. Never before we were ready for them, or before a substantial number of the native populace was enlightened enough to fight on *our* side. You don't waste Men in a war with aliens if you can enlist other aliens to fight on your side." She stared coldly at him. "And you don't decimate entire worlds to the point where they are of no economic value to the Republic. Otherwise they become just so many meaningless numbers added to your total, rather than functioning, economically integrated cogs of a vast human machine."

Gruening shifted uneasily in his chair. "This is not the best time for a political debate," he suggested.

Rawls chuckled aloud. "On Madam Gardener's ship, it's time for anything she wants it to be time for."

Violet turned to Rawls. "Thank you, Linus, but Mr. Gruening is quite right. Our purpose is to determine what actions we will take in regard to Belamaine and especially to Karimon."

They discussed the matter for another hour, at which time her pilot announced that they had entered orbit around Karimon and would be landing momentarily.

"Do you want to meet Jalanopi in his village, or would you rather he came to you?" asked Rawls.

"We're dealing from strength," answered Violet, studying Jalanopi's holograph once more. "Let's leave him a little dignity among his people and go to him."

Rawls nodded, and set about organizing a landing party.

The ship touched down about three miles from Jalanopi's village, and a few moments later a trio of sleek groundcars carrying Violet Gardener and her party emerged from the hold and began driving toward Jalanopi's tree.

"Very pretty planet," commented Violet.

"To tell the truth, I'd have been happy to stay out in the bush another three or four months with Fuentes," replied Rawls with a smile. "It's a lovely world. Exquisite scenery, and some truly fabulous big game."

"I believe I saw an enormous waterfall as we were coming down from orbit," remarked Violet. "It seemed almost four miles wide, though I could be mistaken about the size."

"Yes, I know the place. It's along the Karimona River, an awesome sight. They say you can hear it from as far as twenty miles away."

"Has it got a name?" she asked.

"The natives call it Doratule."

"An evocative name. What does it mean?"

"Thundermist."

She wrinkled her nose. "This is going to be a human world. It ought to have a human name."

"Have you one in mind?"

She was silent for a moment. "Did Johnny Ramsey ever hunt on Karimon after he resigned as Secretary of the Republic?"

"No," answered Rawls. "I believe he confined his hunting to Peponi and one or two other worlds, all closer to the Core."

"All right," said Violet. "Let's call it Ramsey Falls. It's a nice way to honor a good politician—and who knows? If he hears about it, he might take a hunting trip here and write it up in his memoirs. A little publicity never hurts."

"I've been meaning to speak to you about that," said Rawls.

"About Johnny Ramsey?"

He shook his head. "About hunting."

She smiled. "It sounds like Mr. Fuentes has a convert."

"You've never seen game like this, Madam Gardener," he said, trying to control his enthusiasm. "Redmountains twenty feet tall, carnivores like Wildfangs and Nightkillers, behemoths like Horndevils—it's a hunter's paradise." He paused uneasily. "So I was thinking . . . well, you don't really need me to manage the mining concession, and . . ."

"And?"

"I'd like to take a couple of years to set up a hunting industry on the planet. I found that I really enjoyed the time I spent with Fuentes. I think a string of lodges and camps, properly advertised back in the Republic, would quickly return your investment."

She considered the notion for a long moment. "That might not be a bad idea, Linus. It would get us written up in some of the popular journals, it would create a need for hotels and all the other businesses connected with the safari industry; it would probably even make a second spaceport cost-efficient." She paused. "How long will the game hold out?"

"I beg your pardon?"

"How long before you kill it all, or leave so little alive that we have to create parks and start selling the climate and the view?"

"No problem, Madam Gardener," said Rawls confidently. "The game will last forever." He pointed to a trio of gazelle-like creatures grazing a quarter mile away, oblivious to the groundcars. "See those Fleetjumpers there? When I was with Fuentes, I saw a herd of them that was so large it took a full day to pass by."

"Nothing lasts forever, Linus," she replied. "I've been to many worlds like this one. In less than half a century they change from planets with islands of natives in a sea of animals to isolated islands of protected animals in a sea of natives."

"That can't happen here," he assured her. "You can't

imagine the sheer *quantity* of game out there on the plains."

"It happens everywhere," she replied. "Just make sure that we're prepared for it."

"I'll make sure," he said earnestly. "I'd like to run it myself, once we get the mining operation set up."

"I assume you'll want a percentage?"

"I'll earn it," he assured her.

She nodded. "All right. Are you happy now, Linus?"

"Yes, Madam Gardener."

"Then perhaps you'll start concentrating on our upcoming meeting with Jalanopi. I think we're almost there."

The three groundcars came to a stop about one hundred yards from Jalanopi's tree, which had been visible for the past five miles. The king, clad in his headdress, was sitting on his serpentine throne, surrounded by Paratoka and his other advisors. Andrew McFarley stood off to his left, some ten feet away.

Violet waited while the door was opened for her. Then, striding between two of her bodyguards, and followed by the rest of her party, she approached Jalanopi, stopping fifteen feet from him.

McFarley stepped forward.

"Good morning, Madam Gardener," he said. "I am the Reverend Andrew McFarley. Jalanopi has asked me to serve as his translator."

"I'm pleased to meet you, Reverend," said Violet, extending her hand. "How long have you been on Karimon?"

"A little less than two years," he replied.

"And how do you find the climate and the natives?"

"I find both to be admirable."

She smiled. "Do I detect a note of partisanship, Reverend McFarley?"

"I know what you plan to do to this world," he said. "I've seen it before, and I don't like it."

"Reverend McFarley, outside of saving your friend

Jalanopi from his foolishness and implementing a mining concession, even *I* don't know what I plan to do with this world."

"Why don't you just leave them alone?" he demanded.

She arched an eyebrow. "Why don't you?"

"I bring them the word of the Lord," he said. "I don't rape and plunder their planet."

"Just their minds," suggested Violet. "You will bring them guilt and shame. I propose to bring them the more positive benefits of human civilization. We shall see who does the most harm in the long run."

McFarley seemed about to say something else, then evidently thought better of it, and Violet turned to Jalanopi.

"King Jalanopi," she said, shielding her eyes against a sudden gust of wind that brought a cloud of fine reddish dust with it. "I am Violet Gardener, representing the Spiral Arm Development Company. I am delighted to make your acquaintance."

"I am pleased to meet you, Man Violet," said Jalanopi, once her message had been translated. "Welcome to Mastaboni."

Violet turned to McFarley. "Mastaboni?"

"The name of his village," answered McFarley.

"What does it mean?"

" 'The Killing Place'," said McFarley. "It is where his grandfather's people were slaughtered."

She made no comment, and turned back to Jalanopi. "You know why we are here, of course?"

"Yes, Man Violet," he replied. "I know why you are here. You have brought weapons?"

"I have brought weapons," she replied. "And more."

"More?" replied Jalanopi. "I did not ask for anything more than weapons."

"It is a gift of friendship," said Violet.

"And what is this gift?" he asked suspiciously, flicking out his tongue to capture an errant flying insect.

"We wish to be your friends," answered Violet. "Friends do not let other friends suffer needlessly. So along with bringing you five hundred weapons for your own warriors, I have instructed the Spiral Arm Development Company to transfer five thousand members of our private security force to Karimon. Your enemies are our enemies, and we will fight beside you until they have been subdued."

"I requested no help, only weapons," protested Jalanopi.

Violet smiled at him. "What are friends for?"

"How long will your security forces remain on Karimon?" asked Jalanopi.

"For as long as it takes to establish you as the most powerful king of the most powerful nation on the planet."

Jalanopi listened to the translation, then turned to McFarley.

"Does she speak the truth, Man Andrew?" he asked as one hundred feet above his head a Tailswinger family suddenly began screeching at a golden lizard that was scurrying up the huge trunk of the tree.

"Yes, she does," answered McFarley. "But she does not speak the *whole* truth."

"And what is that?"

"You will be the most powerful king of the most powerful tribe on Karimon," said McFarley. "But you must remember that she is not a king, and the Spiral Arm Development Company is not a tribe or a nation."

Jalanopi considered the human's remark for a moment.

"She expects me to be her puppet, then?"

"In essence."

"And I must agree, must I not?" continued Jalanopi, closing his eyes as the warm wind brought another cloud of dust. "For if I refuse, she will then make the same offer to the king of the Fani." He stared at McFarley, who did not answer, and finally he spoke again. "I could kill them all right now."

"Then you will lose the war against the Fani and the

Rakko, a war you are in the process of losing right now. And there will be severe retribution for killing Violet Gardener."

"*How* severe?" asked Jalanopi, still considering his options.

"More severe than I hope you can imagine," answered McFarley. "You have no choice, Jalanopi."

"For the moment," answered Jalanopi. "I will make this treaty because I must, but I will study my enemy and search for weakness, just as the Nightkiller studies the herds of Twisthorns and seeks out the weakest. There must be weakness here as well, and I shall find it."

"You are defeated, my friend," said McFarley sadly. "You have never undergone anything like this before, but for Man—and especially for Violet Gardener—it is an almost daily occurrence. She has seen it all, and has devised ways to combat whatever you may do."

"She has not experienced Jalanopi before," said Jalanopi firmly. "The day will come when she will wish she never had. This I promise you, Man Andrew." He turned back to Violet. "Tell her that I am happy to accept her warriors, and that they will, of course, be under my command."

"She will never accept that, Jalanopi," said McFarley.

"Tell her anyway."

McFarley translated Jalanopi's statement.

"My forces have weapons and procedures that are unfamiliar to you, Jalanopi," replied Violet. "It would be far better for them to be placed under their own command."

"I insist that they obey *my* orders, since they fight for my tribe," said Jalanopi.

Violet stared down at two warring insects next to her foot and considered his demand for a long moment, then looked back at him and nodded her agreement. "If it is that important to you, they will be under your command."

"Are you sure that's a good idea, Madam Gardener?" whispered Gruening.

"Not now, Mr. Gruening!" she said abstractly, without taking her eyes from Jalanopi.

Gruening instantly fell silent.

"Now," continued Violet, "in exchange for our help, and as an act of friendship, you will cede sole mining rights on Karimon to the Spiral Arm Development Company."

"I appreciate your coming to my aid in this minor skirmish with my enemies," answered Jalanopi. "It is truly an act of friendship—" he paused, "—but hardly one that is deserving of my entire mineral wealth."

"We are prepared to pay for what we get."

"I am listening," said Jalanopi.

"First, for the sole right to mine your world, we will give you two thousand more weapons, the highest-powered projectile rifles yet invented by the race of Man," said Violet.

"What of your *other* weapons?" asked Jalanopi.

"Other weapons?"

"The ones Man Andrew has told me about, and that my advisor Paratoka saw when he visited your Republic: laser rifles, sonic pistols, molecular imploders."

"We are forbidden by law to give such weapons to members of any race that has not officially joined the Republic," she answered. "But I think you will find our help and our weapons quite sufficient to your needs." She paused. "In addition, we will give you five thousand credits on the first day of every month, for as long as we remain here."

"They do not yet possess a calendar, Madam Gardener," interjected McFarley.

"How do they determine the seasons?" she asked.

"The long rains and the short rains."

"Tell him that I will give him twenty-five thousand credits on the first day of the long rains and on the first day of the short rains, for as long as Men continue to take minerals out of his hills."

McFarley did some quick mental computing and stared at her. "That's a very small drop in a very large bucket," he said.

"Are you the translator or the negotiator?" asked Violet irritably. "Tell him what I said."

McFarley translated her offer.

"What is your opinion, Man Andrew?" asked Jalanopi.

"It is a drop in the bucket."

"I do not understand."

"It is not enough."

"How much should I demand."

"A million credits before each rain," said McFarley. "The problem is, you've nothing to spend it on."

"I will find something," said Jalanopi, his lips parting. "Oh?"

"Do not the Canphorites manufacture weapons also?" he asked.

McFarley turned back to Violet and relayed Jalanopi's counter-offer.

"*You* had something to do with this," said Violet disapprovingly.

McFarley stared at her without answering, and she continued: "For one thing, they only have three fingers on each hand. I find it highly unlikely they would have developed a decimal system, and without it, how would Jalanopi come up with such a nice, round number?"

"You're a very quick study, Madam Violet," acknowledged McFarley with a wry smile. "It took me almost a month before I realized how they counted things." Suddenly the smile vanished. "You haven't responded to his counter-offer yet."

"Believe it or not, Reverend McFarley, I have no wish to be your enemy or Jalanopi's," said Violet. "Tell him I agree to his terms and will pay him one million credits or its equivalent on the first day of each rain."

"Its equivalent?" said McFarley quickly. "In what—horse manure, chlorine tablets, granite?"

"You are a very distrustful person," said Violet. "This is a bad trait in a Man, and an especially bad trait in a man of the cloth. I will pay the agreed-upon sum in Republic credits or its equivalent currency."

"What's the catch?" asked McFarley.

"There's no catch. I am willing to write all this down in our treaty with Jalanopi. In fact, my investors will insist upon it. All agreements must be documented; I am sure you will be happy to represent Jalanopi if he does not read Terran."

"I will."

"I further assume that the Tulabete have no written language?"

"That is correct."

"Then you will tell him I agree to his terms, and that we will create a document and both sign our names to it. There will be four copies of this treaty. He will keep one copy, I will keep one copy, one copy will remain with the Spiral Arm Development Company, and one copy be filed with the Bureau of Alien Affairs on Deluros VIII."

McFarley presented the proposition to Jalanopi.

"It is the best deal you're going to get," he added on his own. "I think you had better accept it."

"Where are these documents?" asked Jalanopi, looking around, not quite sure what a "document" was.

"They will be created in Madam Gardener's ship once you have agreed. Then she will return, we will go over the treaty line by line and word by word so that there can be no misunderstanding, and then, if both sides are in agreement, you will each put your mark upon each copy."

"And she is bound by the laws of Men to obey the treaty?" asked Jalanopi.

"That is correct," said McFarley.

Jalanopi parted his lips again and emitted a high, hissing sound that McFarley couldn't interpret.

"I am bound by my laws, too," he said at last. "But between us there is a difference: I *make* my laws, and I can change them at my will," he said at last. "This female has much to learn, Man Andrew."

"I get the distinct impression that this female has almost nothing left to learn," said McFarley grimly.

He conveyed Jalanopi's agreement, the human party returned to the ship for an hour, and when they returned they had with them the documents that would legally empower the race of Man to begin mining the mineral wealth of Karimon.

Jalanopi made his mark on the treaties, Violet signed them, and then Paratoka and various humans, including McFarley, signed as witnesses. Before sunset Violet Gardener and her party were on their way to the nearby world of Belamaine and a call had been sent out for five thousand members of her security forces to be transferred from Goldstone to Karimon.

And nothing would ever be the same again.

Nine

It was officially the Spiral Arm Development Company
Security Force, but it quickly became known as The
Column—and an impressive column it was, stretching for
almost three miles.

Jalanopi had gone out to survey the situation on his
northern frontier for himself and had brought McFarley
along to translate. He did not like what he saw and immediately sent for Linus Rawls.

"Man Linus," he said harshly, "I demand an explanation. We agreed to the presence of five thousand Men.
There are at least thirty thousand here, and my advisors tell
me that there is an equal number marching to the south
against the Rakko."

"If you'll read the treaty carefully, as we did," answered
Rawls easily, "you'll see that we promised to provide a
security force of five thousand men, and so we did. There
are three thousand here, prepared to do battle with the
Fani as soon as their orders come through, and two thousand more to the south of us, ready to secure Jalanopi's
kingdom against the Rakko."

"I tell you there is a minimum of thirty thousand soldiers

here!" insisted McFarley, without waiting for Jalanopi to reply.

Rawls looked out across the broad savannah, where his men were encamped for the midday meal.

"You are mistaken, Reverend McFarley," said Rawls. "There are only three thousand members of the security force here. All the rest are functioning as support, not soldiers."

"What's the difference?"

"Only the soldiers will do the actual fighting," replied Rawls. "That was our agreement, and we intend to keep it to the letter. The rest of these men are drivers, cooks, doctors, supply clerks, and the like. Many of them aren't even armed."

"And two or three days from now, when you've defeated the Fani and the Rakko, they all become miners, is that it?"

"Oh, I would think some of them will become farmers," drawled Rawls. "If I were you, I'd be more worried about the battle lasting more than two days."

"With *your* armaments?" said McFarley with a contemptuous laugh.

"We haven't made contact with the Fani yet," noted Rawls. "Our best information is that they're almost two hundred miles north and west of here, and that they're beating up Jalanopi's forces pretty badly."

"When will you meet them in battle?"

"As soon as we're ordered to," answered Rawls. "Read your treaty."

He went off to the mess tent to order lunch.

"You foresaw this, Man Andrew?" asked Jalanopi, when McFarley had explained the gist of the conversation to him.

"Not quite," answered McFarley. "I knew they were duplicitous. I just didn't know what form it would take."

"*I* foresaw it, when they allowed Men to come under my command," said Jalanopi.

"I'm afraid there's not much you can do."

"I can order them to attack."

"I don't know their codes," replied McFarley. "And you may be sure everything will be scrambled."

"What does that mean?"

"It means I can't radio orders to them."

"They are right here," said Jalanopi. "I will give them orders, and you will translate."

"I do not think they will obey you," said McFarley.

"They *must.* It is in their precious treaty. Summon Man Linus; he will support me."

"I doubt it."

"Are you my friend or my enemy?" demanded Jalanopi.

"I am your friend. You know that."

"Then summon Man Linus."

McFarley went off to the mess tent and returned with Rawls.

"What can I do for you, Jalanopi?" asked Rawls pleasantly.

"Bring me the highest-ranking officer among all those present," ordered Jalanopi.

"This is a security force, not an army," answered Rawls. "We don't have officers."

"You are playing with words," said Jalanopi. "Bring me the soldier who commands all the others."

"Certainly," said Rawls. He summoned a stocky, bearded, gray-haired man, who walked over and snapped to attention. "Jalanopi, this is Chester Michaels, the man you wished to speak to."

"Man Chester," said Jalanopi, "you are aware of the treaty I signed with Man Violet?"

"I haven't read it, but I know the gist of it, sir," replied Michaels.

"You know that your army is under my control?"

"I don't have an army, sir," answered Michaels. "I have a security force."

"It is the same thing. You are under my command."

"That is my understanding of the situation, sir," said Michaels.

"Then I order you to attack the Fani."

"Certainly, sir." Michaels looked around the barren savannah. "Where are they, sir?"

"They are to the north and west!"

Michaels shaded his eyes and looked northwest. "I don't see anything, sir."

"They are two hundred miles away," said Jalanopi.

"I'm afraid I'll need a more exact location then that, sir," replied Michaels. "Two hundred miles to the north and west is too vague. It encompasses literally hundreds of square miles, sir."

"Are you refusing my order, Man Chester?"

"Absolutely not, sir," said Michaels. "If you'll pinpoint the enemy's location, I will be happy to lead an attack against them."

"You have machines that can locate them."

"That is true, sir," said Michaels. "They are currently under your command. If you would like to examine them, sir, and thereby locate the enemy, the attack can proceed immediately."

"I cannot read the machines, and while Man Andrew can operate a radio, he tells me that he does not possess the necessary codes."

"Well, that does present a bit of a problem, sir."

"I order you to give him the codes."

"That would be a breach of security, sir. Reverend McFarley is neither a Tulabete nor a member of our force. I would be happy to give the codes to *you*, sir. They are quite complex, but once you have written them down—I assume you know how to read and write, sir?—I cannot legally stop you from turning them over to anyone you choose, including Reverend McFarley."

Jalanopi waited for McFarley's translation, glared at

Rawls and Michaels through his orange cat's-eyes, worked the muscles in his face until it was covered by a clear secretion, and stalked off, followed by McFarley.

"What would you have done if he could read and write?" asked Rawls curiously.

Michaels grinned. "Even if he *did* read and write, he only speaks snake, not Terran."

"Well, enjoy your lunch and get your men ready to move," said Rawls, returning his smile. "I have a feeling that our green-skinned friend is undergoing what we in the trade call 'an agonizing reappraisal'."

"Yes, sir," said Michaels, saluting smartly and returning to the mess tent.

Twenty minutes later Jalanopi ceded control of the column to Linus Rawls, who immediately turned over all operations to Chester Michaels and his aides.

Rawls returned to Mastaboni with Jalanopi and McFarley, where he kept in constant communication with both the northern and southern segments of the column. It took exactly four days for the security forces to subdue the Rakko, and two days after that the Fani surrendered. Eleven thousand inhabitants of the planet had died, with about twice that many wounded; only four Men were killed, three of them by errant bullets from the high-velocity rifles which had been delivered to the Tulabete.

The column regrouped about fifty miles outside of Mastaboni and remained there for a month until Rawls was sure there would be no further uprisings among Jalanopi's enemies. Then the security forces returned to Goldstone, and some of their "support troops" dispersed to other worlds. The bulk of them, over twenty thousand in number, opted to remain on Karimon, filing mining claims, establishing huge farms on the vast plains to the east and west of Mastaboni, starting small businesses, or simply occupying themselves by hunting the vast array of animals that stalked the plains and hills of Karimon.

Violet Gardener returned six weeks after the war, with a treaty from neighboring Belamaine securely tucked away in her safe on Goldstone.

"How are things proceeding?" she asked as Rawls came out to greet her as she emerged from her ship.

"About on schedule," he answered. "The bad snakes have been pacified, and the good snakes are starting to get an inkling of what a credit will buy them. I think within two years' time we won't have to import any food, either; there were more would-be farmers in the column than I had anticipated. We may even be able to start exporting grain in four or five years."

"Good," she replied. "Pirelli, Doxus II, and Castlestone can always use more grain. Nothing grows there except rocks." She paused. "How is our friend Jalanopi taking all this?"

"I think he's adjusting. He is, after all, the king of all he surveys—as long as he doesn't look in any Man's direction," said Rawls with a smile. "How did things go on Belamaine?"

"A bit of a slaughter, I regret to say," answered Violet. "Still, it's in the fold, and that's the main thing. It's not much of a world, really—just endless fields filled with animals and savages, waiting for Men to come and farm it. It has none of the beauty of Karimon."

"You've only been here for a few hours," replied Rawls.

"That's not so, Linus," she said. "In fact, I was here last month. I spent a week touring the Tulabetes' kingdom with your friend Mr. Fuentes as my guide."

"I didn't know that," said Rawls, surprised.

"There's no reason why you should," she answered. "I frequently make unscheduled trips to my worlds." She paused. "Between paying for the security forces and leasing the mining equipment and purchasing the exploitation rights from the Republic, Karimon has already cost me more than two billion credits. I thought I'd like to see what I'd purchased for my money."

"And?"

"As I said, it's a beautiful world. Temperate climate, gravity just a little lighter than Galactic Standard, lovely mountains and rivers, an unlimited source of cheap labor. A Man could live like a king on Karimon, Linus." She paused. "Also, it's perfectly located—halfway between Goldstone and Earth. We can do a lot more than pillage its mineral wealth; I can see us settling and populating the entire planet."

"You *were* impressed, weren't you?" said Rawls, amused.

"Others will be just as impressed," she said confidently.

"First you've got to convince them to come here and see it for themselves," said Rawls. "Just how do you propose to do that?"

"You know that river—the one that eventually goes over Ramsey Falls?"

"The Karimona, yes," said Rawls.

"Fuentes and I followed it from the falls for almost six hundred miles," she said. "Finally we came to a lovely valley, perhaps fifteen miles in diameter, surrounded by hills on three sides, warm by day and cool by night, with the river flowing right through it."

"And?"

She smiled. "That's where I'm going to build my city."

"Your city?" he asked, surprised.

Violet nodded. "I've already designed it. There will be every attraction to appeal to the right kind of colonist: a modern hospital, theater, opera, eventually even a sporting stadium. It's in Fani country, and they're not about to protest, as long as we give them jobs and pay their leaders off with a few weapons that don't function very well."

"You're *really* going to build a city?"

"I plan to break ground next week on the very first structure."

"And what will that be?" asked Rawls.

"I've been living in offices and spaceships for a long time, Linus," she replied. "I'm getting older, slowing down. It's time I had a permanent residence. After I've built it and made it perfect, I'll build the city around it—and when I'm through with that, I'll build the whole planet around the city."

"I'll believe it when I see it," commented Rawls with an amused smile. "Me, I could spend the rest of my life here once we get the hunting concession established. But you—I just can't see you settling down in one spot after all these years."

"I'm *dying*, Linus," she said. "Oh, not very rapidly and not yet very painfully . . . but the day is not that far off when I won't have the energy to keep flitting from one world to the next looking after my interests. I'll need one world to be my headquarters."

"Why not Goldstone?" asked Rawls. "That's where all the action is these days. And from what I saw of the surveys, this world will never be able to produce metals and precious stones to equal what Goldstone is turning out."

"I've already tamed Goldstone," she replied. "And I learned a lot from it."

"And now you want to tame another world?"

She nodded. "Only this time I'm going to make it perfect."

Ten

A thens didn't look like a typical colonial town. Violet Gardener had chosen the name well, and had hired architects to match. It sprouted up from the long grasses in the valley and rapidly spread outward from a central core, white and elegant and pristine.

The animals had been the first problem. Huge Redmountains, fifteen to twenty feet high, some weighing as much as twelve tons, used the valley as a migration route. She offered Fuentes a bounty for each of them, but he was a sportsman, not a killer, and eventually she imported a twelve-man team to eradicate them from the valley.

The Redmountains, for all their size, were no serious threat to Man. They were herbivores and herd animals, gentle and trusting even as they were being decimated, and within a month some seven hundred of them were dead and the rest had deserted the valley forever.

The predators proved more bothersome. There was the Wildfang, a huge catlike creature that weighed some six hundred pounds, could sprint up to half a mile with unbelievable speed, and feared absolutely nothing. And in the evenings there were the Nightkillers, those semi-arboreal creatures that were equally at home on land or in trees. They had huge, many-faceted eyes that could see as well in the dark as in daylight, and they rarely gave any indication that they were in the vicinity before pouncing on their hapless victims. Violet lost her entire team to Wildfangs and Nightkillers during the first three months of the city's construction. The Wildfangs, especially, made a habit of lurking around construction sites and waiting for their breakfast—Men—to come to them. She was about to send for another team when Fuentes, who could not resist the challenge, came and spent another month wiping out the last Wildfangs and Nightkillers in the vicinity, adding considerably to his status as the greatest hunter of his era.

The Rivertooth and the Water Horse still posed serious problems to the Fani females, who insisted on standing waist-deep in the river while indulging in their ritual bathing or fetching water for their families. Not a week went by that a lurking reptilian Rivertooth didn't make off with some female or child, and rarely were there more than forty-eight hours between attacks on native canoes by the huge, ill-tempered Water Horses. But since Men knew enough to stay away from the river and only the Fani were lost, Violet decreed that there had been enough killing of animals and allowed the amphibians to live. She never realized that placing her city in the path of the annual Brownbuck migration would reduce the size of that particular herd from well over a million to just under five thousand in something less than a decade, but even if she *had* known, it wouldn't have made much difference to her. Athens had become her passion, and while it was being constructed all other considerations were secondary to it.

At the foot of the hills, perhaps two miles from Athens, she simultaneously constructed Talami, the natives' quarters named for the village that had existed on the same spot. She had bulldozed the old Talami to erect a new city for the Fani, a city composed of row upon row of small rectangular dwellings, neatly laid out in orderly lines, each equipped with a water source and a power source.

She tore them down a month later when none of the Fani would live in them, preferring their serpentine-shaped dwellings and burrows. Her architects studied them, tried to construct them, but never managed to produce one in which a Fani would consent to live. Eventually she simply gave up, at which time a new Talami, identical to the original Talami in almost every way, grew apace with Athens.

Three days before the four-block central city of Athens was completed, Violet received word of the first mining disaster. Seventeen Tulabete had been buried alive some two hundred feet beneath the surface when a mine wall collapsed; by the time they could be reached, those who hadn't died of other injuries had suffocated.

She flew to Mastaboni in her private aircraft and landed at the newly built airstrip, where Linus Rawls was waiting for her.

"What went wrong?" she demanded as he escorted her to a nearby groundcar. The control tower, which was surrounded by a herd of Fleetjumpers and a crowd of scruffy-looking Tulabete children, glistened new and white in the late morning sun.

"Mine collapsed," answered Rawls. "Had to happen sooner or later. Just bad luck that it happened sooner."

"Are the snakes giving you much trouble over it?"

He shook his head. "We gave five thousand credits compensation to each family."

"They accepted it?" she asked as they began passing the Tulabete's serpentine huts and burrows near the broad new road.

"A year ago they wouldn't have known what a credit was;

today you can see most of the grieving families blowing their money at the company store."

"The benefits of a monied economy," she said wryly. "How much damage was done to the mine?"

Rawls shrugged. "We won't know for a couple of weeks. There's a lot of stuff to clear out."

"Hire more snakes and work them around the clock," said Violet. "I want that mine producing on schedule."

"I don't know that we're going to get *any* snakes back to work until we can show them that the mines are safe."

She stared at him coldly. "I don't recall wording that as a request, Linus. Do whatever must be done, but get that mine operating again."

"Jalanopi may object."

"Pay him off."

Rawls sighed heavily. "We might have a little problem there. He's already figured out that the guns we gave him are virtually useless, and he knows that there's also a limited supply of ammunition. I think it's safe to say that he's not our most rabid supporter."

"He doesn't have to support us. He just has to keep from hindering us."

"I can give him more money," said Rawls tentatively, "but . . ."

"But?" demanded Violet.

"He doesn't have anything to spend it on. Most of the snakes are making next to nothing, but Jalanopi already has enough money to buy everything that's for sale on the whole damned planet." He paused uncomfortably. "We could appropriate some Tallgrazers from the Fani, I suppose."

"Do whatever you have to do," she said, closing the subject. "But get that mine up and running."

"I rather thought I'd leave it to Klein and Schindler," said Rawls. "I've got enough work of my own."

She shook her head. "*This* is your work; the hunting

concession is your reward. You are the most senior member
of my staff on this world, Linus; *you* will make sure the mine
is operational."

"But—"

"No arguments, Linus. I'm delighted that you found
something you want to do, and I'm sure it will turn a
profit—but it will have to wait its turn. The mines come
first."

"If you say so."

"I do."

The next morning McFarley stalked over to her temporary office and demanded an audience with her. She made
him wait until she had finished her breakfast and taken her
various medications, then flooded the room with soothing
music, ordered the walls to become translucent to usher in
the muted rays of the sun, and finally allowed him to be
brought into her presence.

"What can I do you for, Reverend McFarley?" she asked,
looking up from her computer.

"You can shut down your mining operation until it's
safe," he replied, brushing the dust from his outfit.

"It's safe enough now," said Violet, staring idly at the
holographs of her parents that seemed to float just above
the surface of her desk. On the wall behind her was a
framed copy of the treaty she had signed with Jalanopi, one
of the hundreds that were posted in every Spiral Arm Development Company office across the planet.

"You mean it's safe enough for the Tulabete," he shot
back caustically. "I don't see any *Men* working it."

"You didn't see any Men working before the accident,
either. The Men are there to supervise."

"The Men are here to exploit," said McFarley.

"To exploit the mineral wealth of the planet," she
agreed.

"You know exactly what I mean!" snapped McFarley.
"You hire these poor souls for a pittance, provide them

with no protection, pay off their families with another pittance when there's a disaster, bribe Jalanopi to look the other way, and continue working under the same unsafe conditions as if nothing had ever happened."

"Sit down, Reverend McFarley."

He looked around, found the only other chair in the room, and seated himself.

She stared at him for a long minute, studying his face in the muted light, and finally spoke: "You *look* like a Man, Reverend McFarley," she said. "Why is it that you continually take the snakes' side against your own people?"

"Men are not supposed to do what you're doing to these poor, primitive beings!"

"You are wrong," said Violet. "Men do precisely what I am doing. It is our destiny to achieve primacy in the galaxy, Reverend McFarley. Already we have gathered some forty thousand worlds into the fold, and more are joining us every day. Not one of them was better off before it joined the Republic."

"That's a matter of opinion."

"History will prove you wrong, Reverend," she replied, fighting back a wave of the dizziness and nausea that always followed her morning medication. "We will bring these poor unfortunates the gifts of literacy, and technology, and medicine, and eventually even self-government—but Man has spread himself too far and too thin to do it gratis. Each world must pay for itself, and Karimon will pay by providing us with its ores and precious metals."

"If your motives are so pure, why can't you wait until the mines have been made safe?"

"Because I'm not in the philanthropy business," answered Violet. "Karimon has already drained billions of credits from the Spiral Arm Development Company; it has to start showing a return on our investment."

"Rubbish! You have tens of billions of credits in your various banks. How much could waiting an extra month or two cost you? What harm is there in seeing that no Tula-bete will ever again die in an avoidable disaster?"

"I'm operating on a much tighter schedule than the Republic," she said. "This planet could be an oasis of human civilization in the vast emptiness of the Spiral Arm. Its mineral wealth and farmland could make it the premier world of this sector. I can foresee the day when Athens becomes the financial and cultural center of the entire Arm. That is my vision, Reverend McFarley, and I will bring it into being during my lifetime."

"And a month or two makes that much difference?" demanded McFarley.

"It might," she said bluntly. "I have a lot to accomplish in the Spiral Arm, and Time is always the one irreplaceable commodity."

"And what about the thousands of Tulabete who might die for this vision of yours?"

"I am not a monster, Reverend McFarley," she replied. "Of course I hope that no one dies, and I will do my best to protect them—but if a handful *should* die to achieve Karimon's destiny, then their heirs will reap the benefits that much sooner."

"How much comfort do you think they will derive from that?" he asked sardonically.

"Precious little," she admitted.

"Well, then?"

"These are not Men you are talking about," said Violet. "They are aliens who eat insects, wantonly brutalize small animals, have yet to discover the wheel or the lever, and live in burrows. Would you have them remain at this stage of social evolution forever?"

"Certainly not—but I would not *force* change upon them."

"Oh?" she said sardonically. "Then may I presume that you have not attempted to spread the word of Our Lord Jesus Christ among them?"

"That is not the same thing."

"Of course not. *You* are doing it, not I." She smiled. "I believe the word for that is 'hypocrite'."

"I resent that!" he snapped. "I am attempting to bring comfort and solace to them, not to exploit them!"

"Nonsense," she said, suddenly weary. "I have had this argument and fought this battle many times before." She waited until another wave of dizziness had passed. "Let me suggest, Reverend, that in all the time you have been here, you have not made a single convert."

"No, I have not," he admitted defensively.

"Has it occurred to you that this is because they do not share human values?"

"They share a desire to live," said McFarley. "That is enough."

"To live, and to eat, and to procreate," said Violet. "So do the beasts in the field and the insects that the Tulabete feed upon."

"There is a difference," said McFarley. "The Tulabete are intelligent beings."

"No, Reverend McFarley," said Violet firmly. "They are *sentient* beings. As we bring them the benefits of human civilization, we will turn them into intelligent beings. We will teach them to *use* their minds, to read and write, to work with sophisticated machines, to run an economy that is acceptable to other societies, and to farm their land rather than ignore it."

"You are trying to turn them into something they are not," said McFarley.

"I am turning them into something they would have eventually become without our interference," said Violet. "And I will save them untold generations of ignorance and suffering and disease." She paused again. "I will turn them into a race that will live its potential lifespan. Before we arrived, there was not a wheel on the entire planet; I will turn them into users of tools, so that eventually they need never perform the kind of labor to which you object so strongly. They are totally without power: electric, solar, fusion, or any other kind; I will create dams and power sources so that the most remote village will have light at night." She looked across her desk at him. "And once I have done these things, maybe *then* you might have more success convincing them that our God is worth worshiping."

"I'm not sure that you and I worship the same God," said McFarley.

"I can live with that if you can," replied Violet.

"I don't know if *they* can," he said.

"I know a little something about them," said Violet. "Karimon was *not* Eden when you arrived, and you did not find a bunch of innocents living in a state of grace. They go to war, they kill and torture their enemies, they worship half a hundred gods. They are not a batch of Adams and Eves waiting for us to leave so that they can return to lives of peace and innocence." She paused and stared at him. "Their society has been evolving slowly, but it has been coming closer and closer to what we would term civilization each day. All I am doing is speeding up the process."

"By swindling them out of their natural resources and appropriating their land?" demanded McFarley.

"No one is swindling anyone, Reverend McFarley," she replied calmly. "We have paid their government for the right to establish our mines, and we have appropriated no land that was under cultivation."

"It was *their* land nevertheless—and as for paying their government, you have taken a completely unsophisticated leader and paid him a pittance to let you pull billions of credits out of his land."

"We have a treaty, Reverend McFarley," responded Violet. "If you feel it was unfair, why didn't you inform Jalanopi of your objections?"

"He had no choice, and you know it," McFarley shot

back. "If he hadn't signed, he'd have been overrun by the Fani and the Rakko, and you'd have dealt with them."

"Then you agree that he's better off for having signed the treaty."

"He'd be better off if you had never landed on Karimon."

"I doubt it," said Violet. "He'd probably have been killed by an enemy or a subordinate in the next year or two, and even if he survived, he'd spend the rest of his life sitting beneath that ridiculous tree wrapped in a blanket and making pronouncements that had no effect five miles away. I have made him the richest and most powerful snake on the planet, and as long as he continues to abide by the treaty, he will remain so."

McFarley struggled to keep his temper in check. "You've got all the answers, haven't you?"

"No, Reverend McFarley," she replied. "Only God has all the answers. All I have is a dream that I plan to realize."

"No matter what the cost."

"I expect it to show a profit."

"You don't know what I'm talking about, do you?"

"I know precisely what you are talking about," she said. "Do you think you're the first Man who has turned his back on his own race and tried to thwart me? Eventually most of them have come to the realization that what I am doing is for the good of both Men and aliens."

"Well, this is one man who will never agree with what you're doing," he said firmly.

"Doubtless you would have preferred to see Karimon become a satellite of the Canphorite empire."

"I would have preferred that neither Men nor Canphorites exploit Karimon."

"One or the other was bound to."

"I don't know why," he said stubbornly.

"Then you are a fool." Violet got to her feet. "And I have

already spent enough time listening to your foolishness. This interview is over."

"You won't reconsider your decision?"

"If a member of your congregation—assuming you ever *have* a congregation—were to collapse and die in the heat of religious fervor, you wouldn't stop doing God's work, would you? Well, I won't stop doing Man's work."

"You haven't heard the last of this," promised McFarley.

"I'm sure I haven't," replied Violet. "But perhaps, before we speak again, you will take a long look in a mirror. You are a Man, Reverend McFarley, as much as you may wish you weren't. You may be tolerated by the snakes, but you will never be one of them. You do not look like them, you do not think like them, you do not share their values or even their gods. What possible good can come of denying your own humanity? Whether you approve of them or not, changes are coming to Karimon. It will become a modern world, a working member of the Republic. You can make the transition from savagery to civilization easier, or you can make it more difficult, but you cannot stop it." She paused and stared at him once more. "I'd like you to think about that before we have our next conversation."

She dismissed him with a wave of her hand and went back to conversing with her computer. After lunch, she received assurances from her engineers that the collapsed mine could be reopened the next morning and she took her private plane back to Athens, where she checked into the one room of the hospital that was already operational for her monthly blood transfusion.

She floated above the floor on her airbed, one tube carrying her own blood to an atomizer while another delivered a fresh supply of the life-extending fluid into her veins. She marveled, as she always did, that medical science had kept her alive and functioning this long, at the same time wondering what demons within her could so pollute this fresh blood that within four weeks it would be as useless and diseased as that which was now being drained from her. McFarley, she decided, would call it the curse of ambition. She preferred to think of it as the price of greatness. From time to time she wondered whether time would prove her or McFarley correct, or whether her condition was simply the result of an indifferent God in an indifferent universe.

She was always surprised when she emerged from the transfusion feeling weak rather than vigorous with her renewed blood supply, and she elected to recuperate in solitude at the small cottage she had built for herself, overlooking the Ramsey Falls.

She arrived in late afternoon, spent the few remaining hours of sunlight strolling through the countryside accompanied by a trio of bodyguards, then returned to the cottage, where her personal chef had prepared her dinner. Later, under the light of Karimon's two moons, she sat on the raised porch outside her front door and watched as huge Redmountains and majestic Twisthorns and light-footed Fleetjumpers came down to the Karimona River to drink. The air was cool and crisp and clear, and she felt, for a pleasant few moments, as if she were the only person on the planet.

She spent two days and two nights at the Falls, renewing her depleted energies, and was fully prepared to spend another week there before returning to Athens.

Then she received a message from Rawls that jolted her back to reality.

Eleven

"Strike?" she repeated. "They don't even know what a strike *is!*"

Rawls' holographic image hovered above her computer, looking more annoyed than worried.

"They do now," he replied wryly. "I have a feeling that a certain gentleman of the cloth has been giving them a crash course in labor relations."

"That man is getting to be more trouble than he's worth," she said grimly. "Place him under house arrest and restrict him to his quarters while we get this situation sorted out."

"On what charges?" asked Rawls.

"Find one and make it stick."

"He hasn't broken any Karimon laws, and human laws don't apply here."

She was silent for a moment as she considered the situation. Finally she made her decision.

"Put the whole place under martial law," she said. "Send for the security force from Athens to back you up. I'll let them know the request is coming through; they can be there in three hours." She paused. "Arrest McFarley for breaking some violation. Treat him with courtesy, and make sure he's comfortable, but keep him isolated. I don't want him talking to any of the Tulabete."

"I'll need some legal basis for declaring martial law," noted Rawls.

"The basis is planetary security. We have received word that the Canphorites may attack at any moment. And of course, we can't have them disrupting our production of vital material for the war effort, so you have the authority to conscript all able-bodied snakes and put them to work in the mines."

"I'd hate to defend this in a Republic court," remarked Rawls.

"The Republic has nothing to do with this," answered Violet. "Karimon isn't a Republic world. It is an independent planet that has signed a treaty with a private company."

"What if there's resistance?"

"There won't be."

"But if there is . . . ?"

"Then take Jalanopi into protective custody, and do the same with any other snake that has the authority to call a strike. Treat them with every courtesy, but don't let them near any of their people." She paused again. "I'll be there sometime tomorrow to take charge."

"Maybe you'd better stay where you are," said Rawls, "or go back to Athens. Things could get ugly here."

She shook her head. "They haven't had time to organize," she replied. "Remove Jalanopi and McFarley and you'll find that there won't be any trouble." She grimaced and added, "*This* time."

Twelve

The strike lasted for three days.

The Tulabete, who didn't quite know why they had to work in the mines in the first place, seemed equally unaware of why they suddenly had to stop. Rawls jailed the five who seemed to be the ringleaders, though he was sure they were taking their orders from Jalanopi, then shut down all the services that the Tulabete had grown used to. When this didn't have the desired effect, he had his security forces take one hundred Tulabete males to the mines, and released them only when they had produced their day's quota. The next day he took two hundred, the day after that three hundred, and since there were less than six hundred able-bodied males in the area, the strike was virtually over.

He waited another week to make sure there were no further problems, then released Jalanopi and the ringleaders with a stern warning that further agitation would result in further confinement.

Two days later he paid a visit to McFarley's church, where the Reverend had been held incommunicado since the strike began. A guard let him in, and he found McFarley sitting on the steps leading up to the pulpit, reading a bible in the dim light that filtered in through the high windows.

"Good morning, Reverend McFarley," said Rawls.

"What are you doing here?" said McFarley suspiciously.

"I bear glad tidings," said Rawls with a smile. "The state of emergency is over, and Mastaboni is no longer under martial law. You're free to go."

"You broke the strike," said McFarley. It was not a question.

"Strike?" repeated Rawls. "What strike?"

"Don't play games with me," said McFarley. "I was confined to my church because of the strike in the mines."

Rawls frowned. "I don't know what you're talking about, Reverend. You were confined for your own safety because of a very real threat of invasion by the 5th Canphorite Fleet. Fortunately, the Republic's Navy was able to frighten them off."

"How long did it last?"

"They just turned away this morning, so I would estimate that we were in a state of emergency for twelve days."

"You know what I mean," said McFarley irritably. "How long did the strike last?"

"You keep mentioning a strike," said Rawls. "There was a mild disturbance when the mine collapsed, but everyone was back to work just as soon as the mine could be reentered. I have nothing but admiration for the grit and determination of your parishioners."

"What about Jalanopi?"

"I give up," said Rawls. "What *about* Jalanopi?"

"Is he alive?"

Rawls chuckled. "Of course he's alive. He's probably eating bugs beneath that stupid tree of his. You're welcome to visit him."

"This isn't the end of it, you know," said McFarley, getting to his feet and brushing some dust from his clothing.

"I tend to agree with you, Reverend," said Rawls. "You

never can tell when the Canphorites will threaten us again. We'll simply have to remain in a state of preparedness."

"Where's Violet Gardener? I want to speak to her."

"She's in the hospital at Athens," answered Rawls. "I'm told it's nothing serious. I'm sure she'd be happy to speak to you once she's released. That will be sometime tomorrow morning, I believe."

McFarley looked around the church. "You say I'm free to go now?"

"We'd never keep you against your will," Rawls assured him.

"You just did, for the better part of two weeks."

"That was for your own safety, Reverend," said Rawls. "*You* may think you're a snake, but we know better, and Men always protect their own."

"How comforting," said McFarley caustically.

"I'm glad you appreciate it, sir," said Rawls.

"Are my movements to be restricted in any way?" asked McFarley.

"Absolutely not, sir. You are free to go wherever you please."

"Including off the planet?"

"Certainly. We have no desire to keep you on Karimon." Rawls paused. "In fact, it might be better all the way around if you were to leave. You were doing noble work here, sir, but it's time to turn it over to the experts."

"Thank you, Mr. Rawls," said McFarley, making no attempt to mask his dislike of the man. "Then if you will step aside, I'd like to go outside."

"I can drive you to your ship if you like, sir."

"I think I'd like to visit my friend Jalanopi first," answered McFarley. "If I find you've harmed him in any way, I have every intention of reporting it to the Bureau of Alien Affairs on Deluros VIII."

"That's certainly your privilege, sir," said Rawls. "If

Jalanopi tells you he was physically mistreated, I will personally seek out and punish the man responsible for it."

McFarley seemed about to say something else, thought better of it, and walked down the aisle and out of the church. Rawls nodded to the guard at the door, who stepped aside to allow the Reverend to pass by.

"Follow him," said Rawls. "I want to know every place he goes and every snake he sees."

The guard saluted and left, and Rawls, wondering if he would *ever* get a chance to sit beside a fire and plan the next day's hunting, put through a call to Violet Gardener.

"How are you feeling?" he asked as her image, surrounded by a sterile hospital environment, appeared over his computer.

"I'll be all right," she replied, displaying an arm that was attached by tubes and wires to half a dozen sleek new machines. "We've got a new medic here from Earth who specializes in exotic blood diseases, so he's doing some tests."

"Can he cure you?"

She shook her head. "Nothing can cure me, Linus. But possibly he can see to it that I don't tire so easily. There's a lot of work still to be done, and I can't live on amphetamines forever." She shrugged. "That's neither here nor there. Why have you contacted me?"

"I released McFarley twenty minutes ago."

"And?"

"He's talking about leaving the planet. I don't like it. Men like him don't give up that easily."

Violet frowned. "I agree."

"What do you think he's up to?"

"I don't know."

"Do you want me to keep him here?"

"No," she said with a sigh. "He'll just foment more trouble, and eventually we would have to do something very unpleasant to him."

"He's meeting with Jalanopi right now. I can't imagine he's going to talk the snakes into another strike, not after we broke the first one so easily."

"No, he's brighter than that," agreed Violet. "He's got something else in mind."

"The Bureau of Alien Affairs?" suggested Rawls.

"I doubt it. We're developing a primitive planet and we haven't harmed anyone. The mining accident was just that—an accident. They'd back us to the hilt."

"But does *he* know that?"

"If he doesn't, he should."

"Maybe this is his first alien planet."

"I'm sure it is," said Violet. "Men like McFarley, they decide they're all that stands between alien Edens and human corruption, and they become more alien than the aliens they're misguidedly trying to help. Once they land on a planet, they stay there."

"Well, then, what do you want to do?" asked Rawls.

"I suppose we'll just have to wait. The next move is up to him." She frowned. "Time is so precious. If there's one thing I hate, it's *waiting*."

"Perhaps it won't be too long," he reassured her.

And it wasn't.

Thirteen

S even uneventful weeks and two blood transfusions
later, Violet Gardener was summoned from her house
in Athens to Mastaboni.

"What's up?" she asked Rawls, when she was finally able
to raise him from aboard her private plane.

"The other shoe just dropped."

"Explain yourself, Linus."

"McFarley's back, and he's got a couple of high-level
officials from Deluros VIII with him. They've been speaking to Jalanopi all morning."

"Who are they?"

"No one that we've dealt with before. A man named
Willis Gaunt, from the Bureau of Alien Affairs, and a
woman named Katherine Njobe from the Department of
Cartography." He paused. "I ran a check on them, and
they're legitimate."

"Have you any idea what they've got in mind?"

"None . . . except that we're probably not going to like
it much."

"I *already* don't like it," she said. "If the Republic is
willing to accept all these worlds we've brought into the

fold, you would think they'd finally be willing to let us simply do our job, instead of constantly throwing obstacles in our path." She sighed wearily. "All right. I'm due to land in less than an hour. Have someone there to meet me."

"I'll meet you myself."

"No," she said. "I want you to stay at your computer. Find out everything you can about Gaunt and Njobe. Where they've lived, where they were employed before they got their current jobs, if any complaints have been filed against them. See if you can run a financial check, too."

"You're not giving me a lot of time," he said.

"Do what you can," she replied, ending the connection and silently cursing her one true enemy, Time. Jalanopi, McFarley, these bureaucrats, the entire Spiral Arm, all were nothing but irritants. But just as Rawls had a limited amount of time to probe for weaknesses with his computer, so, too, did she have a limited amount of time to pursue her vision. The blood tests had shown some promise, but it would take more time—her nemesis again—to study the results, to create a formula, to effect a change in her condition.

And the Republic which she was trying to serve was the greatest waster of time. If it didn't assimilate Karimon today, it would do so tomorrow, or next year, or next century. She felt like the ephemeral servant of an eternal master, which, if it blinked its eyes, would miss the entirety of her lifetime. The only way to prove she had existed at all was to make a mark, leave something behind so people would know that Violet Gardener had been here, had lived and breathed and *accomplished* something with her brief span of years.

She was still dwelling on such thoughts as her plane glided in for a gentle landing, then accelerated and shot skyward at the last moment.

"What's the matter?" she demanded.

The pilot looked back at her and grinned. "Horndevils

on the runway. This isn't exactly Earth or Sirius V. The sound of the engine scattered them; we won't have any problems on our next approach."

She looked out the window as a dozen of the huge, two-ton beasts lumbered off in fright. *Before I die, I will look out at this same spot and see nothing but cultivated farmland, land that will feed the millions of Men who will emigrate here to make their lives and their fortunes.*

The plane touched down, one of Rawls' assistants escorted her to a groundcar, and a few moments later they reached Mastaboni, which had changed considerably in the two months since she had last seen it. The human community, formerly a row of assay and claims offices and a pair of hastily erected rooming houses, now comprised three long blocks, with stores and restaurants and a pair of small hotels lining the main street, and perhaps three hundred quickly erected geodesic domes forming an adjacent residential area. There was even a small office building, and some entrepreneur had set up a groundcar dealership next door. Eight or nine large, substantial homes were being constructed half a mile away, overlooking the river. The embryonic human city was still surrounded by miles and miles of empty, uncultivated scrubland, an occasional Fleetjumper or Twisthorn still wandered through the streets, and it hardly compared to her spotless, shining Athens, but the sight of it comforted her nonetheless. Change was movement from one point in Time to the next, and when you stopped moving, so did Time.

"I've lost my bearings," she said. "Where is Jalanopi's tree?"

"About three miles downriver," said her driver. "They're not going to leave that damned tree, and nobody wanted to live next door to them, so the town kind of developed right here. We don't go among the snakes unless we're invited, and they don't come here. Works out just fine all the way around."

"Well, I've been invited. Let's pick up Linus and pay Jalanopi and his guests a visit."

They walked to a small shop, not yet opened to the public, that displayed a vast array of hunting gear and weaponry in its windows. The door scanned them, identified them, and slid back to allow them inside, where Rawls sat behind a small desk.

"How are you feeling?" he asked.

"Annoyed as hell," she answered.

He grinned. "Okay, you're fit for duty. Let's go." He got up from his desk and led her out to a groundcar, leaving his assistant behind.

"What did you manage to find?" asked Violet as they left the new city behind them and headed south.

"So far, not much," answered Rawls. "They seem to be exemplary civil servants. If there's any hint of impropriety, I haven't been able to find it yet. Of the two, I'd watch out for Gaunt."

"The Alien Affairs representative?"

Rawls nodded. "He seems to be a passionate advocate of alien causes, and he's got a hell of a legal staff behind him."

"What about Njobe?"

"She's been in Cartography for sixteen years. I still don't know what the hell she's doing here."

"Well, we'll find out soon enough," said Violet.

Halfway there Rawls had to stop to allow a small herd of Redmountains to finish crossing the road.

"They're awesome, aren't they?" remarked Violet, staring at the huge beasts. "I can't imagine why you and Fuentes take such pleasure in killing them."

Rawls made no answer, and after another moment they were once again speeding along the road. A few Tulabete children waved at them as they went past, and soon they came to a halt some fifty yards from Jalanopi's tree.

Jalanopi himself, wearing his ceremonial headdress, sat

upon his wooden throne, flanked on one side by Andrew McFarley and Paratoka, and on the other by Willis Gaunt, a slender man dressed in a dust-covered white outfit, and Katherine Njobe, a smallish woman with short black hair and a much more sensible khaki garment.

Rawls helped Violet out of the groundcar and accompanied her to the little group, then stood aside as she came to a halt directly in front of Jalanopi.

"Good morning, King Jalanopi," she said. "I understand that you wish to speak with me."

"I will let others speak for me, Man Violet," answered Jalanopi in broken Terran. He gestured toward the two emissaries of the Republic. "These are Man Gaunt and Man Njobe."

Violet turned to face them. "Welcome to Karimon," she said. "I trust you will enjoy your stay."

"We do not plan to remain here very long, Madam Gardener," said Gaunt, his diction precise and clipped. "We are here for business, not pleasure."

"There is no reason why you can't combine both," replied Violet. "Karimon has many scenic wonders, and if you are a sportsman, I'm sure Mr. Rawls can arrange a hunting or fishing vacation for you."

"I am afraid not."

"Then perhaps we can at least entice Miss Njobe to sample the beauties of our world," said Violet pleasantly.

"May we get down to business, Madam Gardener?" said Gaunt. "It is precisely to determine whose world this is that I have come all the way from Deluros VIII."

"I could have sent you a copy of our treaty and saved you the voyage," said Violet. She turned to Katherine Njobe. "Might I ask what a representative from Cartography is doing here?"

"All in good time," said Gaunt. "Miss Njobe and I have agreed that I should speak first."

"As you wish," said Violet with a shrug.

"Some weeks ago, Reverend Andrew McFarley visited the Department of Alien Affairs with some disquieting information," said Gaunt.

"That's not surprising," replied Violet. "Reverend McFarley finds most things disquieting. I suspect it goes with his profession."

"Please let me continue," said Gaunt severely. "Reverend McFarley brought to our attention the fact that you had conscripted native labor to work in your mines, and—"

"They are not *my* mines," Violet interrupted him. "They are the property of the Spiral Arm Development Company."

"Of which you are the majority stockholder," he replied.

"Nor were any Tulabete conscripted," she continued. "Everyone who works in the mines has been paid, and the Spiral Arm Development Company can produce records to prove it."

"Let us cut straight to the heart of the matter," said Gaunt. "A mine collapsed, the laborers refused to work until their safety could be guaranteed, and you incarcerated Jalanopi, Reverend McFarley, and five members of the Tulabete community. Do you deny that?"

"Certainly I deny it," answered Violet. "Karimon was under threat by a Canphorite fleet, and Jalanopi was placed in protective custody for his own safety, as was Reverend McFarley."

"And the other five?"

"Suspected Canphorite sympathizers. They were released as soon as the threat was over."

"On what authority did you declare martial law?" continued Gaunt.

"The treaty that Jalanopi signed with the Spiral Arm Development Company gives us the authority, in fact the duty, to protect his people and assure his continued sovereignty."

"Reverend McFarley says that Jalanopi was manipulated

into signing this treaty because you interfered with the internal politics of Karimon, and that had he not signed it, his nation would have been defeated by other nations that you yourself had armed. Jalanopi supports Reverend McFarley's explanation."

"Jalanopi had no objection to that treaty when it was all that stood between him and military defeat," answered Violet. "I don't see any reason why it is invalid now."

"Madam Gardener, it is invalid because my department has ruled it to be invalid," said Gaunt. "I only wish I had held my current position when you bludgeoned Goldstone into accepting your terms. I have reviewed that treaty, and unfortunately it is too late for me to disallow it, but I promise you that I cannot and will not allow you to subjugate or exploit either the Tulabete or any other alien races. Do I make myself perfectly clear?"

"You make yourself perfectly clear, but I do not think you established a legal basis for your actions," replied Violet. "I have a legal treaty that was signed by both myself and Jalanopi, and the fact that he no longer wishes to abide by it does not make it any less legal."

"That is a matter for the Department of Alien Affairs to decide."

"No, Mr. Gaunt. If anything, it is a matter for the courts to decide. I have been this route before, on both Doxus II and Sugarmoon, and I assure you that the courts will support our right to be here."

"I have reviewed your entire career, Madam Gardener," said Gaunt. "In the cases of Doxus II and Sugarmoon, you had the support of the Bureau of Alien Affairs. I assure you that this is no longer the case."

"Your support has always been welcome, but it is hardly necessary," said Violet. "I repeat: I have a valid, legal treaty with Jalanopi."

"Not as of this moment," said Gaunt sternly. "If you wish to go to court to reverse my ruling, you are certainly free to. The Bureau will fight you every step of the way. I should imagine it will take the better part of thirty years to get a reversal, perhaps longer—*if* you get one at all. If I were you, I would channel my efforts into helping aliens rather than exploiting them."

"Mr. Gaunt," said Violet, "pardon my bluntness, but you are a desk-bound bureaucratic fool. I *am* helping to elevate the natives of those worlds controlled by the Spiral Arm Development Company—and I am doing it without bombing them into submission, as the Republic has done on so many other worlds. I have not installed a puppet government—another favorite Republic ploy—and I have not found it necessary to appeal to the Navy to support the handful of Men who have emigrated here. I am doing what your cherished department *ought* to be doing, and I resent your blind, hostile ignorance as much as your illegal interference. Have I made *my* position perfectly clear?"

"Your position was clear to me the first time you exploited the innocent natives of the first world you set foot on," said Gaunt with open hostility. "It is the conclusion of the Department of Alien Affairs that you manufactured the conditions that led Jalanopi to sign the treaty with your company, that you willfully misled him about the extent of the powers the treaty allowed you, that you broke a legal strike of native workers, and that you illegally incarcerated one Man and six Tulabete, including King Jalanopi, to further your company's financial gain." He stopped for breath and stared directly into her eyes. "The treaty is invalid. You have legal recourse if you wish to pursue it, but until such time as my decision is reversed in a court of law, you will be criminally libel for any action you take on Karimon based on rights granted to you by the treaty." He paused. "I will allow all Men one month to make their personal accommodations with King Jalanopi or leave the planet." He turned to Jalanopi. "Is that acceptable to you, King Jalanopi?"

"Yes, Man Gaunt," said Jalanopi, who had been listening to McFarley's translation of the conversation, his own comprehension of Terran not being up to the task.

"I ask you, Madam Gardener, not whether you agree with my ruling, but whether you understand it?"

"I understand it," said Violet.

"And will you abide by it?"

She stared at him without saying anything.

"I repeat," said Gaunt. "Will you abide by my ruling?"

"I don't answer insulting questions," said Violet. She turned to Katherine Njobe. "What has the Department of Cartography to do with all this?"

"We have been speaking as if Jalanopi is the ruler of the entire planet," said Njobe. "But this is not the case. He is the king of the Tulabete, but there are other nations here as well. When Cartography was informed of the Bureau of Alien Affairs' ruling, we were instructed to create a map delineating the various nations on Karimon." She paused, and smiled uncomfortably. "The Republic realizes that you have a considerable investment on Karimon and suggests that you might wish to make an accommodation with one of the other nations rather than abandon the world entirely." She shifted her weight uneasily. "Such an accommodation would of course require the approval of the Bureau of Alien Affairs."

Violet smiled in amusement. "That's the Republic for you," she said. "While they're letting Mr. Gaunt and his department slap my right hand, they're telling me to dig in with my left and save them the trouble of conquering Karimon fifty or seventy years from now."

"In essence," agreed Njobe.

"It's a moot point," interjected Gaunt. "Given your prior record, I think I can guarantee that my department will look with disfavor upon any treaty you may sign with any alien race. There has been no complaint from the neighboring world of Belamaine, and so we are not free to inter-

vene there, but before I leave here this afternoon you will
be given an official edict requiring the Spiral Arm Development Company to submit all future treaties to the Department of Alien Affairs before they can be enacted." A smug
smile crossed his face. "I hope you are satisfied with the
empire you have built upon the shoulders of oppressed
alien races, because it will extend no farther."

"We shall see," said Violet. She turned once again to
Katherine Njobe. "How long will your work require you to
remain here, Miss Njobe?"

"Perhaps three days, possibly four," she replied. "My
understanding of the political structure of Karimon is that
the actual borders are in a state of constant flux. I will
create a broad generalized map to which the the various
nations agree and then station two members of the Department of Cartography on Karimon to refine it. Hopefully,
with the aid of the various local governments, they can
create a definitive map within half a year."

Fat chance, thought Violet. *Not a one of these snake rulers
has ever even seen his boundaries.*

Aloud, she said, "I have an apartment in Mastaboni and
a house in Athens. They are at your disposal for the dura-
tion of your stay here."

"Thank you," she said.

"I will provide you with a guide for the Tulabete's country, and will supply you with a security team for those
borders that are not considered secure."

"That is most generous of you, Madam Gardener."

"We have no disagreement with the Department of Cartography," replied Violet. "In fact, I hope you will join me
for dinner in Athens prior to your departure."

"If I have the time."

"Mr. Gaunt, have we any further business to discuss?"

"We have not," said Gaunt.

"Then, if you don't mind, I'll take my leave of you." She

turned to McFarley. "Are you satisfied, Reverend McFarley?"

"Totally," replied McFarley with a triumphant smile.

"Good," she said.

"What are you staring at?" he asked.

"I just want to make sure I remember that smile," she replied pleasantly.

Then she turned and walked back to her groundcar.

Fourteen

V iolet flew back to Athens as soon as the meeting was over and summoned Rawls there the next morning. He arrived at her newly completed mansion just before noon and was ushered into her private office. It was decorated with certificates and citations from the Republic, holographs of herself in the company of both human and alien leaders, and various awards she had won for her accomplishments over the years. The holographs of her parents sat on her desk, and floating some four feet above the floor was a three-dimensional display of the Spiral Arm. Those planets she had opened and brought into the fold glowed a brilliant green, those she still needed to assimilate to bring her dream to fruition blinked a bright blue at regular intervals.

She sat behind an imported desk made of shining alloys, her various computers and vidphones hidden from sight.

"Much nicer than your office at Mastaboni," said Rawls, surveying his surroundings. "I don't see the treaty, though."

"It's invalid, in case you've forgotten already," she said wryly.

"I haven't," he replied. "Do you mind if I sit down?"

"Please do," she said, as he commanded a chair to float over to him. "I trust that Mr. Gaunt has taken his leave of us?"

"Yesterday."

"Good. I have developed a serious dislike for him."

"I have a feeling that it's mutual."

"Doubtless," she agreed.

"Well," said Rawls after a brief silence, "what's our next step?"

"We're certainly not going to go to court," she replied. "I couldn't afford the time even if I were in perfect health and assured of twice my normal lifespan."

"I suppose we could just ignore the ruling," suggested Rawls. "I can't imagine that the Navy would actually be ordered to attack Men who are developing an alien world."

Violet shook her head. "That's stupid, Linus," she said. "We're dealing with a fanatic who has the support of one of the most powerful departments in the government. He'd make it a point of honor for the Navy to do just that." She snorted contemptuously. "Hell, it might even catapult him to elective office. I'd hate to have *that* on my conscience."

Rawls chuckled. "You just might have a point there." Suddenly he leaned forward, serious again. "So what *do* we plan to do?"

"We plan to obey Mr. Gaunt's edict to the letter."

"You're not seriously considering leaving the planet," said Rawls firmly. "I know you better than that. You've never backed away from a fight in your life."

"Who said anything about leaving?" replied Violet. "Karimon is my home now. I plan to live out my life here, hopefully in peace and tranquillity."

Rawls leaned back comfortably. "You've got it all figured out. I knew it wouldn't take you a whole day to come up with a solution." He paused. "What's our plan of attack?"

"What would *you* do, Linus?" she asked.

"Me?"

She nodded. "One of these days there's going to be a crisis while I'm in the hospital or visiting some other world. You've been with me longer than any of the others. I'd like to think you can get your mind off killing helpless animals long enough to take charge if you have to."

Rawls shifted in his chair and considered his options. "Well, you can't appeal to Gaunt," he said. "That's obvious. And McFarley would sooner dance on your grave than help you across the room. That leaves Jalanopi." He paused, frowning. "But you've got to cut him loose from McFarley, and you've only got a month to do it."

"That's right."

"Wait a minute," he said. "There's Katherine Njobe, too. She's still on Karimon." He frowned again. "But what the hell can *she* have to do with anything? She's just a map-maker."

She turned to stare at her display of the Spiral Arm. "Linus, Linus," she said wearily. "It's as plain as the nose on your face, or the horns on one of your trophy animals. *Think!*"

He lowered his head in thought for a moment, then looked up. "I'm sorry. I was a little slow today, wasn't I?" He smiled. "It doesn't have a damned thing to do with mapmaking. It was her offer, right?"

"Certainly."

"That's what stumped me for a minute. There isn't a damned thing worth pulling out of the ground up in Fani country."

"You know it, and I know it . . ." said Violet, returning his smile.

"But Jalanopi doesn't know it, and neither does McFarley!" concluded Rawls triumphantly. "So we sign another treaty, this time with the Fani, and we make a lot of noise and fuss about moving our whole operation up there. We close down the company stores and the native infirmary, we shut off the power, we do everything we can to make Jalanopi think that he's lost our money, our weapons, everything, to the Fani."

"I think it should work," said Violet. "The Republic practically begged us to stay."

"There are a couple of problems," said Rawls. "Even if Jalanopi wants us back, there's no way the Department of Alien Affairs will okay any new agreement you sign with him." He paused. "And after what Gaunt said, I don't see how you're going to slip a treaty with the Fani past him."

Violet smiled. "There's a big difference between signing a treaty with the Fani and letting the Tulabete know we are *willing* to sign it." She paused. "As for Jalanopi, why would we want to sign a treaty with him?" she continued with false innocence. "We'll be hellbent on moving our base of operations to Fani, remember? Jalanopi's caused us a lot of trouble with our own government; we're not going to give him so much as a credit."

Rawls looked puzzled. "Then I don't quite see . . ."

"Put yourself in Jalanopi's place, Linus," she said. "He'd like us off the planet, but we're not leaving. Furthermore, we're about to spend all our money with the Fani. Not only don't his people know how to locate or work a mine without instruction—and McFarley isn't the one to tell them how—but even if they managed to pull some ores out of the mines we've already started, they have no market for them. We own the only spaceships on Karimon, and McFarley wouldn't begin to know where to go to get a price for anything they wanted to sell." She paused. "All right. You're Jalanopi, and you know all this. You see the Fani becoming rich and powerful, and your own mines deserted by the one race that could reestablish your primacy on the planet. What would you do?"

"I'd look for an investor," said Rawls. "A human investor."

"Right."

"But there aren't any. McFarley doesn't have any money, and everyone else on the planet works for us, or spent everything they had to emigrate here."

"Wrong," she said.

He stared at her curiously. "Who am I missing?" Then, suddenly, he grinned. "Will she do it?"

"*You* ran the financial check on her," said Violet. "What do you think?"

"Katherine Njobe: thirty-seven years old, unmarried, spent her whole career in Cartography," recited Rawls. "Net worth: seventy-two thousand credits."

"Not much to show for fifteen years, is it?" suggested Violet. "Especially if I can show her a way to make a million credits in one month."

"Sounds good to me," said Linus. "How do we work it? Set up a dummy corporation in her name, filter a few million credits into it, have her pay it to Jalanopi as a show of good faith for signing a new treaty . . ."

"And then have her sell us the rights she's purchased," concluded Violet. "She'll have a legally binding treaty with the Tulabete, and we will deal directly with her corporation and not with Jalanopi at all, thereby obeying Mr. Gaunt's dictum to the letter."

"What if she says no?"

"Then I will gently explain to her that I will fly to Goldstone and return with the first Man who *doesn't* say no, and the only difference is that someone else will make a million credits that could have been hers."

Rawls lit a smokeless cigarette and shook his head sadly. "That poor snake," he said at last. "He'll never figure out what's happened."

"He'd be a poor snake if we let the Republic run us off the planet," Violet corrected him. "I'm going to make him the king of the most powerful country on a major planet. If he'd thought things through and stopped listening to fools like McFarley and Gaunt, he'd realize that he's much better off with us than without."

"I wonder . . ." said Rawls.

"What do you wonder?"

"If he wasn't happier before we arrived. Maybe his kingdom was just a tree and a patch of barren ground, but his word was law and he took orders from no one."

"Of course he was happier before we arrived," she said irritably. "Just as Men were happier when all they had to do was fill their bellies and keep warm and dry. They didn't have neuroses, they didn't fight wars, they didn't worry about nonessentials." She paused. "But on the other hand, they lost more than half their children in infancy, they succumbed to every disease that came around, they had no language, no history, no art—and they were hunted by everything that was bigger and stronger. They may have been happier, but they weren't better off. You learn to take the bad with the good, Linus."

"I suppose so," he agreed. "But it does lead to another question."

"Oh?"

"Which are we—the bad or the good?"

"That all depends," said Violet.

"On what?"

"On who writes the history books."

Fifteen

Two weeks had passed when Linus Rawls drove up to Jalanopi's tree, got out of his car, and walked over to where the Tulabete king and the human minister were awaiting him.

"Good morning, Jalanopi," said Rawls, bowing his head slightly. "Morning, Reverend."

"I had rather hoped we had seen the last of you, Mr. Rawls," said McFarley distastefully.

"Well, that's what I'm here to speak to you about," said Rawls easily. He turned to Jalanopi. "I know you've been learning Terran. Are you comfortable enough with it for me to speak directly to you, or would you rather have Reverend McFarley translate?"

"You may speak to me, Man Rawls," said Jalanopi. "If I do not understand, I will ask Man Andrew."

"Fine," said Rawls. "Let me know if I'm going too fast for you."

"I will do so." Jalanopi stared at Rawls out of his orange cat's-eyes. "Why are you here, Man Rawls?"

"I'm here to talk a little business with you," replied Rawls, pulling a large Antarrean cigar out of his tunic and lighting it.

"We are not required to do business with Violet Gardener or her Spiral Arm Development Company anymore," interjected McFarley heatedly. "I thought that Mr. Gaunt of the Department of Alien Affairs made that quite clear."

"I'm no longer working for her," said Rawls. "I'm here on my own behalf."

"A falling out among thieves?" suggested McFarley.

"Let's say a reassessment of goals," answered Rawls. "She has hers, I have mine."

"I do not wish to deal with *any* Men," said Jalanopi.

"Oh, I think you do," said Rawls, unperturbed. "I very much think you do." He shrugged. "But if you don't want to listen to me, well, that's your problem. Thank you for your time, and I'm sorry to have bothered you."

He had started to leave when Jalanopi said, "Wait."

McFarley turned to Jalanopi. "Why have you stopped him?" he asked in the Tulabete dialect.

"Let us hear what he has to say," answered Jalanopi. "I do not like his attitude. He seems very sure of himself."

"You do not have to listen to him," warned McFarley. "Remember: we have the Department of Alien Affairs on our side."

"True," said Jalanopi. "But it cannot hurt to listen. I want to know why he speaks with such confidence." He turned to Rawls. "I will hear your proposal, Man Rawls," he said in Terran.

"Thank you," said Rawls. "I don't suppose it's any great secret that I want to set up a safari company on Karimon. I had taken some tentative steps in that direction before our little contretemps two weeks ago." He paused. "I'd still like to start my company, and I'd like to lease the area that you call the Baski Plains."

Jalanopi understood the gist of it, but turned to McFarley for a precise translation.

"What is that to me?" he answered at last. "I am not required to enter into any transactions with you."

"Hear me out," said Rawls. "I am prepared to pay you a fee of one hundred thousand credits, renewable annually, as well as ten percent of my gross profits. This is not a treaty, as Reverend McFarley will tell you. It's a straight business deal. The land will remain yours; all I want is the exclusive right to hunt on it."

"I am not interested in what you want, Man Rawls," said Jalanopi, "nor do I trust you."

"Look," said Rawls, "if it's Violet Gardener you're worried about, I'll agree to a stipulation that none of her people will be allowed to cross the Baski Plains."

"They are leaving in twelve more days," interjected McFarley. "Why would they want to cross the Baski Plains?"

"Hadn't you heard?" asked Rawls. "She's moving her operations to Fani."

McFarley and Jalanopi exchanged surprised glances.

"No," said Jalanopi. "We had not heard."

Rawls nodded. "Yeah, she's pulling everything she's got out of Mastaboni—every Man, every machine, every generator. I guess she's got to leave you the roads, even if there won't be any vehicles here to use 'em."

"She cannot treat with the Fani," said McFarley. "Mr. Gaunt assured us of that."

"Mr. Gaunt is cooling his heels back on Deluros VIII," Rawls pointed out. "Besides, I think she took his warning to heart. She's offering the Fani a much more favorable treaty. Something like fifty million credits a year, free hospitals and schooling, more weapons than you can shake a stick at—weapons that *work*, not the kind she foisted off on the Tulabete—and she's agreed to pay the miners a hell of a lot more than she was paying them here." He paused. "She's had a couple of weeks to cash in a batch of political favors she's owed back on Deluros. My understanding is that she went over Gaunt's head and has gotten the Bureau of Alien Affairs' approval." He stared at McFarley and Jalanopi in open surprise. "You really didn't know?"

"This is the first I've heard of it," said McFarley, frowning.

"How many weapons?" asked Jalanopi.

Rawls shrugged again. "I don't know. Twenty, thirty thousand. Maybe more."

"Why have you left her service?" demanded McFarley suspiciously.

"Despite what you may think, we parted on friendly terms," answered Rawls. "She's a driven woman; she won't stop until she's put together her string of worlds in the Spiral Arm, and she'll die before she's finished. I took a long hard look at the situation one day and realized that I'm *not* a driven man. I have enough money to live comfortably for the rest of my life, and it suddenly occurred to me that I'm nearer the end than the beginning. It's time to start enjoying the fruits of my labor, and during the time I spent hunting with Fuentes, I discovered what I enjoy the most."

"Then why start a safari business? Why not just go out and hunt for the rest of your life?"

Rawls smiled. "I may not be a driven man, but I'm not a *stupid* man, either. I haven't the skill or the reputation to get contracts from the huge Republic museums like Fuentes can, but I see no reason why I shouldn't make a profit on my hobby if I can."

There was a momentary silence, which was broken by Jalanopi.

"What of Athens?" he asked. "She cannot move an entire city to Fani country."

"You're not dealing with some amateur," said Rawls. "This is Violet Gardener we're talking about."

"What's your point?" asked McFarley.

Rawls grinned. "Since she couldn't move Athens to Fani country, she moved Fani country to Athens."

"I do not understand," said Jalanopi.

"The Fani border was officially moved two hundred miles south last week, and somewhere out there is a Republic mapmaker who's about five million credits richer than she was the last time you saw her."

"I don't believe you," said McFarley.

"I have copies of the map in my office back in Athens, with the Department of Cartography's seal on them," said Rawls. "I'll have one sent to you."

"That's illegal!" shouted McFarley.

"Since it falls within the domain of the Department of Cartography, it's perfectly legal," replied Rawls. "Oh, you could challenge it in court, or get Mr. Gaunt to do it for you, but Katherine Njobe can tie it up for as long as Gaunt can tie up the treaty. We'll all be dead and buried before any of it gets resolved."

"Then I will go to war and reclaim my land," said Jalanopi.

Rawls looked amused. "With what? The weapons you've got will kill more Tulabete than Fani."

McFarley stared at him for a long minute. "Why have you told us all this, Mr. Rawls?" he asked at last.

"Because you asked, and because it's in my best interest that you realize I'm the only source of Republic credits you've got. If Jalanopi wants to buy weapons, or bring back any of the conveniences his people have grown used to before they get annoyed with him for sending Violet Gardener away, you might as well deal with me."

"We have much information to evaluate," said Jalanopi. "I will give you my answer in ten days."

"I'm afraid I'll need it by tomorrow," said Rawls, deciding the time had come to bait the hook and dangle it before them. "I have a partner who's anxious to move quickly. If we can't get a hunting concession here, we'll have to deal with the Fani or the Rakko." He paused. "I'd much prefer the Baski Plains. Fuentes says it's the best hunting area on the planet."

"Who is your partner?" demanded McFarley. "Violet Gardener?"

"I told you before," said Rawls. "I am no longer associated with Violet Gardener."

"Then who is it?"

"I don't suppose there's any harm in telling you," said Rawls, after pretending to weigh the question for a moment. "It's Katherine Njobe. She saw no reason to keep working on salary after her little windfall last week, and she wants to invest her money on Karimon. *I'm* perfectly willing to wait ten days, but she's never had this kind of money before, and as the old saying goes, it's burning a hole in her pocket. She wants everything to get started yesterday." He paused and smiled. "You know, the crazy thing is she doesn't even *like* hunting. Thinks it's immoral to go around shooting animals for anything but food. But she wants her money to start working for her, and she doesn't like the thought of being one of Madam Gardener's minority stockholders." She chuckled. "Probably afraid Violet will find some way to do to her what she did to the border."

"I see," said McFarley thoughtfully.

Rawls looked at both faces, human and alien, trying to hide their thought processes from him, and decided that his job was done.

"I've got to go back to Athens and close out some accounts—it's my last official act as a Spiral Arm Development Company employee—and I probably won't be able to get back until tomorrow evening," he said. "Katherine is due to land at Mastaboni later this afternoon. Since she's putting up the bulk of the money, and she's the one who knows the exact dimensions of the Baski Plains, she's empowered to finalize an agreement with you."

"We will consider meeting with her," said Jalanopi.

"Fair enough," said Rawls. "We've had our differences in

the past, but I'm sure you'll see that my business proposition can benefit both of us. I look forward to a long and prosperous relationship with you."

"We shall see," said Jalanopi.

"Just consider the alternatives," said Rawls. "That's all I ask."

As he drove back to the airport, he was certain they were doing just that: considering the alternatives. And long before Katherine Njobe arrived, they would realize that the only alternative to becoming an economic and military backwater while the Fani were prospering through their mythical treaty with the Spiral Arm Development Company was to make the best deal they could with the cartographer.

It was not the first time in his life that he felt a twinge of sympathy for anyone who was foolish enough to stand in the path of Violet Gardener's dream.

Sixteen

On the 183rd day of the year 1826 G.E., Jalanopi, king of the Tulabete, signed an agreement giving Katherine Njobe's newly formed Karimon Development Corporation limited farming and homesteading rights and unlimited mining rights to the kingdom of the Tulabete, as well as a hunting concession in the Baski Plains, in exchange for a fee of five million credits per annum to be paid in perpetuity to Jalanopi and his heirs.

On the 186th day of the year 1826 G.E., the Spiral Arm Development Company purchased one hundred percent of the stock of the Karimon Development Corporation, including all of its assets and liabilities, for the sum of one million credits, and Katherine Njobe was given a seat on the board of directors of the Spiral Arm Development Corporation.

On the 304th day of the year 1826 G.E., Katherine Njobe submitted her maps of Karimon and the neighboring world of Belamaine to the Department of Cartography.

On the 316th day of the year 1826 G.E., the Department of Cartography approved Katherine Njobe's recommendation that the names of Karimon and Belamaine, the sister planets that specialized in mining and agriculture, be changed to Rockgarden and Flowergarden in honor of Violet Gardener, whose efforts on behalf of the Spiral Arm Development Company had brought so many new worlds into the Republic's eager embrace.

And Violet Gardener was two steps closer to the realization of the dream that burned so fiercely within her.

III

FUENTES'
GLORY

Seventeen

Fuentes, his rifle cradled in his arms, crawled across the sunbaked ground, trying to ignore the sweat that rolled down his forehead and into his eyes. After he had progressed some five yards he stopped and peered ahead once more.

The small herd of Brownbucks was still grazing about forty yards ahead of him. Twelve—no, make that eleven females, nine of them with young, and one male. About three hundred yards to his left were another half dozen males, bachelors who were biding their time until one felt capable of challenging the herd bull.

He wished they would all go away.

Because one hundred yards past the herd was his prey, a huge Redmountain that had so far remained unaware of his presence. It was a magnificent beast, standing fully fifteen feet at the shoulder, covered with coarse reddish hair, its long narrow ears tight atop its head, twitching constantly, listening for danger. The eyes—small, blue, distrusting, peeking out from beneath the rudimentary horns on its forehead—weren't of much use to it, but it was said those ears could hear a bush rustle a mile away. And the huge nostrils, set at the end of its enormous, oblong head, could smell water from fifty miles away.

The Redmountain had no natural enemies, not until the natives of Rockgarden had developed weapons, but it was almost as if Nature had anticipated this, for no animal on the planet was better equipped to pinpoint danger, and none was so quick to flee from it.

Which, concluded Fuentes, was what made them worth the effort in the first place. Merchants within the Republic paid good money for the horns, which were then transformed into jewelry . . . but Fuentes had more than enough money. It was the challenge he craved, and that was why he hunted Rockgarden, as he had hunted Peponi and Serengeti and a dozen other worlds before he had landed on this one.

He really should have been out dispatching a family of Blue-and-Golds, those oddly striped herbivores of the northern plains, to fill a commission for the Natural History Museum on Far London. In fact, he had a lot of commissions still to fulfill, but Bandakona, his tracker, had spotted this particular Redmountain late yesterday afternoon, and he had dropped everything else to go after it.

Slowly, carefully, he withdrew a small cloth bag filled with cigar ashes from one of his many pockets and tapped it gently, then watched the ash float gently past him, away from the Redmountain.

Fuentes sighed. The wind was right, the sun was so bright that the Redmountain couldn't tell him from a tree stump, not at this distance . . . but if he stood up, he would panic the Brownbucks, and the second they took off the Redmountain would flee into the nearby thornscrub. It wouldn't hide him, but it wouldn't have to: no Man could keep up with a Redmountain, and only a hunter with a death wish would walk alone into the shoulder-high bush, where he'd be at the mercy of any carnivore that chose to stalk him. There was no visibility, no room to maneuver, too many chances of hanging himself up on the six-inch thorns.

He put the ash bag back into his pocket, then froze as the Brownbuck bull suddenly raised its head and stared in his direction. An insect crawled up his shirt, attracted by the scent of his perspiration, and bit him painfully on the side of his neck. He grimaced, but made no other movement, and after what seemed an eternity the bull went back to its grazing. Fuentes waited another ten seconds, then carefully moved his hand up to his neck, found the insect, and pulped it between a thumb and forefinger.

He looked ahead again and saw that the Redmountain's grazing was slowly taking him farther and farther away. Fuentes estimated the Redmountain's distance at two hundred fifty yards. For a moment he considered leaping to his feet, yelling to scatter the Brownbucks, and taking a quick quartering shot as the Redmountain raced off toward the thornscrub. It was possible, of course—he'd made more difficult shots in his career—but the likelihood of dropping the Redmountain with the first shot was minimal. Probably he'd have to go for a lung shot; with the Redmountain racing hell-for-leather in the opposite direction, there was too much chance of having the bullet deflected by a massive hip or leg bone . . . and even a lung shot would be unlikely to kill it before it reached the thornscrub, and then he'd have to follow it into the bush, where the advantage would be all with the Redmountain.

No, he'd just have to wait where he was, inch forward whenever he could, and hope that the Brownbucks would disperse or the Redmountain would move off in a new direction. Otherwise, it would simply be another unsuccessful hunt; he'd had hundreds before, he'd have hundreds in the future.

He looked behind him. There was Bandakona, his tracker, laying motionless some sixty yards away. The Tulabete saw Fuentes staring at him and looked at the hunter questioningly. Fuentes shook his head and motioned the tracker to remain where he was.

Then his attention was taken by the Brownbucks. Suddenly they seemed nervous and uneasy. They would graze for a moment, then suddenly look around with wild, staring eyes. The herd bull snorted a few times and walked a few steps in Fuentes' direction, its ears tight on its head, flicking constantly.

Fuentes knew that he had done nothing to alert the Brownbucks to his presence, and a quick glance back showed him that Bandakona had remained absolutely motionless. No, something else was disturbing the herd. Possibly a Wildfang or a Nightkiller in the tall grass.

Even the Redmountain was getting uncomfortable now. It bellowed, that resonant, low-pitched bellow that, once heard, could never be forgotten, and began looking around restlessly.

Fuentes noticed some sweat on the stock of his rifle and slowly, gently wiped it off with his sleeve. If there *was* a carnivore out there, and the herd suddenly broke and ran, he might, just might, be able to get off two aimed shots before the Redmountain made it to the thornscrub.

Then the Redmountain looked straight in his direction, bellowed again, turned on its heel, and raced off. An instant later the Brownbuck raced off after it.

"Fuentes!" cried a voice, and he turned to see a Tulabete racing across the flat dry grass toward him.

"Damn it, Bandakona, what the hell got into—?"

Fuentes stopped, puzzled, as Bandakona stood up, looking every bit as disgusted as the hunter.

"Fuentes!" cried the running Tulabete again, and now Fuentes could see that it was Ramaloki, one of his camp attendants.

Fuentes stood, hands on hips, and waited for the Tulabete to reach him.

"You'd better have a damned good reason for frightening off that Redmountain," he said at last.

"Message you," panted Ramaloki, who had only recently mastered a very rudimentary Terran.

"It couldn't wait?"

"Big message. Very important."

"All right. What is it?"

"You come back to camp, you see and hear."

"Why don't you just tell me?"

"Can't. Violet Gardener not to confide."

"Violet Gardener?" repeated Fuentes. "Are you sure?"

"Yes. Very sure."

Fuentes sighed, slung his rifle over his shoulder, and began the two-mile walk to where he had parked his groundcar. Once there, he waited until Bandakona and Ramaloki climbed onto the roof—their favorite seating area—and followed the barely discernible track back to his camp, which had been pitched in a small clearing beside a stream. Three of his assistants were working on skins he had taken the day before, scraping the insides with knives to remove the last vestiges of flesh and fat, and his cook, a native with an unpronounceable name from a tiny tribe that was distantly related to the Fani, started making a pot of coffee the instant his groundcar arrived.

A small, slight woman was sitting on a chair in front of his bubble tent, and he had to stare at her for a moment before he realized that it was Violet Gardener. She had lost some thirty pounds from her stocky frame in the three years since he had last seen her, and she now supported herself with a cane. Her hair was almost totally white.

"Good morning," she said. "I'm sorry to disturb your hunt, but it's imperative that I speak to you."

"I'm always happy to speak to you, Madam Gardener," said Fuentes, handing his rifle to one of his bearers, who took it off to clean and oil it. "Shall we go into my bubble?"

She nodded, turned with some difficulty, and had barely

reached the entrance before he caught up with her and helped her through.

"Won't you sit down?" he asked, pulling up a chair for her.

"Thank you," she said, seating herself gently and breathing an exhausted sigh.

"I almost didn't recognize you," said Fuentes.

"Incurable blood diseases will do that to you," she replied wryly. Suddenly she smiled. "At least I don't have any trouble keeping my weight down these days."

"You don't look well, Madam Gardener," said Fuentes. "Whatever you have to say, you could have done it via our camp video receiver. You didn't have to come in person."

"I think I did," she replied. "I have a proposition to put to you, and I cannot take No for an answer."

He eyed her warily. She may have been old and weak and sickly, but she was still Violet Gardener.

"How long have you been out here in the wilderness?" she asked, returning his stare.

"Four or five months," he said. "Possibly six. Time doesn't have much meaning out here. I get into Athens during the rains, to ship out my trophies, deposit my commissions, and pick up new assignments."

"But for all practical purposes, you just stay for a few days and then come out to the bush again?"

He nodded, wondering what was coming. "That's right."

"So you're not aware of the political situation."

"*Is* there a political situation?" he asked. "I thought you secured the rights to exploit Rockgarden almost six years ago."

"I did."

"Well, then?"

"We have a problem on our hands," said Violet, shifting painfully on her chair, trying vainly to find a comfortable position.

"The Republic?" asked Fuentes. "Most of my contacts on Deluros VIII are dead or retired."

She shook her head. "The problem is right here on Rockgarden," she replied.

"Who's causing it?"

She sighed again. "Part of our agreement, the operative part that allows us to function here, is that we have been paying Jalanopi an obscene amount of tribute each year for the right to mine and homestead his land."

"He's demanding more?"

"No."

"Well, then?"

"He wants all Men to leave Rockgarden immediately."

"He did that once before, and it didn't work."

"Before, he hadn't spent twenty million credits on Canphorite weapons," noted Violet grimly. "He's got a fully equipped army. They've taken over some of our outposts on the Rakko border."

"How big an army?"

"Who knows? At least thirty thousand, possibly four times that many, not counting collaborators and fifth columnists in every native village."

"All right," said Fuentes. "You've got an armed native uprising on your hands. I'm sorry to hear about it. But why does this concern *me*? I live out here in the bush; I didn't even know what was going on until you informed me."

"Fair question," acknowledged Violet. "Straight and to the point." She paused. "I want you to take command of our armed forces."

Fuentes laughed. "Me? I've never spent a day in uniform in my life."

"That's not important."

"Then why are you joking about it?"

"I'm not joking. We need a hero to rally around, and you happen to be the only hero we've got."

"Why don't you just do the reasonable thing and ask the Republic to send the Navy?" said Fuentes.

"We could," admitted Violet. "But once you let the Republic in, it's damnably hard to make them go away again." She shook her head. "No, we have the manpower and the weaponry to put down this uprising. What we need is a bona fide hero that Men want to follow, a hero who will inspire them to do what they have to do."

"I'm no hero," protested Fuentes. "I'm just a hunter."

"You are a hunter with four best-selling books circulating through the Republic. They've written two biographies of you, and even made a syndicated holo show of your adventures. They've—"

"Those weren't *my* adventures," interrupted Fuentes. "Some scriptwriter dreamed them up."

"It makes no difference," said Violet firmly. "They're yours now." She paused. "You have been honored on Earth and Deluros VIII. One of your hunting companions was Johnny Ramsey, the most popular Secretary the Republic ever had. There's not a man on Rockgarden who doesn't know your face. You're T. J. Fuentes, the greatest hero on Rockgarden, maybe in the whole Spiral Arm, and you're the man I want for the job."

Fuentes spent a moment considering his reply. "I'm flattered, Madam Gardener," he said at last. "But I don't know the first thing about military strategy."

"You think Jalanopi does?" she shot back.

"At least he knows his territory."

"So do you," said Violet. "Better than any Man. Perhaps even better than Jalanopi himself."

"I'm not qualified to command men in battle."

"Then I will surround you with officers who are, and you can rely on their advice. But I need *you* to rally the people and lead our men into battle."

"And if I say no?" he asked.

"Then we'll lose an outpost a day, and our colonists will

be tortured and killed, until I can find someone else to lead us."

"How many colonists have we lost so far?"

"Thirty-seven."

"That's not very many."

"I know," said Violet. "But I want you to know *how* they died."

She handed him a trio of cubes, each with a holograph taken at the scene of the carnage. Fuentes, who had seen death every day of his adult life, winced as he stared at the first two and returned the third without looking at it.

"When and where do I report for duty?"

"Tomorrow morning, at Government House, in Athens."

"I'll be there," he promised.

Eighteen

Fuentes sat in his bubble, examining his weaponry: laser pistol, sonic pistol, plasma rifle, molecular imploder.

He shook his head sadly. If there were four less sporting weapons in existence, he didn't know of them. He missed his projectile rifle, just as he was sure he would miss the *thunk!* of a bullet striking home.

He sipped his coffee and studied the map once again. No one knew quite where Jalanopi was, but Paratoka, Jalanopi's most trusted advisor, had the main body of Tulabete forces encamped on the Karimona River, about eighty miles north of the Ramsey Falls. It was good terrain for them: heavily forested, too damned hilly for Violet's engineers to have gotten around to building roads yet, lots of meals on the hoof, plenty of water, a couple of hundred villages where any wounded snakes could find aid and succor.

The problem was, he didn't know *why* they were there. There were no human habitations within forty miles, and the snakes had no vehicles. They were hundreds of miles from Mastaboni, almost a thousand miles from Athens.

Whenever he hunted a new world, he always gave himself a few months to study his prey, to learn how it thought, before going out with rifle in hand to take his trophies. But now he had eight thousand Men under his command, almost a third of the human population of Rockgarden, and they—and Violet Gardener and the politicians—were itching for battle, hungering for a victory to brag about.

He looked out the open entrance of his bubble, at the hustle and bustle of the encampment. There were so many Men! It made him uneasy. He was used to being virtually alone, accompanied only by an alien camp staff, neither knowing nor caring what day of the week it was, or even where he was. For more years than he cared to think about, his life had been structured around two necessities: a source of water and a source of trophies. He begrudgingly carried a video transmitter, but he had never once sent a message on it; he used it only to receive the rare transmission from civilization.

And now he was surrounded by officers awaiting his orders, by farmers and miners turned soldier who had probably been handling these strange weapons all their lives, by radio and video operators who were in constant contact with Athens and Mastaboni, by a small army of chefs and orderlies who were required to tend to the larger army that looked to him for leadership.

How had it happened? One moment he was lying on his belly in the dry grass, waiting for a clear shot at a Redmountain, and then suddenly he was a commanding general, wondering not only why he and he alone was qualified to lead his Men against Jalanopi, but also what Jalanopi had gone to war for in the first place. Normally taciturn, he had become positively close-mouthed. Normally given to a drink before supper, he now consumed almost a pint of alcohol each evening. Normally given to walking twenty and thirty miles under the blistering sun of Rockgarden, he now rode in the back of his command vehicle, surrounded by officers and communications equipment that were more alien to him than the Redmountains and Wildfangs that he hunted.

A uniformed man entered his bubble, stood before him, and saluted smartly.

"Yes?" he said.

"Colonel Marston requests permission to speak to Commander Fuentes, sir."

Fuentes sighed. "Then just say, 'I want to talk to you, Fuentes,' " he said. "And skip the salute. And the sir."

"But—"

"You know I'm the boss here, don't you?" asked Fuentes.

"Yes, sir."

"And I know you know it. And there's no one else around to impress. So forget the pomp and ceremony and just tell me what's on your mind, Mr. Marston."

"Yes, sir . . . ah, yes, Fuentes," said Marston with an expression of disapproval.

"That's better. Now let's have it."

"We caught a Tulabete spy about three miles from here, sir," said Marston. "We thought you might like to be present for questioning."

Fuentes nodded and got to his feet. "Where is he?"

"It's a she," said Marston, stepping aside as Fuentes walked past him and out into the open. "We've got her in the guardhouse." He paused. "We haven't been able to get a word out of her yet."

"Let's go," said Fuentes, turning to his left. He walked with the same easy, ground-eating stride he had developed over the years, and Marston had to trot to keep up with him.

When he reached the guardhouse, two soldiers saluted him, and one opened the door of the lightweight titanium structure for him. He stepped inside, waited until his eyes became accustomed to the poor light, then turned to Marston.

"Where is she?"

"Cell number three, sir."

"Open it."

Marston walked to the third cell and hit the combination that caused the door to slide into the wall. Seated on the chair was a female inhabitant of the planet, her jaw swollen, her left eye blackened and shut. Her hands were cuffed behind her, and she sat on a small, uncomfortable stool.

"Turn her loose," said Fuentes.

"You mean take off the cuffs, sir?" asked Marston.

"I meant what I said. Take her back to where you found her, set her free, and give her our apologies."

"But, sir—"

"Look at the tattoos on her legs, and at the totem on her necklace," snapped Fuentes. "Can't any of you fools tell a Fani from a Tulabete?"

"She's a Fani?" asked Marston, surprised.

"Of course she's a Fani. *That's* why she wouldn't talk to you. She doesn't understand the Tulabete dialect."

"But she looks just like a Tulabete!" said Marston defensively.

"And you and I probably look alike to her," said Fuentes.

"How will I convey our apologies to her, sir?" asked Marston.

"Take my personal chef along with you," said Fuentes. "He speaks some Fani."

"Yes, sir," said Marston, saluting.

"And Colonel Marston," said Fuentes.

"Sir?"

"Next time, *look* first. We're here to fight the Tulabete. We don't need a war with the Fani, too."

Marston took the Fani female by the arm and left without another word, and Fuentes, dreaming of empty places and silent nights, returned to his bubble, opened his bottle a few hours earlier than usual, and poured himself a tall drink.

Nineteen

I t was an hour before dawn when Fuentes gave the signal to halt.

The woods were silent, all the predators having fled before the approach of his army. He gave the signal to his chief lieutenants, who began dispersing in a huge semicircle. Suddenly a Tailswinger screeched, and one of the soldiers instantly silenced it with a sonic pistol.

Fuentes checked his timepiece. Marston's men should have positioned themselves about four miles to the south. He'd give his own men twenty minutes to circle the Tulabete encampment, and then he'd call for the predawn attack.

It had been worked out in minute detail by his advisors, a classic example of military encirclement. The Karimona River was running fast and deep at this time of year, and they would be attacking from three directions, with the river itself cutting off any possible retreat. Paratoka was supposed to have close to six thousand Tulabete here; a quick, decisive victory might convince Jalanopi to call off the war and sue for peace.

Nonetheless, Fuentes felt uneasy. Maybe this was the way

Men fought against each other, or against the Canphorites and Lodinites, but the Tulabete were creatures of the wilderness, even more at home in it than Fuentes himself. *He* couldn't be caught in a trap like this, and he had some difficulty believing that *they* could. Just the absence of predators' growls and coughs should have told them something was amiss, as should the fact that no avian or Tail-swinger screeched a second time.

He'd left three thousand men back at his main encampment, going through drills for the benefit of any spies Paratoka might have sent up there—*real* spies, not poor Fani females who didn't even know there was a war going on—and had come down here with one hundred boats silently riding the swift river current. One boat had capsized, one had been attacked by an enraged Water Horse, but the other ninety-eight had made it intact, and he now had a force slightly larger than Paratoka's own, and far better armed, almost in position to strike.

His advisors were manning the communication devices, making sure each unit was properly placed, and still he felt uneasy. They may have been primitives, these Tulabete, but they weren't stupid, and only stupid soldiers allowed themselves to be completely surrounded in the bush.

Still, he wasn't able to put his doubts into the form of valid objections, objections that his lieutenants would understand, and so he stood, his back against a small tree, peering ahead into the darkness, trying futilely to spot a flickering light from a Tulabete campfire.

Finally the moment came for him to signal the attack, and still he waited. It *felt* wrong, and he hadn't lived this long in the wild by not paying attention to his instincts.

"Sir?" said an advisor, crawling over to him. "Is something wrong?"

"I don't know," said Fuentes.

"The men are all in position, and it will be light in

another eight or ten minutes, sir," said the advisor. "If we wait much longer, we lose our advantage."

Fuentes waited silently for another moment, and finally nodded.

"All right," he said. "Pass the word."

"Thank you, sir."

Timepieces were synchronized, communications were passed, and ninety seconds later thousands of Men stormed the Tulabete camp.

It was deserted.

Fuentes arrived with his advisors five minutes later.

"I was afraid of this," he muttered.

"How could they have known?" said one of his advisors bitterly.

"We must have a traitor in the ranks," said another.

"We don't have any traitors," said Fuentes.

"Then how could they have known, sir?"

"The same way I'd have known."

The man stared at him, but made no reply.

Fuentes saw two soldiers approaching a hut.

"Tell those men that no one enters any dwellings," he ordered.

"But sir," said an advisor, "they may have stockpiled some weaponry in—"

The explosion drowned out the rest of his sentence, and more than one hundred Men fell to the ground. Most lay still; a few writhed weakly.

"Medic!" screamed an officer.

As the sun came up, three more dwellings exploded, and Fuentes, leaving only his explosives experts behind, ordered a retreat to the boats.

"But shouldn't we try to pick up their trail, sir?" asked an advisor.

"They're long gone," said Fuentes. "They've got a ten- or twelve-hour head start on us, and they've had time to lay a booby trap every half mile. I've lost over three hundred

Men here without even sighting the enemy. I think that's enough for one disaster, don't you?"

"Then we're just going to turn tail and run?"

"That's right."

"I request permission to take a party out after them," insisted the advisor.

"Permission denied," said Fuentes. "You and your brethren are military men, and I'm sure you know what you're doing in a conventional military situation, but you're overmatched here. As long as I'm still in charge, I'm going to do what I should have done in the first place."

"And what is that, sir?" asked the advisor sullenly.

"I'm going to fight this war the way it *should* be fought," answered Fuentes.

Twenty

F uentes leaned against the corral rail and looked at the herd of Blue-and-Golds.

"Well," asked Alex Hawkins, standing beside him.

"How many have you got?" asked Fuentes.

"Maybe a hundred here, probably four hundred more roaming the north pasture."

"And they've all been broken to bridle and saddle?"

"That's right."

"You showed remarkable foresight, Mr. Hawkins."

"Foresight, hell," chuckled Hawkins. "I took one look at your armored column when it moved through four months ago, and I knew you couldn't sneak up on a deaf man with it." He paused and lit a small, thin cigar. "So I asked myself, what are these guys gonna need if they really plan to fight the Tulabete? And I said, they're gonna need some way to approach 'em without alerting every living thing within ten miles. Well, I'd been raising Blue-and-Golds for meat—I've got a contract with a couple of restaurants, plus your pal Rawls' safari camps—and I figured, hell, they're half-domesticated anyway, so why not see if they can be broken for riding? Could be worth even more to me that way."

"It was a very smart move."

"I knew sooner or later you'd need something to ride, and I figured, well, they could import horses or some other riding animals, but they're not native to Rockgarden. Those that disease don't kill right off will alert every avian and Tailswinger around—whereas if you ride through the bush on Blue-and-Golds, animals that *belong* there, hell, none of the other animals figure to raise any kind of a ruckus at all, and you don't need to carry any special feed with you. They'll eat whatever the land's got to give 'em."

"How much are you asking for the batch?"

"Well, I've got to keep at least a half a dozen stallions and maybe sixty mares to form the nucleus of a new herd," said Hawkins. "And then I have to figure my expenses. I mean, hell, they put fifteen of my wranglers in the hospital at Athens." He lowered his head in thought for a moment, then looked up. "Twelve hundred credits apiece, in lots of fifty."

"I'll take all that you have."

"Just like that?" asked Hawkins, amused. "You don't want to argue price?"

"The government's paying for it," said Fuentes. He pulled out a pocket computer, dictated his agreement, sealed it with both thumbprint and voiceprint, and ordered it to supply a hard copy, which he handed to Hawkins. "Just transmit this to the Department of Defense at Athens. I'll need an accurate count of them before I leave, and they'll deposit the money in your account within ten days."

"When will you take them away?"

"I'll be back in an hour with my men."

"Hey, Fuentes!" called Hawkins as Fuentes walked to his armored groundcar.

"Yes?"

"I ain't got more than a dozen saddles and bridles."

"I ordered five hundred in Athens. They arrived at my camp this morning."

"Then you knew all along you were buying my Blue-and-Golds."

"That's right."

"Maybe I should have asked for more money."

"But you didn't."

Hawkins shrugged. "Well, what the hell, I sure as hell ain't gonna go broke on the deal."

Fuentes returned an hour later with a dozen Men and herded the Blue-and-Golds back to his camp. Four hundred thirty-six hand-picked men and women, each of whom had had some experience riding horses or other animals, were waiting for them. Within an hour all of the Blue-and-Golds had been saddled and mounted. A few were initially skittish, but Fuentes gave his team a full week to get used to working with their animals, and by the end of that time they were as well behaved as any cavalry mounts back on old Earth.

Each night he had one of his aides contact his base camp and find out where the enemy's warriors were located. Finally, on the eighth day, when he decided his team was ready for battle, he pinpointed the nearest of Jalanopi's armies, a force of about four thousand Tulabete that was encamped at the foot of the Tenya Mountains some forty miles to the east of him.

"Summon the troops," he ordered another aide, then went out to the center of the camp and waited for them to assemble.

"Your training period has ended," he announced when the last of them had arrived, and they were all lined up at attention. "Tomorrow morning we will ride to the Tenya Mountains, where we expect resistance from one of Jalanopi's armies. They have Canphorite weaponry, but I think we can anticipate that not one in ten of them will have mastered it, whereas you have all demonstrated proficiency with your own weapons."

He paused, and accepted a small box from one of his

aides. "Our Blue-and-Golds will allow us to traverse any type of terrain without calling undue attention to ourselves. They are of this world, and I think I can guarantee that this will not be a repeat of the fiasco that took place two months ago at the Karimona River.

"Some of you," he continued, "may question just how easy it will be to approach the enemy, even mounted on native animals. Each of you, upon returning to your bubbles, will find a box identical to this on your bunk." He held the box up, then opened it. "Each box contains an outfit identical to *this*"—he produced a form-fitting blue-and-gold–striped bodysuit—"and from this day forth, you will wear your camouflage suit at all times. I guarantee that at eight hundred yards, you will be indistinguishable from your mounts, especially since we will not be marching them in formation, and once you are closer to the enemy than eight hundred yards, I trust you will know what to do and there will be no further need for camouflage or secrecy."

There was a murmur of surprise at the sight of the outfit.

"Let me impress upon you once again that once I pass the word that we are nearing the enemy, only myself, Colonel Nichols, and Colonel Calthrop are empowered to lead the team. One of us will always be in the vanguard, and your animals will follow us at their own speed and in their own way. Should they appear in any recognizable formation, our advantage will be lost. Is that understood?"

There was a general nodding of heads.

"Are there any questions?"

"What are we to do with our prisoners, sir?" asked a young woman. "Since we've been living off the land, we don't have any provisions for them, or even any extra Blue-and-Golds for them to ride once they've been captured."

"The answer to that should be obvious," answered Fuentes. "We cannot afford to have any survivors escape and inform the rest of Jalanopi's armies that we have employed the strategy of approaching and attacking on Blue-

and-Golds." He paused and looked around at his troops. "If there are no survivors, there are no prisoners. Is there anyone who does not understand what I am saying?"

Silence.

He dismissed them then and had them awaked about an hour before sunrise. The camp was bustling with chefs and aides-de-camp and grooms rushing all over, but Fuentes got them moving by daybreak.

"We might as well find out what kind of stamina these beasts have when they're carrying full loads," he announced about a mile out of camp. "Let's take them at a trot or a slow canter for the next few miles and see how they hold up."

Within two miles even the fittest of the Blue-and-Golds were covered with lather and panting heavily.

"Well, that's that," he remarked. "They've got a fine turn of speed for a little more than half a mile, enough to take them well clear of a Wildfang or a Nightkiller, but they can't remain in motion all day like the Fleetjumpers or the Brownbucks."

He had his team dismount and walk beside the Blue-and-Golds for the next mile. Then they were back in the saddle, making their slow, easy way to the foothills of the Tenya Mountains. They didn't seem to be making much progress, but nightfall found them only ten miles from their destination.

Fuentes made each member of the team responsible for his mount. They attracted a family of Wildfangs early in the evening, but the scent of Men drove them away. A Nightkiller made a run at one of the Blue-and-Golds just before dawn and fell to the laser pistol of one of the camp guards.

They were off again just before sunrise, and Fuentes cautioned them to let their mounts graze and proceed at their own pace.

"Do you think they can see us yet, sir?" asked a female

aide when the bulk of the Blue-and-Golds were within two miles of the enemy's camp.

Fuentes nodded. "They've got to have lookouts posted higher up the mountain. Yes, they can see us all right."

"Then shouldn't we pass the word to charge?"

"No. The animals would be exhausted long before we reached our destination. Let's just let them keep grazing and edging closer." He paused. "Our only problem will come if one of the Tulabete comes out to shoot some meat for his camp."

"What do we do then?"

"Kill him as quickly and silently as possible."

But no Tulabete came to meet them, and when they were finally able to see the camp, Fuentes pulled out his sonic pistol, the predetermined sign for a charge, and a moment later more than four hundred humans, wearing striped outfits that matched their steeds, were riding hell-for-leather into the middle of the Tulabete stronghold.

Laser weapons hummed, sonic pistols destroyed with silent sound, plasma rifles hissed, and the surprised Tulabete began dropping in huge numbers. Here and there members of Fuentes' team fell to the Canphorite weapons, but the boldness of the daylight attack had caught the Tulabete by surprise, and the scene passed from attack to carnage to a simple mopping-up operation in a matter of ten minutes.

Finally silence reigned, and one of Fuentes' lieutenants approached him with the news that all but two hundred of the enemy were dead. A pair had fled up the mountain, but posed no immediate threat.

"They pose a very definite threat," Fuentes contradicted her. "We can't have them coming down after we leave and alerting the remainder of Jalanopi's soldiers to the method of our attack."

"What of the two hundred prisoners, sir?" she asked.

"I told you when we began this enterprise that we could

not afford to take any prisoners," said Fuentes. "Execute them."

"Have you any preference?"

"Preference?" he repeated, confused.

"The form of execution, sir?"

He shook his head. "Just do it as quickly and painlessly as possible."

She saluted. "Yes, sir."

He gave orders to confiscate all the Canphorite weapons, then entered his opposite number's hut, hoping to find some hint as to what they were doing here in the mountains, what their next target might be. He found nothing, but remained for almost two hours, long enough for the executions to be completed.

When he emerged he found his team's leaders waiting for further orders.

"Even the dead can inform the living," he said. "I want you to turn your molecular imploders on the corpses until there's nothing left of them. Then do the same to the huts and all other signs that there was ever an army or a battle on this spot." He paused. "You," he said to one of his aides, "get me my rifle."

"You mean your plasma weapon, sir?"

"I mean my *rifle*," said Fuentes.

She returned with it a moment later and handed it to him. He took it from her, thrilling to the feel of it in his hands after all these months.

"I should be back within two days," he said. "Set up camp out on the savannah about ten miles west of here and wait for me."

"Where are you going, sir?"

"Up there," he said, jerking his head toward the mountain. "There are two Tulabete up there, remember?"

"It's a huge mountain, sir."

"I'll find them," he replied confidently.

"They may be armed."

"I hope so," he said, walking toward the mountain, rifle in hand.

"Shouldn't we send a party out with you, sir?"

He stopped in his tracks. "There's nobody on this team who can read a trail or shoot a weapon as well as I can. The bush turns to dense forest about a quarter mile up the mountain. I won't risk human lives unnecessarily."

"We just don't want you to risk your own, sir."

He smiled. "Risk it? Hell, I'm reclaiming it."

"I don't understand, sir."

"No, I suppose you don't."

And with that, he started off again toward the mountain, his stride a little springier, his eyes a little brighter.

After five months of engaging in the follies of Men and aliens, Fuentes was going hunting once again.

Twenty-one

F uentes followed the trail, spotting a patch of crushed grass here, a piece of shed skin hanging from a thorn branch there. They were running aimlessly, panicked, using up too much energy. He knew from his long association with the Fani and the Tulabete how far they could run under normal circumstances . . . but the Tulabete were plains-dwellers, and the higher they climbed, the more difficulty they would have as the air became thinner. They'd drop, exhausted, in another mile and a half, possibly less.

He surveyed the landscape, the contours and ridges of the mountain; he'd hunted it a year ago, and he knew it fairly well. They'd never make it up past the treeline, nor would they want to. They'd feel safe in the forest and would wait for his team to depart. That meant they'd need a vantage point, a place from which they could observe his cavalry's departure. And water, of course; they couldn't know how long the Men would remain in the area, and they'd have to have water.

His keen eyes sought out and found the three likeliest spots from which the two Tulabete could watch their camp without being spotted from below. One had the wrong kind of shrubbery, a dryland bush that required minimal water; it would never have grown up there if there had been an ample supply. That narrowed it down to the other two sights, one quite steep, one a much easier climb. They couldn't know they were being followed, and they'd be exhausted by now, so he opted for the latter.

When he was half a mile away from it, he left the more obvious route and began silently climbing up through the bushes and trees that clung to the mountain. After a few moments he hit a thick grove of thornscrub and stripped down to his shorts and shoes, leaving his outfit and his socks behind. He'd rather have his body take the scrapes and wounds from the thorn than give himself away by a sound of ripping fabric.

The site was empty when he arrived half an hour later, but that didn't surprise him. He had analyzed where they'd go, but they would arrive only after some trial and error. He felt he had at least an hour before they showed up, and he spent the time creating a blind behind the thick bushes and then waited patiently inside it.

And it was an hour later, almost to the minute, that two Tulabete cautiously approached the site, obviously exhausted from their exertion. He waited until they were almost on top of him, then fired his rifle once and instantly trained it on the second Tulabete as the first dropped to the ground. His finger was tightening on the trigger when he recognized the Tulabete's insignia, and instead of firing, he stood up.

"Don't move!" he said in Tulabete.

"Go ahead and kill me, as you killed all the others," answered the Tulabete in excellent Terran.

"I have no intention of killing you," said Fuentes, stepping out of the blind. "You are Paratoka, Jalanopi's most trusted general. You are worth more to me alive than dead."

"Jalanopi will not ransom me," answered Paratoka.

"Jalanopi will not be given the opportunity to ransom you," answered Fuentes. "You possess much valuable information. We want it."

"I will not speak under torture," said Paratoka.

"No, you probably won't," answered Fuentes. "But you will tell us what we want to know under the influence of certain drugs."

"I will tell you nothing."

"You're welcome to think so, if it brings you comfort," said Fuentes. "Now," he added, prodding the Tulabete with the tip of his rifle, "let's climb back down the mountain and find out which of us is right." Suddenly he stopped and fired a shot in the air.

"What was that for?" asked Paratoka.

"My men know I came up here after two of you. If they spotted you before they saw me, and they hadn't heard that second shot, they might think you had murdered me and be tempted to kill you themselves."

They began climbing down the mountain. After some forty minutes of silence, Paratoka turned to Fuentes.

"Do you really have drugs that will force me to tell what I know?" he asked.

Fuentes nodded. "Your central nervous system is different than ours, so they're not the same drugs, but every sentient being is susceptible to *some* truth serum. If the medics in Athens haven't isolated it yet, your presence will give them a reason to redouble their efforts."

"I cannot let you give such drugs to me."

"You should have thought of that before you went to war."

"You should not have come to our world, and we would not have *had* to go to war."

"I never caused you any trouble," replied Fuentes. "I've always dealt fairly with Jalanopi."

"If it was just *you*, we would have had no cause for war.

But your people have virtually enslaved the Tulabete, and as Athens expands you are doing the same to the Fani. You plunder our hills, you take away our land, you make us work for you so that we can pay the taxes that you impose, and each of you lives in more luxury than Jalanopi." He paused. "Is it any wonder that we have gone to war?"

"I'm no politician," answered Fuentes. "The reasons you took up arms are your business. Ending the war as quickly as possible is mine."

"You may win this battle, and the next one, and the one after that," said Paratoka. "But in the end we will win the war. It is our world, and you are the intruders."

"It's my observation that God usually favors the side with the best weapons."

"Then your god is a fool."

"We shall see," said Fuentes, as the trail narrowed and they found themselves walking at a steep angle down a precarious path.

"No, Fuentes," said Paratoka. "*You* shall see. I cannot go to Athens with you. I will not betray my people."

And with that, he calmly stepped out into space and fell some three hundred feet into a gully.

It was then that Fuentes began to wonder if the war would ever truly end as long as a single Tulabete or Fani remained alive.

Twenty-two

Fuentes spent the next day and night alone in his bubble, considering the implications of Paratoka's death, the fanaticism of a man—*snake,* he corrected himself—who would rather throw himself off a mountain than betray an army that was obviously doomed to defeat.

When he emerged after breakfast the next day, he was a changed man, a man who knew what had to be done. The snakes must be taught, now and for all time, that resistance was futile, because if that lesson wasn't driven home, promptly and unequivocally, they might have continual war until the last snake was killed. He didn't care what happened to the planet—it would never be an untouched wilderness again, and if he survived the war he knew that he'd be heading off in search of another paradise, hopefully a few years ahead of the colonists—but he was a Man, and he knew that it was his duty to do what he could to see that Men didn't get thrown off the planet, because if it could happen on Rockgarden, it could happen on Flowergarden and Goldstone and Peponi and Walpurgis III and all the thousands of other worlds on which the race had gained a toehold.

So Rockgarden wouldn't be Paradise anymore, which was simply evolution, to his way of thinking. As long as he could stop it from becoming Inferno, he'd have done his job, fulfilled his obligation to the race, and then he could move on. He was a realist, and in this case, outnumbered hundreds to one by the snakes, he'd settle for stopping the slide at Purgatory.

That afternoon he studied the map again. There were twenty-seven Tulabete villages between the Tenya Mountains and the Fani border. Twenty-seven lessons to be learned by the snakes, before they became so powerful that only their extinction could prevent the slaughter of every Man on the planet.

This time the Blue-and-Golds marched in formation. They came out of the savannah and burned the first three villages they came to. Those snakes who remained to fight were killed; those who fled were left alone, to spread the word of what happened to innocent snake bystanders when Jalanopi dared to take up arms against Man.

The fourth village he bypassed entirely. Let the snakes wonder about that, let them search for fifth columnists among their own, let them destroy every last member of the village simply because Fuentes had seen fit not to attack it.

He leveled the next nine, burning crops wherever he found them. He then bypassed two more, and followed that by destroying every Tulabete village all the way to the Fani border.

Then, because he didn't want a war with the Fani at some future date, he marched his squad through the heart of Fani country. They killed no one, destroyed no dwellings or farmfields, killed only those animals they needed to eat . . . but they represented an irresistible force, and when he returned to Tulabete land three weeks later, he did so with the confident knowledge that those Fani who harbored thoughts of revolution had seen the future and didn't like the shape of it.

Jalanopi was waiting for him, enraged at the slaughter and destruction of twenty-four Tulabete villages. His forward scouts brought word of Jalanopi's presence back to him, and drawing upon a lifetime's bushcraft, he and his squad melted into the night and reappeared thirty miles behind Jalanopi. He waited until he had been spotted again, then began a zigzag retreat across the western hill country, never getting more than forty miles ahead of Jalanopi's army, never allowing the Tulabete to get within ten miles of him.

This cat-and-mouse pursuit continued for almost a month, as he drew Jalanopi closer and closer to the main body of his own army. He knew that the humans' weapons of destruction would work to best effect on a broad, flat field, so he gradually led Jalanopi to the Baski Plains, a broad savannah some three hundred miles long and fifty miles wide. Jalanopi followed him up to the edge of the Plains, then halted, not willing to expose his army to the superior firepower of his enemy.

Fuentes tried feint after feint, but to no avail. Jalanopi was willing to fight a guerrilla war, but he was no fool, and he knew that the humans had had ample time to reinforce their army and add to their weaponry.

Fuentes even came up with the stratagem of driving a wild herd of Blue-and-Golds to within a quarter mile of Jalanopi's main encampment and laying a trap for the retreating Tulabete, but Jalanopi spotted the ruse and held his ground. Fuentes then considered sending his cavalry in an earnest charge in the hope that Jalanopi might consider it another trick, but as well-armed as his squad was, he couldn't ask them to face nine thousand entrenched Tulabete.

And so the standoff continued, until a single radio message from Athens changed everything.

Twenty-three

Fuentes approached the airbed that floated gently some three feet above the hospital floor and wondered what was keeping its occupant alive other than her indomitable will.

Violet Gardener lay on her back, attached to half a dozen monitoring devices. Tubes and pumps constantly recirculated fresh blood through her veins, machines performed the functions of her heart, her lungs, her pancreas, and her liver. There was so much medical paraphernalia crisscrossing the bed that the patient herself seemed almost an afterthought.

"I came as soon as I heard," said Fuentes softly.

"It had to happen sooner or later," replied Violet weakly. "Even the best machine can run only so long on rotten fuel, and my body was never the best of machines even on its good days."

"There's nothing they can do?"

"They've been doing it for thirty years," she said wryly. "The stockpile of miracles finally ran out."

"What if they shipped you to Deluros?" asked Fuentes.

"This is my world. I'd rather die here."

"Has anyone told you . . . that is . . . ?"

"Two days, maybe three," she answered. "If it's any longer than that, I won't know about it: I'll be too heavily drugged because of the pain."

"I'm sorry," said Fuentes. "I wish there was something I could do."

"There is," whispered Violet.

"What?" asked Fuentes, suddenly alert.

"If I have to die, and I do, then I want to die knowing that Rockgarden is once again safe for colonization. This world can be the center of human commerce and culture in the Spiral Arm. That has been my dream. Now you have to take the next step toward making it a reality."

"We're not going to lose the war, Madam Gardener," he assured her.

"That's not enough," she said with something like her old strength. "I want to die knowing that we've *won!*"

The effort left her weak and gasping for breath.

"Two days . . ." mused Fuentes.

"One more thing," she said in a barely audible whisper.

"What is it?"

"If Jalanopi surrenders, so much the better . . . but if he should die, I want him buried next to me."

"He's your enemy."

"We have to live with the snakes," she said. "We must triumph over them, but we must also be magnanimous in victory. Bury us side by side. It will be a gesture they understand—two leaders who respected each other."

"I'll see to it," said Fuentes, as a nurse entered the room, took some new readings, and changed some of the medications that were dripping slowly into Violet's body.

"Thank you," said Violet, just before fading into unconsciousness.

Fuentes remained with her for a few more minutes, then had a driver take him back to the airport, where he rode a small military plane back to his encampment, wrestling with the problem of how to keep his promise to Violet Gardener. The two sides had been at a standoff for close to a month. Eventually the humans' superior firepower would win the war, but first it would become a battle of attrition. He had nothing against wiping out Jalanopi's entire army with saturation bombing, but they were dispersed in small groups, and the landscape precluded the possibility of a successful mission. He'd kill two hundred thousand trees and level forty hills and pollute the Karimona River before he killed half of Jalanopi's warriors, nor did he have the military capacity to deliver a tenth of the bombs required before Violet Gardener died.

When the plane landed, he went directly to his bubble and spent another fruitless hour trying to devise some strategy to defeat an army that had stood against him for half a year, in less than two days' time. Finally he called in his most trusted advisors, put the question to them, and rejected one half-baked suggestion after another.

The consensus, after three hours of brainstorming, was that it couldn't be done, even without allowing for a safety factor. Besides, Violet Gardener, if she hadn't expired already, was almost certainly in a coma by now; what difference could it make to her whether they won in two days or two weeks or two months?

"I gave her my word," said Fuentes at last, closing the matter.

His aides walked out, one by one, and then, on a hunch, he sent for Bandakona, his former tracker who now served as his personal aide. The Tulabete arrived a moment later, and Fuentes gestured for him to sit down.

Bandakona was even more apolitical that Fuentes. He had lived in the bush all his life and felt loyalty neither to his own race nor to the race that now employed and protected him. All he wanted was for the war to end, not out of any humanitarian reasons, but so that he and Fuentes could go back to hunting once again.

"Bandakona," began Fuentes, pouring himself a drink but not offering any to the tracker, whose metabolism couldn't handle alcohol, "I need your advice."

"You want, I give."

"You know that Jalanopi's army is dug in forty miles to the north of us."

"Yes," said Bandakona, nodding his head and pointing to the north. "In forest."

"For almost a month I have been trying to lure him out onto the Baski Plains, but I have been unsuccessful. Now it is imperative that we meet in battle in the next two days. How can I get his army to meet mine?"

Bandakona, whose Terran was too limited to comprehend some of the terms used, merely stared at Fuentes, who then translated his question into Tulabete.

"You cannot entice his army out of the forest," answered Bandakona in his native tongue, "for he knows that you have more men and better weapons. You must go in after him."

"We couldn't *find* him in that forest, let alone fight him," said Fuentes, shaking his head. "My men would be just as likely to shoot each other by mistake."

"No," said Bandakona. "You do not understand."

"Then explain to me, please."

"What I said: *you* must go in after him."

"I just told you why we can't."

"Not *we*," said Bandakona. "*You*."

Fuentes frowned. "I don't understand."

"You must enter his camp alone, or at most accompanied by myself, a Tulabete."

"I'll be an easy target the second I enter the forest."

"He will not have you killed. You are too important. He will want to know your mind."

"All right," said Fuentes. "So I enter his camp. Then what? He takes me prisoner. What good does that do?"

Bandakona parted his lips in a reptilian smile. "No, Fuentes," he said. "Go back to 'Then what?' "

"All right," said Fuentes. "I walk into his camp. Then what?"

"Then you challenge him."

"I *challenge* him?"

"In front of his own army. He cannot say no, for this is how he became king, and how he retains his kingship."

"Are you saying that if I win, I become king of the Tulabete, and can order the armies to disperse?"

"No," answered Bandakona. "You are not a Tulabete, so you cannot become king. But you one make condition: if he wins, all Men will leave Rockgarden. If you win, the Tulabete surrender and return to their villages."

"You're sure he'll do it?"

"He has no choice. If he does not accept your challenge, he is no longer king."

"You mean I could have done this at any time, and he'd have accepted the challenge?"

"Yes."

"Why the hell didn't you tell me before?" demanded Fuentes.

Bandakona looked at him, puzzled. "You never asked," he replied.

Fuentes considered the proposition. "I'm fifty-four years old," he said at last. "I don't know how you measure age, but that's not young for a Man. Jalanopi's almost a foot taller than I am, and he must outweigh me by close to one hundred pounds."

"That is another reason he will fight you," agreed Bandakona.

Fuentes sighed. "What chance have I?"

"Depends."

"Depends on what?" asked Fuentes quickly.

"If he chooses weapons, you have a chance."

"If *he* chooses weapons?" repeated Fuentes. "Why can't *I* have the choice of weapons?"

"Because you are not the king."

"What if I bring a weapon anyway?"

"Then you will be killed before you have a chance to fight him."

"I see," said Fuentes. Suddenly he got to his feet. "Let's go," he said.

"Right now?"

"If I think about it, I'll find five hundred reasons not to go."

"Violet Gardener was right," said Bandakona as they walked to the corral.

"About what?"

"You are a great warrior."

"Only if I win," said Fuentes grimly.

After they saddled their Blue-and-Golds, Fuentes summoned six of his officers to the corral.

He briefly explained the situation to them, then concluded: "I'm telling *you* this precisely because you are not settlers or colonists. You came to Rockgarden to serve in the military, and you have no vested interest in this planet. If Jalanopi defeats me in fair combat, you *must* find a way to disperse the troops and keep my word to him. I'm acting with the full power and authority of Violet Gardener."

"We'll go with you, sir!" said the youngest of them.

He shook his head. "Bandakona says if anyone except himself accompanies me I'll never make it to Jalanopi alive."

"Can you trust him, sir?"

"Jalanopi?"

"Bandakona. After all, he's a Tulabete."

"I've trusted him with my life many times in the past. He has never given me cause to regret it."

"How do you know they won't slice you to ribbons once you get there?"

"If they do, Bandakona will tell you so."

"If they don't kill him, too."

"Sir," said another lieutenant. "You really must take some of us along as observers. With all due respect to your special relationship to Bandakona, I do not believe that the Men will disperse because a Tulabete says Jalanopi defeated you in fair combat."

Fuentes considered the statement, then nodded. "You have a point. All right. Colonel Montgomery and Major Williams, get your mounts and join me."

Bandakona walked over to Fuentes. "The Tulabete will not like it, these two coming with you."

"I'll instruct them to leave their weapons behind, but we have to have a pair of credible observers. That young man was right: none of my troops will believe you."

Bandakona shrugged, and made no reply.

A few moments later Colonel Montgomery and Major Williams, a young woman who had been promoted twice by Fuentes for bravery and initiative in the face of the enemy, rode up to him.

"Do I understand that we are to be observers at a personal combat between you and Jalanopi?" asked Montgomery incredulously.

"That's right."

"And that this fight will decide the outcome of the rebellion?"

"So I have been led to believe."

"Why in the world aren't you sending Carruthers, or one of our other martial-arts experts?" persisted Montgomery.

"According to Tulabete tradition, it can only be decided by personal combat between the two leaders."

"I take it Jalanopi's met you?"

"Many times," said Fuentes. "No doubles, no ringers."

"Pity."

"I agree," said Fuentes grimly. "On that happy note, let's go off and end this war one way or another."

He turned his Blue-and-Gold to the north and urged him to a ground-eating trot.

Twenty-four

F uentes led his little party into the forest. He was aware that the Tulabete were watching his every move, though Montgomery and Williams couldn't spot the tell-tale signs. Bandakona brought up the rear. Fuentes waited until he was more than halfway to Jalanopi's camp, then slowly unbuckled his gunbelt, held the holster and weapon above his head for his unseen observers to see, and let it drop to the ground, ordering the two officers to do the same.

"Let me discharge it first," said Williams, referring to her laser pistol. "Then it won't be any use to them."

"Don't," said Fuentes sharply. "If they hear it start to hum, they'll turn you into a pincushion."

"But there aren't any Tulabete around," she protested.

"You'd be surprised."

"How many?"

"More than fifty."

"Well, I'll be damned!" she muttered, and followed Fuentes' example with her own weapon. Montgomery hesitated for a moment, and then dropped his sonic pistol to the forest floor.

"Good," said Fuentes. "You're not supposed to be accompanying me at all, but that should convince them you've only come as observers."

Bandakona, who disdained human weapons, hurled his spear into a tree and dropped his knife to the ground.

They rode in total silence for two more hours, and finally reached a large clearing that had five Tulabete dwellings that seemed to have been hastily erected some time ago and were already falling into disrepair. Some sixty Tulabete were in the camp, and Fuentes dismounted and held one hand up in the air to show he was unarmed, while he held his Blue-and-Gold's bridle with the other.

"Dismount, please," he said to his officers.

Montgomery and Williams did as he said, and stood by their mounts.

A Tulabete, wearing the insignia of an officer, approached them.

"I have come to speak to Jalanopi," said Fuentes in the Tulabete dialect.

"I speak for Jalanopi."

"Do you also fight for him?" asked Fuentes.

"I fight in his army," said the officer, not understanding the implication.

"I am tired of fighting his army," said Fuentes. He raised his voice so that everyone could hear it. "I have come here to challenge Jalanopi in personal combat. If he chooses not to meet me, he is a coward, and I will claim victory before all of his people."

"I will give him your message," said the officer.

"You do that," said Fuentes. He turned his Blue-and-Gold's reins over to Bandakona and waited, hands on hips, for Jalanopi to appear.

Finally a vast number of soldiers approached, with Jalanopi, wearing his ceremonial headdress and walking with his characteristic limp, at their head. He came to a halt some ten feet from Fuentes.

"We meet again," said the Tulabete.

"We meet again," said Fuentes.

"You were a hunter of animals, Man Fuentes," said Jalanopi. "How did you come to be a persecutor of my people?"

"It happened when you became a torturer and murderer of *my* people," replied Fuentes.

"Your people have no right to be on Karimon."

"That's what I have come here to decide," said Fuentes. "If you win, Men will leave your planet. If I win, we stay. Either way, the war ends."

"You are a fool, Man Fuentes," said Jalanopi. "With my own hands I have slain a Nightkiller and killed four Tulabete, all stronger than you, who aspired to my throne."

"I believe you."

"You slay animals from great distances. You do not pit your strength against them."

"That is true," acknowledged Fuentes.

"Why, then, have you challenged me?"

"I promised Violet Gardener the war would end before she died. She will die in the next few days."

"The war will end," agreed Jalanopi. "And your race will leave Karimon forever."

"The name of this world is Rockgarden," said Fuentes, removing his hat and tossing it to Bandakona, "and nobody's leaving it. Choose your weapons."

"You hope, perhaps, that I will choose rifles at four hundred yards?" asked Jalanopi, parting his lips and hissing.

"It makes no difference to me," said Fuentes with an air of indifference. "But before we begin, I want you to instruct your people that they are to disperse and return to their homes after I kill you. Their weapons will of course be confiscated, but they will not be punished for having followed you."

Jalanopi nodded curtly to his lieutenants. "It is done.

And these two, and the traitor who holds your hat, will tell
your army to return to the stars from which they came when
I place my foot on your neck and claim victory?"

"They will."

"Then it is agreed, and now I will kill you, as I have killed
all the others who thought they could defeat Jalanopi." He
paused and drew himself up to his full seven-foot height.
"We will fight with no weapons at all."

Fuentes stared at the glistening scales on Jalanopi's massive, muscular body and wondered at his own audacity.
Aloud he said, "That is acceptable."

Jalanopi spread his arms wide, and his soldiers backed
away, forming a huge circle of perhaps seventy feet around
the two combatants. Then the king of the Tulabete lowered
his head and charged the slim, gray-haired man.

Fuentes sidestepped the charge and kicked Jalanopi's
game leg as the huge Tulabete passed by him. Jalanopi
stumbled, fell briefly to the ground, and was up on his feet
instantly.

Twice more Jalanopi charged, and twice more Fuentes
narrowly avoided him and went after his bad leg. But at the
end of the three charges, Jalanopi showed no sign of pain
or frustration, while Fuentes was panting heavily.

This time Jalanopi approached Fuentes slowly if not cautiously, his massive arms spread out to catch the human if
he tried to sidestep or avoid him. Fuentes backed away
slowly, then at the last moment reached down, grabbed a
handful of powdery dirt, and hurled it into Jalanopi's eyes.
The Tulabete brought his hands to his face, and Fuentes,
mustering all his strength, hurled himself, head and shoulder first, at Jalanopi's game leg. The *crack!* was loud
enough for every soldier gathered in the circle to hear.

He felt no pride in his accomplishment. He had merely
done as the predators he had hunted all his life had done:
find the weak link and attack it. Besides, his shoulder was
throbbing so badly he could barely lift his arm, he was

having difficulty catching his breath, and the huge being on the ground wasn't dead yet.

"I have no wish to kill you," panted Fuentes. "If you will surrender, I will let you live."

Jalanopi's answer was to lunge forward and deliver a powerful blow that was aimed at Fuentes' head but landed on his shoulder as the Tulabete lost his balance at the last instant. Nonetheless, the force of it sent Fuentes rolling across the ground, and he scrambled to his feet just before Jalanopi, dragging his broken leg behind him, could catch him.

Fuentes felt the energy leaving his aging body and realized that he could take no more chances. Instinct and a bit of wrestling and kickfighting had gotten him this far, but now he had to finish the job, and he doubled up his fists and began circling Jalanopi, always keeping just out of the Tulabete's reach, feinting now and then, and stepping in to deliver his devastating punches only when the Tulabete's leg caused him to turn too slowly or to struggle to keep his balance. He saw a rock on the ground, a large enough rock to do some serious damage, but to use it he would have to get close enough so that Jalanopi might be able to take it away and use it against him, and he decided to wait until the Tulabete was further weakened.

It was a slaughter, but a slow slaughter. Within ten minutes Jalanopi's face was bleeding in half a dozen places, and one of his eyes was swollen shut. Five minutes later the other eye closed, and blind and crippled, the Tulabete still refused to yield, hurling himself blindly at where he thought Fuentes was standing.

Twice Fuentes pleaded with Jalanopi's lieutenants to surrender on behalf of their king, and twice they merely stared at him as if he were quite mad. Finally, nearing exhaustion himself, he picked up the large rock he had spotted earlier, cautiously circled around behind Jalanopi, and brought it down on the back of the Tulabete's head with all his remaining strength. Jalanopi grunted and plunged forward on his face. Fuentes dropped to his knees, brought the rock down twice more, and the Tulabete Uprising was officially over.

Twenty-five

V iolet Gardener and Jalanopi, king of the Tulabete, were buried side by side beneath Jalanopi's tree two days later, and Fuentes, who would have preferred to be left alone, was forced to undergo a triumphal parade through the streets of Athens, the conquering hero of the Tulabete War.

"Thanks to you and you alone," said the mayor of Athens during the ceremony in which Fuentes received the medal which had been created expressly for him, "Rockgarden has truly become a planet for Men. Never again will the duplicitous, cowardly snakes take up arms against us. Never again will they have the courage to challenge our primacy. This is truly a glorious and historic day."

It took all of Fuentes' self-control not to laugh aloud at that statement.

Three weeks later he landed on the jungle world of Ascardi II and went hunting for Greendevils, the huge carnivorous amphibians that were coveted by so many museums within the Republic.

He never returned to Rockgarden.

IV

WILCOCK'S CASTLE

Twenty-six

I t was twenty-seven years after Violet Gardener's death that Richard Wilcock stumbled upon the castle.

Progress during the preceding quarter century had been steady, but not phenomenal. Six hundred thousand Men now lived on Rockgarden, all but a handful of them colonists who had made the commitment to live out their lives there. Fully a third of the planet was under cultivation, and far from importing food from the neighboring world of Flowergarden, Rockgarden exported almost half its produce to the other mining worlds in the vicinity.

Athens was the cultural center Violet Gardener had envisioned, populated by more than four hundred thousand Men, and the neighboring shantytown (shanty*city*, actually) of Talami had grown apace, housing more than two million snakes, most in the employ of the men who lived in Athens.

Fuentes had lived long enough to write two memoirs of Rockgarden, one of the war and one of his hunting experiences, and Linus Rawls' son and two daughters now managed an enormous safari operation, catering to the wealthiest sportsmen and tourists in the Republic.

Faniland and Tulabete Country were crisscrossed with networks of roads and powergrids, the desert continent on the other side of the world was finally being exploited, and Mastaboni and Athens both boasted large up-to-date spaceports.

There was still land to be had, too—millions of square miles of it, and there was no shortage of immigrants willing to spend their savings to purchase it. There were planets such as the university world of Aristotle, where people came to study; and planets such as Peponi, where the rich and the idle came to pursue their pleasures; and planets such as Buddha II and Luther and Inshallah IV, where people came to practice their religions; but the people who came to Rockgarden came to work, to plow the earth, to extract the metals from the hills, to form a merchant class that catered to the needs of those who farmed and mined.

Richard Wilcock was no different from most of them. He had come to Rockgarden with his parents at the age of fifteen, had spent four years on their farm outside of Mastaboni and another seven as a mining engineer until he had accumulated enough money to buy a homestead. It was his misfortune to be in the market for land during one of the periodic inflationary spirals that tended to hit the colony worlds, and rather than pay the exorbitant prices being asked for farmland near Mastaboni, he packed his few belongings in his groundcar and headed south to the still-undeveloped Rakko Country.

He drove more than two thousand miles, the last seven hundred without roads or even tracks, shot his own dinner each night, made rudimentary maps of the area through which he traveled, even learned the Rakko dialect well enough to make himself understood. The journey took him the better part of eight months, but finally he found the property he was looking for: it was a large plateau, perhaps six miles in diameter, buttressed up against huge rocky outcroppings which were not quite mountains but more than hills, to the south and west. A river flowed across the eastern side of the land, and the climate seemed temperate.

He surveyed the property, staked his claim, discovered to his delight that he was able to afford such a remote piece of land, and spent the remainder of his money buying the farming machinery he needed. It was all secondhand, since the shipping costs exceeded the cost of the equipment itself, but it worked, and, filled with the pride of ownership, Richard Wilcock set about the business of establishing the farm he had always dreamed of owning.

He knew that his situation wasn't unique on the planet, that other young men and women who could not afford the more desirable land in nearby Faniland and Tulabete Country would be looking about for less expensive locations, and that within a handful of years there would be a hundred or more farms down in Rakko Country. The roads would follow, then the first small trading centers, then the huge granaries, and finally a city or two. He planned to be ready when they arrived.

The only problem was that, despite the land's flat surface, there were an awful lot of rocks in it, most of them just beneath the surface. They slowed down his equipment, broke his blades, pierced his tires. They were not big rocks—most of them could easily be lifted with one hand. But there were so *many* of them, the more he pulled out, the more there seemed to be.

Curious, he dug straight down some twenty feet, and still the profusion of rocks continued. Wilcock had no degrees in agriculture or geology, but he thought he knew good virgin farmland when he saw it, and he'd never come across anything like this.

Finally, in frustration, he contacted Mastaboni, gave them his coordinates, and chartered a plane to take some soil samples back for analysis to determine if he could expect to continue finding myriads of these rocks in what he had fondly hoped would be rich, fertile soil.

The plane returned three days later with his soil samples and Professor James Ellery.

Wilcock walked out to the grass landing strip, and was surprised to see the big, burly, bearded Ellery emerge from the plane, a huge pack on his back.

"Richard Wilcock?" said Ellery.

"Right."

Ellery extended his hand. "I'm James Ellery of Gardener University."

"But that's in Athens," said Wilcock, frowning. "I sent my samples to Mastaboni."

"And they consulted with experts in Athens," said Ellery.

"Well? What's the verdict?"

"This soil can't contain those rocks."

"They sent you all the way here to accuse me of faking a sample?" demanded Wilcock heatedly.

"Not at all," replied Ellery. "Since such stones don't occur naturally in such soil, they sent me here to find out who put them there." He smiled. "I'm from the Department of Archaeology."

"You think someone *put* them there?" repeated Wilcock.

"We're quite certain of it," answered Ellery. "The only questions are who and why."

"How long do you think it will take you to find out?"

Ellery shrugged. "I have no idea."

"I have to warn you: I'm not really equipped to handle a guest." He smiled apologetically. "In fact, I'm still living in a camping bubble."

"Oh, that's quite all right. I can camp out until my staff gets here."

"Your staff?"

"I'm just the advance guard, so to speak."

The pilot waved to Ellery, who waved back as the little plane sped by them on its takeoff.

"Well," said Ellery energetically, "suppose you show me where I can find these stones?"

"Just dig straight down," answered Wilcock.

"Right where I'm standing?"

Wilcock snorted disgustedly. "Anywhere within two miles of where you're standing."

"Excellent!" exclaimed Ellery.

"Have you eaten lunch yet?" asked Wilcock.

"I haven't even had breakfast," admitted Ellery. "I've been too excited."

"Well, come on back to my bubble and I'll fix something for us to eat."

"Lovely place here," said Ellery, looking around as they walked the mile to Wilcock's camp. "Well-protected from the elements, dependable source of water, altitude of forty-seven hundred feet so the summers don't get too hot. I can see why you chose it." He paused. "I wonder who chose it before you?"

"You're absolutely sure that somebody did?" said Wilcock dubiously.

"Those rocks don't belong here, and certainly not in that quantity," said Ellery.

"And you base your hopes or theories or whatever they are on that?"

"Not entirely," answered Ellery. "Though the rocks are certainly a strong indicator."

"But not the only one?"

Ellery shook his head. "No."

"What else is there?"

"There are also some things that *should* be here, but aren't," said Ellery.

"What?" asked Wilcock, surprised.

"Trees."

"Trees?"

Ellery nodded. "Given the conditions, there should be trees here, Mr. Wilcock. But look out across the valley; not a single one as far as the eye can see."

"That's one of the reasons I chose it," explained Wilcock. "I didn't want to waste the first few months deforesting the land."

"Someone did it for you."

"How can you be sure?" asked Wilcock as they arrived at his camp and Ellery gratefully took off his enormous backpack. Wilcock led his visitor past the sheds that housed his equipment and over to his bubble. He gave a brief order to his kitchen computer, then pulled up a pair of chairs for himself and Ellery.

"You drove here, Mr. Wilcock," said Ellery. "You went though hundreds of miles of Rakko Country and stopped when you found what seemed to be a flat empty field of tillable land. I *flew* here, and once we pinpointed your location I had my pilot fly in increasingly larger concentric circles, always using the river as a starting point. There are perhaps twenty other valleys just like this one within a radius of seventy miles, and each of them is covered with trees. Also, I studied the animals we saw: we passed over Redmountains, Horndevils, Twisthorns, Fleetjumpers, three species of Brownbucks—all browsers. We didn't see a single Blue-and-Gold or Brownbison, or any other grazer. The reason we didn't see them is they are not native to this area, and the reason they're not native to this area is that there is no savannah. There are forests, and scrubland, and some swamps, but *you* have the only grassland for a hundred miles." He paused. "Do you know how unusual that is, Mr. Wilcock?"

"Evidently not."

"Well, let us say that it would be enough to get me here, even without the rocks."

"What do you expect to find?" asked Wilcock, walking to the kitchen area for a moment and returning with a sandwich for Ellery and canisters of beer for each of them.

"Some evidence of a prior civilization."

"You mean a snake civilization?"

Ellery sat down on a folding chair. "Oh, I doubt it. The

snakes hardly strike me as a race of sentient beings that has reverted to barbarism."

"Then what?"

"There are more than ten thousand sentient races in the galaxy, Mr. Wilcock," said Ellery, "and more than eight hundred of them achieved space flight before we did. I suspect one of them posted a colony here sometime in the past."

"That's an awfully farfetched conclusion to draw based on a few rocks and a lack of trees," said Wilcock skeptically.

"Oh, there are other reasons too," said Ellery, sipping his beer.

"Such as?"

"The soil samples you sent."

"What about them?"

"Very poor in nutrients."

"I don't understand," said Wilcock.

"You may think you're the first young man who set out for Rakko Country to make his fortune, but in fact there have been about forty others. Many of them have sent soil samples to Mastaboni or Athens, so that experts could analyze them and suggest the best combinations of crops and fertilizers." He paused and took a bite of his sandwich. "In every case, their soil samples contained far more nutrients than yours did."

"So I picked a spot with poorer land."

"True—but there has to be a *reason* why it's poorer."

"And what do you think the reason is?"

"I should think that would be obvious from everything else we've discussed," answered Ellery. "This land was overused."

"I just run in luck, don't I?" said Wilcock disgustedly. "I spent every credit I've got buying what looks like the most idyllic farmland on the planet, and there are so many rocks I can't plant anything, and even if I could, the soil couldn't support it."

"Not to worry, Mr. Wilcock," answered Ellery. "If we find what I think we're going to find, the government will be more than happy to resettle you elsewhere."

"Why should the government give a damn whether someone lived here hundreds or thousands of years ago?"

"If my theory is correct, we are not the first race to colonize Rockgarden. Someone else was here first."

"So you said—but that doesn't tell me why the government should take an interest in it?"

"I should think that would be obvious to you, Mr. Wilcock," said Ellery with a smile. "They may come back." He paused. "They may even think that Rockgarden belongs to them."

Twenty-seven

E llery's crew arrived a week later, by which time the archaeologist had thoroughly examined the site and was able to tell them where to begin work.

At first the digging seemed haphazard, and Wilcock, an interested spectator now that he knew the government would recoup his losses, thought that Ellery had been wrong, that, all his arguments to the contrary, this was simply a patch of ground with a lot of rocks buried in it.

But after a month it became apparent that they were indeed unearthing an ancient structure that had been made entirely of stone. There was a main area, surrounded by walls some forty feet high, that Ellery called the Castle, filled with large courtyards, labyrinthian passageways, cisterns, and grain storehouses. But as the scope of the dig continued, they found stone fencing extending entirely across the valley floor. Whoever or whatever had built this forgotten structure hadn't done it overnight.

The bubbles that had temporarily housed Ellery's staff of thirty soon became more permanent structures, and doubled and redoubled within five months. The Rakko themselves began coming to the valley to watch the dig, and many of them hired on as servants or laborers on the project, and a village of huts and burrows sprang up a mile away from the humans' houses.

Each night, after dinner, Ellery would preside at a meeting where his staff described what they had discovered that day and discussed its meaning, and Wilcock sat in rapt fascination, assimilating what he could.

After the initial work had disclosed that the structure was made entirely of millions of stones carried from the rocky outcroppings some fifty miles away from the valley, the brunt of each discussion concerned the builders of the Castle. About half of the crew felt that it had indeed been created, perhaps a millennium ago, by the Rakko or a related tribe, but Ellery and a number of others insisted that the structure was far too sophisticated, that the Rakko—and indeed every other tribe of snakes—gave no indication of being a once-powerful civilization that had fallen into barbarism, but rather appeared to be a primitive race that was just now, with an enormous boost from Man, emerging from it.

The problem facing those on Ellery's side of the question was quite simple: what had become of the builders? If they were Rakko, they were still in the area . . . but if they were Men or another starfaring race, why was there no sign of them? They had found the skeletons of a few snakes, but not enough to imply they had been the only inhabitants; more likely, concluded Ellery, they were laborers or servants, possibly even slaves. If some plague or war had wiped out the builders, where were *their* remains? And if they had migrated elsewhere, where had they gone to?

"Back home," suggested Ellery when Wilcock, who was still struggling to comprehend some of the terminology, asked the question again one day at breakfast on the veranda of the permanent structure Wilcock had built for himself while all the digging was going on.

"Then why didn't the Department of Cartography have

a map of the planet, or even a name for it, before Violet Gardener opened it up?" persisted Wilcock. "*We* haven't reverted to barbarism since reaching the stars. There should have been a record of it."

"*We* never colonized Rockgarden prior to Violet Gardener," answered Ellery. "I gave up on that hypothesis weeks ago. This is simply not the kind of structure Men would build, not even Men who had been stranded here without weapons and were desperate to protect themselves from hostile snakes." He shook his head. "No, it had to be some other race."

"Then where are they?"

"Either they're dead, in which case we will come across their remains someday, if not here, then wherever they migrated to; or they went back home, wherever *home* may be."

"I still don't know why the place couldn't have been built by the Rakko," said Wilcock. "It would answer the question of what happened to them."

"Not really," said Ellery. "If they built it, why did they desert it? It was virtually impregnable, it had a supply of water, it had cultivated land. Only something catastrophic could have made them leave." He paused. "Have you seen any signs of a catastrophe?"

"No," said Wilcock. "But perhaps a disease . . ."

"Would you leave a city and go back to subsistence farming and living in burrows if a disease struck?"

"I'd want to get away from it."

"You'd be carrying it with you."

"But if I was so primitive I didn't know that," said Wilcock, "if I had no notion of medicine or hygiene . . ."

"Then you'd also be too primitive to have built the castle," answered Ellery with an air of finality. He got to his feet. "No, it has to have been another race, a race about which we know nothing."

"Perhaps they were a native race—not snakes, but some other race—that became extinct," suggested Wilcock.

Ellery chuckled. "And didn't leave a trace of themselves anywhere on this entire planet except right here?"

"You won't know that until you dig up the whole planet," replied Wilcock stubbornly.

"I'm glad you're showing such an interest in our work, Richard," said Ellery. "But perhaps you should leave the hypothesizing to the experts."

"I didn't mean to annoy you," said Wilcock. "It's just very difficult to watch what's being dug up every day without becoming curious."

"I'm not annoyed," said Ellery. "But I really must get back to the site. We'll speak again later."

He walked off, leaving Wilcock to ponder the unanswered questions of the Castle while Tbona and Mbani, the two Rakkos he had hired as servants a few weeks earlier, cleaned up the breakfast table. He watched them idly for a few minutes as they carried plates and trays off to the kitchen, scrubbed the table, and swept and washed the veranda floor.

He was still daydreaming when Tbona approached him gently.

"Man Richard," he said in the Rakko dialect.

"What?" asked Wilcock, startled.

"Do you wish your tea now?"

"Oh, yes, thank you, Tbona."

Tbona disappeared into the kitchen and returned a moment later carrying a tray on which sat, in neat order, a cup and saucer, a tiny pitcher of cream, and a pot of steeping tea.

"You do not go to the dig today?" asked Tbona.

"Oh, I'll get by there a little later," answered Wilcock.

"My two brothers were hired yesterday," said Tbona.

"I'm glad to hear it," said Wilcock.

"Yes," said Tbona. "They will live with me at the far end

of the valley. I have not seen them in many days. It is good that we are all together again."

"I'm sure you will all be very happy," said Wilcock, pouring himself a cup of tea.

"I am happy, because I like to work in the house." He paused. "They are not very happy."

"Well, if I hear of anyone else needing houseboys, I'll recommend your brothers," said Wilcock, adding some cream and stirring his tea.

"Oh, no," said Tbona. "They do not like houseboy work."

"Why do they work here at all if they are not happy?"

"They are working over by the fences," answered Tbona, pointing toward a spot at the edge of the valley, "and they wanted to work at Castle Karimon."

"Is that what you're calling it—Castle Karimon?"

"That is what we have always called it," answered Tbona.

"You mean, since Professor Ellery discovered it," said Wilcock.

"No—always."

"Just a moment," said Wilcock, putting down his tea and staring at Tbona. "Are you trying to tell me that you knew about the castle before I arrived?"

"Yes, Man Richard," answered Tbona. "And always it has been called Castle Karimon, by my father and his father too."

"Have you told this to Professor Ellery?"

"No."

"Why not?"

"The Men who work at the dig, they do not talk to the Rakko, except to give orders." He paused and parted his lips. "That is why I like being your houseboy. You are nicer than the others."

Wilcock frowned. "Bring Mbani here for a moment, please. I'd like to speak to him."

"Have we done something wrong, Man Richard?"

"No."

Tbona went into the house and emerged a moment later, followed by Mbani.

"Mbani," said Wilcock, "what do you know about Castle Karimon?"

"Nothing, Man Richard," answered Mbani.

"You've never heard of it before?"

"Oh, everyone has heard of it," said Mbani. "But I know nothing about it."

"How long has it been here?"

They each shrugged.

"Forever," said Tbona at last.

"Who lived in it?"

"Great kings," said Mbani with complete assurance.

"Rakko kings?"

Again they shrugged.

"Snake kings?"

"Yes, great snake kings," said Mbani.

"What became of them?"

"I do not understand."

"The kings who lived in Castle Karimon," said Wilcock. "Where are they now?"

"They are dead, Man Richard."

"What about their descendants?"

"What is a descendant?"

"What happened to their sons and grandsons?" amended Wilcock.

"They have been dead for more rains than you can count, Man Richard," answered Tbona.

"What killed them?"

"Who can say?" replied Tbona. "Wildfangs, Nightkillers, sickness, hunger, war. What kills any of us?"

"Would you be willing to repeat to Professor Ellery what you have said to me?" asked Wilcock.

"He will not listen," said Tbona.

"Why do you think not?"

"I have learned a little of your language," said Tbona. "Not enough to speak, but enough to understand some things. And I know he thinks that the snakes are not smart enough to have built Castle Karimon."

"Will you tell him anyway?"

"Will he beat us?" asked Mbani.

"Of course not."

"Many of the Men on the dig beat snakes."

"You are *my* servants. I will not permit anyone to beat you for following my orders."

"Will he beat *you*, then?" persisted Mbani. "You have been good to us, Man Richard. If he kills you, we will have to work on the dig, or perhaps for another Man who will beat us."

"No one is going to beat anyone!" snapped Wilcock in frustration. "I just want you to tell him what you told me."

"If that is your order, Man Richard," said Mbani unhappily.

"It is my order," said Wilcock with a sigh.

"Then we shall do so," said Tbona. "But it will make no difference."

"It might."

Tbona shook his head. "For Man Ellery to believe us, he would have to admit that we could build such a castle, and he will not do that."

"Why should that bother him?" asked Wilcock. "He's a scientist. If he finds his theory is invalid, he will move on to the next theory."

"But he is also a Man."

"I don't understand."

"If he admits that Castle Karimon was built by my people," said Tbona, "then he must agree that it is ours and he must give it back to us." He stared at Wilcock, and suddenly Wilcock could see the bitterness in his servant's face and hear it in his voice. "Do you think he will do that?"

Twenty-eight

W ithin three years the entire area had been fully excavated, the crumbling walls of Castle Karimon had been reinforced, and the debate over the structure's origins continued unabated.

Wilcock was absolutely certain that the structure had been built by the snakes. Once, perhaps a millennium ago, they had migrated south—long before the tribes called Rakko, Tulabete, or Fani existed—and built this outpost in the wilderness. They had traded with snakes who lived even farther south, and they had prospered; at one point, some four thousand snakes had lived within the huge enclosure. It was a thriving city, perhaps the first ever on the face of the planet, and it had survived for centuries.

But the exhaustion of the soil, which had led Ellery to conclude it had been overfarmed, was to Wilcock the key to why the city had been abandoned. It was neither war nor pestilence nor a reversion to barbarism: it was the simple fact that after a couple of centuries the land could no longer feed the city's inhabitants, and it was this that eventually caused them to leave in search of more fertile land.

It seemed a simple and elegant conclusion, and Wilcock

found that a number of archaeologists had arrived at it independently. But Ellery and other senior members of the team insisted that snakes simply could not build a city of such complexity, that its design and construction were forever beyond their capabilities.

The argument wasn't confined to Wilcock's property. It extended to Athens and Mastaboni, where the daily newstapes presented arguments on both sides of the question. Wilcock himself "wrote" a book about his discovery of the city—which is to say, he sat down with a ghostwriter and poured out his thoughts, findings, and reminiscences into a recording device—and offered his conclusion, which was that what he had found was an ancient city built by the natives of Rockgarden. Even the name lent force to his argument, he said, for the Rakko had no word for the world they lived on, yet they called the place Castle Karimon— and since Karimon was the Tulabete and Fani name for the planet, he decided that the word had existed in some previous language that had split up into the three major dialects sometime after the desertion of the city.

Dozens of linguists then leapt into the fray, most of them claiming that Wilcock didn't know what he was talking about, and that he should leave the evolution of nonhuman languages to those who studied them for a living.

Early on, the government had expressed its willingness to reimburse Wilcock for his trouble and offered him a farm in Faniland, but he decided not to part with his valley. He had become fascinated with Castle Karimon, and to support himself—the land, after all, wasn't producing any income—he built a small hotel for tourists and visiting scholars who wished to explore the ruins. Then, because Violet Gardener had done her groundwork properly and forced the snakes to convert to a monied economy, he built a smaller, less elegant second hotel, about two miles away, for the occasional snake that wished to see the castle.

And then, seven years after first stumbling onto the valley, Richard Wilcock contracted an exceptionally virulent tropical disease. He was shipped to Athens, and for three weeks it was touch and go, but eventually the doctors effected a cure. When he emerged from the hospital, he had lost almost half his body weight, all of his hair, and most of his health, and had been told that he was inviting certain death if he returned to the valley. His immune system had been seriously compromised, and he was informed that he would have to spend the rest of his life in the city as a semi-invalid.

His immediate response was to ignore the advice of his doctors and return to his home in Rakko Country. For three months he seemed fine, and then the disease struck again.

He died on the plane that was flying him to the hospital.

He left behind no wife or children, no relatives of any sort. His book had made enough money to pay for his funeral and satisfy his various debts. He was, in truth, a relatively unimportant man who had not made much of a mark on Rockgarden during his brief life. All he had really done was find a tract of land laden with rocks and call in the experts.

But if his life left no lasting marks on Rockgarden's history, his death was another matter altogether.

Twenty-nine

R ichard Wilcock died intestate. He made sure there was enough money in his estate to pay his creditors, but having no heirs, he never saw any purpose in making a will.

The government waited the mandatory two rains for any claimants to Wilcock's estate, which for all practical purposes meant the valley that held Castle Karimon, and then set in motion the legal machinery to reclaim the land.

At the same time, one Milton Jnoma, one of the first members of the Rakko tribe to receive a higher education, and the very first to hold a law degree, petitioned the court to award the land to the members of the Rakko nation as a whole, with himself and a select committee of Rakko elders as executors.

The land, he claimed, housed a historical artifact of vast importance to the Rakko. Using Wilcock's book as evidence, he argued that the Rakko or their progenitors had built Castle Karimon, and since the land was worthless as farmland, the government could have no objection to turning it over to his people, who viewed themselves as the spiritual heirs to the ancient city.

James Ellery immediately stepped forward as a friend of the court, arguing that Wilcock had been mistaken and that the structure had been created not by snakes but by aliens. He brought in seventeen experts who agreed with his conclusion, which was simple and to the point: no snake society in the history of the planet, up to and including the current one, had the sophistication and expertise to create such a structure.

Jnoma suggested that it was even more difficult to obtain a law degree than build a stone castle, and pointed out that he had graduated fourth in a class of fifty, ahead of forty-six Men. Was Ellery saying that none of those forty-six Men had the sophistication to build a stone wall?

The trial went on for two weeks, with witnesses on both sides contradicting each other so thoroughly that at last the judge threw her hands in the air, ruled that insufficient information existed to determine who had built Castle Karimon, and put the land in a government-administered trust until such time as the original builders could be identified beyond any reasonable doubt.

That settled the matter . . . for six days.

Then Jnoma asked for another hearing, based on new evidence. He had located Wilcock's two houseboys, Tbona and Mbani, who were willing to testify that Wilcock, after returning from his hospitalization in Athens, had expressed the desire that the Rakko eventually take possession of Castle Karimon and indeed the entire valley.

The judge refused to allow their statements to be read into the record, as snakes did not have the same rights or status as Men under the constitution of Rockgarden, and hence their testimony could not be used to contradict any human testimony.

That night there were riots in Athens, Talami, Mastaboni, and even the small snake colony just beyond Ramsey Falls, and suddenly, by the next morning, Castle Karimon had become a planet-wide symbol of equality for the snakes. Tulabete who had never been to Rakko Country, as well as Fani who had never even seen a Rakko, began picketing the government buildings, demanding that Castle Karimon be turned over to the Rakko. Richard Wilcock, whose name had been unknown to them a week earlier, was mourned as the one unprejudiced Man on the planet, and rumors were rife that the government had actually had him assassinated before he could legally turn the land over to his two Rakko servants—who had been elevated, in the snakes' minds, to his two staunch Rakko friends and co-workers, and who themselves had become legal martyrs to the cause when they were not permitted to speak in court.

Eventually one leader emerged, as one leader usually does in such cases. His name was Robert Gobe, he was a Fani who had spent some years off-planet, studying in the better schools of the Republic, and upon his return he inflamed his followers with a series of fire-breathing speeches demanding that the government turn Castle Karimon over to the snakes' keeping, that anything less was not only an insult and an injustice but was the equivalent to an official government position that the snakes were nothing but animals in the eyes of the ruling race.

Gobe's problem was that the snakes *were* nothing but animals in the eyes of the ruling race, and especially in the eyes of their legal system, and he was arrested after a week of less-than-gentle suggestions that he moderate his rhetoric.

Since he was a Fani, it was decided to incarcerate him in Tulabete Country, far from his followers, and so he was shipped off to jail in Mastaboni. When he arrived there, the government found, much to its surprise, that a crowd of almost ten thousand worshipful Tulabete had surrounded the jail.

Gobe stood at the door to the jail and raised his hand for silence.

"They can lock me away," he said, "they can starve and

beat and humiliate me, just as they can jail and beat and humiliate you, but they cannot make us less than we are. Castle Karimon is ours, and justice must eventually prevail." And then, as they dragged him off, he decided to say one last thing to solidify his bonds with this particular audience: "Jalanopi's tree still stands!"

Very few of the Men on the scene understood the reference, but the cheer from the Tulabete could be heard for miles in every direction.

Thirty

R obert Gobe was locked away without a trial and kept incarcerated for two years.

He put the time to good use, laboriously writing a book entitled *Karimon Will Be Ours,* which included not only the moral justification for returning Castle Karimon to the snakes, but a long and detailed section cataloguing the abuses his people received at the hands of their human rulers, and finally, a truly frightening account of the regular beatings he had received since his arrest.

Somehow he managed smuggle the book out, a few pages at a time. The government caught wind of it just before it went to press in Talami, arrested everyone involved in the project, and destroyed the plates.

What they did not know was that a second copy of the manuscript existed, and that it was being printed on Earth even as they were confiscating all the primitive printing presses in Talami. Copies soon spread throughout the Spiral Arm, the human press took up the snakes' cause, and within another year the Secretary of the Republic, half a galaxy away on Deluros VIII, wrote a strong letter of protest to Rockgarden concerning the treatment of the snakes in general and Gobe in particular.

The government of Rockgarden, with their race still out-numbered hundreds to one by the snakes, decided that since the problem wouldn't go away on its own, they would solve it in the most efficient way possible. Robert Gobe was finally charged with inciting to riot and insurrection, was found guilty, and was hanged from Jalanopi's tree the next morning.

Those protesting his treatment—and there were many—were arrested on the spot. Some were beaten, some were released unharmed, and some were never seen again. The protests became less frequent and less violent, Wilcock's castle was made off-limits to snakes, and within a month things were back to normal on Rockgarden.

Except that the name Karimon, which had virtually vanished from the language prior to Violet Gardener's death, was once again in fashion when Men were not around and the snakes spoke, with renewed purpose, among themselves.

V

PETERSON'S
LAKE

Thirty-one

E mily Peterson stood atop a bluff, overlooking the
Punda River as it flowed through a small valley in the
northern sector of Faniland.

"Well?" asked her foreman.

She continued looking at the river for another moment,
then turned her attention to the holographic map that her
pocket computer projected in the air just in front of her.

"I think we'll do a series of five small dams, rather than
the two larger ones," she said, instructing the computer to
make notes on the map. "The river is too small for any
commercial traffic, and it'll do less damage to the fish and
wildlife this way. After all, we're doing it for *their* benefit in
the first place." She shook her head in wonderment.
"You'd think if they were going to gazette a new national
park, they'd choose an area that isn't subject to annual
droughts—or at least that they wouldn't import four hundred Redmountains that have to drink eighty gallons of
water apiece every day."

"Well, that's the government for you."

"I think we'll also create a number of permanent lagoons," she added, displaying them on the map. "The

Punda is very narrow here, and it's the only water for fifty miles in the dry season. No sense making the predators' job *too* easy."

"Good idea," replied her foreman. "They can rename it the Punda Pools National Park. It's got a nice ring to it."

"All right, Alexander," she said, deactivating the computer. "Go on back to the hotel, tie in to our office computer in Athens, and start running a cost analysis."

"Aren't you coming back with me?"

She shook her head. "I want to look around a little more and pinpoint exactly where I want those dams."

"All right. I'll see you later, then."

He turned and walked toward his groundcar, and Emily spent the next two hours walking beside the Punda, her experienced eye examining the landscape, the flow and depth of the water, the routes the animals would have to take to reach the lagoons she planned to create.

Suddenly she heard something moving in the bush. For just a moment she realized that she was alone and unarmed in the midst of an untamed wilderness area, but even as she was looking for a convenient tree to climb she decided that no animal would approach that clumsily.

"Alexander, is that you?" she said. "I thought I told you to start running a cost analysis."

"No, it isn't Alexander," said a voice, and a moment later a middle-aged man, lean and wiry, with a deep scar on his chin, came into view. "They told me I'd find you here," he said, and then smiled. "But nobody told me how big 'here' was."

"Have you any idea how ridiculous you look?" asked Emily, chuckling at his elegant city outfit. "What in the world is John Blake doing out in the bush?"

"Looking for you," he said, brushing the dust from his clothing. "Isn't it against the law to be walking around on your own in a national park without a communicator?"

"Is that another of the many laws you've passed this

year?" she asked, as a small herd of Fleetjumpers peered at him and then leaped off in the opposite direction.

"Probably," he said. He shrugged. "What the hell. I was never very good with a compass anyway. Even if I had raised you, you couldn't have told me how to find you."

"How *did* you find me?"

"I pulled up next to your groundcar and started walking along the river." He paused. "Thank heaven you were going south rather than north, or I might have been walking forever."

She laughed. "All right, now that you've found me, what's so important that you had to fly all the way out from Athens? Has the Wildlife Department changed their mind about the dams, or did you simply cut their budget again?"

"Neither," he replied. "The dams will be built—but if I have my way, they won't be built by you."

She frowned. "Oh?"

"I've got a more important job for you," he continued. "Quite possibly the most important job on the planet."

"I've been listening to your speeches," answered Emily. "I thought the most important job on the planet was keeping the snakes in line."

"It is."

"I run a construction company, not a prison," she answered.

"Then hear me out," said Blake. "The snakes are Rockgarden's problem, and we'll solve it ourselves. The one thing we do not need is someone coming in and telling us what we must or must not do."

"So the Republic's finally gotten into the act," said Emily.

"The Republic has no business telling us what we have to do," insisted Blake. "We are not a member world."

"I may not agree with all your policies," replied Emily, "but I agree with *that*. Rockgarden's problems are Rockgarden's, not the Republic's." She looked out over the river,

where a trio of Twisthorns had just come down to drink.
"What have they demanded?" she asked.

"Equal rights for all sentient beings," answered Blake.
"One being, one vote."

"I assume the government has refused?"

"Give every snake the vote and they'd kick us off the
planet by sundown," he said. "Of course we refused."

"Well, that's very interesting, John, and more than a
little bit disturbing—but what has it got to do with me?"

"The Republic won't bring military force to bear," he
said. "They've overextended themselves throughout the
galaxy, and they're very sensitive to charges of militarism
these days." He paused. "But they have no compunction
about using economic force to make us comply with their
edicts."

"What have they threatened?"

"Nothing specific yet . . . but we are not without our
sources of information. When dealing with planets like
ours, their first step is always to cut off sources of energy."

"Planets like ours?"

"Rockgarden is very poor in fossil fuels, and those minimal amounts that we have are in environments that are very
difficult to work. We've been depending on shipments of
fissionable materials from the Republic for ninety percent
of our power."

"Then why don't we simply use our own fissionable materials?" asked Emily.

"It's never been cost-effective to mine and refine them."
He paused. "More to the point, given the current situation,
we can't afford to let any fissionable material fall into the
hands of the snakes."

"Then what *do* you want?"

"We want to convert to a safe power source that will last
as long as Rockgarden—and we want to do it fast."

She stared at him, puzzled, as he took out his own computer and had it create a map of the continent.

"Here is the Karimona River, all forty-six hundred miles of it," he said, tracing a winding strip of blue with his forefinger. "And *here*," he said, "is the Zantu Valley, three hundred miles long, eighty miles wide, with the Karimona passing right through the middle of it."

"So?"

"I want you to build a dam," said Blake. "I want that dam, plus the Ramsey Falls, to supply all the power that Rockgarden can use for the foreseeable future."

"I don't think you understand what you're asking," replied Emily. "To create that much power—"

"—you'd have to turn the Zantu Valley into a lake three hundred miles long, eighty miles wide and four thousand feet deep in the middle," he concluded for her.

"Precisely."

"The government has just voted to use the Zantu Valley for that purpose."

"What about all the snakes who live there?"

"We'll move them."

"And the animals?"

"We'll move them, too—as many as we can."

Emily stared at the map for a long moment. "What kind of timetable are we talking about here?"

"Our target date is five years from now."

"It could take me three months just to develop some feasibility studies and to cost it out."

"It is feasible, because it *must* be feasible," said Blake firmly. "As for money, that's no object. You will be given everything you need, and you yourself will emerge from the project an extremely wealthy woman."

"It's a hell of an undertaking," said Emily, still studying the map.

"That's why I came to *you*," said Blake. "But you must remember that this is a matter of paramount importance. This dam *will* be built and this lake *will* be created. You are my first choice, but your refusal will not halt the project."

"I quite understand," replied Emily. "Let me speak with my associates, and if we decide that your project is feasible, then I will accept your commission."

"That's all I ask."

"I don't think you realize half of what you are asking," said Emily.

"I beg your pardon?"

"At a time when relations between the races have never been more strained, you propose to move perhaps a million snakes from their tribal homeland and turn it into a lake. At a time when our hunting and tourist industries are in decline, you are proposing a project that will almost certainly kill off ten to twenty million game animals. In the middle of a drought, you are proposing a project that will lower the Karimona River, the lifeblood of the entire continent, by perhaps fifty percent. And while you're doing all this, you're also thumbing your nose at the Republic."

"Suppose you let *me* worry about all that," said Blake.

"I just hope *some*body in Athens is worrying about it," said Emily seriously.

Thirty-two

The surveys took five months. The cost analysis took another three. The creation of a work force, a million strong, mostly snakes supervised by Men, took another two. Every problem, and there were many, was pinpointed, analyzed, and solved.

Except one:

The seven hundred thousand Fani who lived in the Zantu Valley were relocated, or hired onto the work force.

The two hundred thousand Fallani, a Fani subgroup, who lived in the Zantu Valley, were relocated.

The seventy-eight thousand Golomba who lived in the Zantu Valley were relocated.

That left twenty-two thousand snakes of the Polombi tribe, impoverished even by snake standards, who made their meager living by fishing in the Karimona River. Their entire culture was based on the river; even their god, a huge four-armed fire-breathing deity, was a river god.

And they refused to leave.

"They are a royal pain in the ass," complained Blake at his weekly meeting with Emily Peterson in her Athens headquarters. "I've offered the entire tribe one thousand credits apiece and the guarantee of a new homeland, and they simply won't budge."

"Obviously they prefer their old homeland," replied Emily.

"Their old homeland is going to be submerged under trillions of tons of water in another couple of years," answered Blake. "What they like isn't important."

"It is to them."

"If I have to move them forcibly, I will," said Blake. "I would just prefer to find a less controversial solution."

"I don't know why you've come to us with your problem," said Emily. "I was hired to create a lake and build a dam. *You* were supposed to take care of the political aspects of the situation."

"I thought the creator of the Peterson Dam might care to have some input," said Blake coldly.

"I didn't ask for this to be called the Peterson Dam," responded Emily. "In fact, I expressly asked you *not* to use my name. You insisted on it so that the snakes' anger would be directed at me rather than the government—but I'm telling you now that I will not be held responsible for whatever you finally do to or with the Polombi."

"You could help by hiring at least some of them to work on the project," said Blake.

"We catch fifteen or twenty of them every night, doing their damnedest to *sabotage* the project," answered Emily.

"I wasn't aware of that."

"Well, now you are."

"We'll have to put a stop to it."

"I wish you luck," said Emily. "They think they're doing the bidding of Gantamunu, and that he'll protect them."

"Who's Gantamunu? Their king?"

"Their god."

"Wonderful!" spat Blake. "Just what I need. A bunch of religious zealots trying to destroy the project."

"They're a bunch of innocent primitives who can't understand why you are destroying their river."

"I've had interpreters explain it to them again and again," complained Blake. "They'll be better off for it. Once we create Lake Zantu, we plan to stock it. In fifteen years, we'll be pulling a hundred tons of fish out of it every day."

"Well, that's one reason your arguments don't work," said Emily.

"I don't understand."

"Why don't you go look at the absolute poverty in which they live?" she suggested. "Not one in five of them will be alive in fifteen years."

"If they'll move, we, give them all the medical attention they need."

"Probably they'd prefer spiritual attention, which is what you're taking away from them."

"How? They can build churches or whatever they use for worship wherever we relocate them."

"Gantamunu is a river god," said Emily. "If you destroy the Karimona River, you destroy *him*."

Blake shook his head in disgust. "And the Republic wants *them* to run this planet!"

Thirty-three

M atunay, the king of the Polombi, walked along the
moonlit bank of the Karimona River.

Here was the spot where he was born, over there the
place where he underwent the Adulthood Ritual, half a
mile back the spot where his father had died and he himself
had become king. This mound of dirt was where he had
taken his first wife in marriage, that tree over there where
he had hidden as a youth when a Water Horse attacked
him, three hundred yards upriver the spot where a Rivertooth had killed his daughter.

This was more than land, it was a history book of his life
and his people. What audacity the Men had to think that
Gantamunu would sit idly by and let them destroy it, bury
it under untold fathoms of water!

And their reasons made no more sense than they themselves did. They were doing this for power.

Power?

Power was what he had in his arm when he hurled his
spear into the water and came up with a fish. Power was
what a king wielded when he sat in judgment of his people,
or made war or peace with the neighboring tribes.

And power was what the mighty Karimona possessed, with a current so strong that only the greatest of his people could swim against it. Power to make the crops grow, power to flood the landscape, power to take the breath from even a king's lungs and fill them with water.

Power was Gantamunu, and now these foolish Men had pitted themselves against him, against the most powerful god of all.

Well, let the Fani and the Fallani and Golomba do Man's bidding and move away from the source of all life. Their gods were evidently not strong enough to oppose the Men who dared to try to change the shape and course of the Karimona, but Gantamunu feared neither Man nor god. He might not protect the Polombi, for he was a harsh god, but he would protect his river.

Balator, who was Matunay's personal shaman, had suggested that instead of making the usual sacrifices of fish and fruit to Gantamunu, the Polombi would find favor in his eyes by destroying the Men's work. Of course, there were so many Men and so much work that they couldn't stop all progress, but they could cut a line here, break a support post there, overturn a supply raft, even throw mud in the delicate equipment the Men set such store by.

And so they did. For months they went unnoticed, or at least unhindered, but lately the Men had taken to posting guards up and down the river at all their work sites. Already twenty-nine Polombi had been killed, and sixty-seven more had been taken off to prison, which was worse than death for a being that had spent all its life under the brilliant sun of Karimon.

Matunay was of two minds concerning the sabotage. He approved of it, certainly, but he saw no reason for any Polombi to die when it was obvious that Gantamunu would not allow the completion of the project. After the first of his people were killed and incarcerated, he did not order his warriors to continue the practice, but on the other hand he did not forbid it, and the boldest of his young warriors continued a campaign of harassment, while he waited patiently for Gantamunu to drive the aliens from his river.

On this particular evening, two of his warriors had staggered into camp, exhausted, to report that they had overturned yet another raft, but had lost three companions in the process. One had been shot, one had been captured, and the third had drowned. Upon receiving the news, Matunay walked in silence along the river bank, trying to sort matters out in his mind. Finally, unable to do so, he returned to his throne—a small tree stump covered with the hide of a Water Horse—and summoned Balator, his shaman.

Balator, whose skin was shedding, arrived a few minutes later, looking like some moldering corpse risen from the grave. He grunted a greeting to his king, then squatted down next to the throne to await Matunay's bidding.

"I am troubled, Balator," said Matunay.

"What troubles you, my king?"

"Tonight five of our warriors went down the river to overturn a raft that contained the Men's supplies," said Matunay.

"Did you send them, my king?" asked Balator.

"No, but I did not stop them," answered Matunay. "They were seen by the Men who guard. Two escaped, and three did not."

"I am sorry to hear that, my king."

"They are warriors; that is the chance they take."

"Then this is not why you summoned me?"

"Let me continue. One of the warriors was shot and killed, and one was captured."

"That is only two, my king," said Balator. "What became of the third?"

"He drowned."

"Ah," said Balator.

"That is why I must speak with you, Balator," said Matunay. "They were acting on Gantamunu's behalf. Why would he drown one of his chosen people? Why does he not drown all the Men, and all the Fani and Tulabete and Golomba who work for them?"

"We shall see," said Balator. He reached into a pouch that hung about his neck and pulled out a number of bones and shining stones. He stared at them for a moment, muttered a brief chant, and rolled them on the ground, then repeated the process thrice more.

"What do the signs tell you?" asked Matunay.

"Gantamunu is pleased with you, my king," said Balator, "as he is pleased with all the Polombi."

"Then why did my warrior drown in Gantamunu's river?" persisted Matunay.

"Soon Gantamunu shall strike, and the Men shall know the full extent of his power and his fury," answered Balator. "But before he does this, he must feed deeply and build his strength, for though they are his enemies, the Men are themselves brave and strong. Every Polombi, every Man, every Fani, every Tulabete, every fish that dies in the Karimona lends its essence to Gantamunu. Every Brown-buck that dies beneath the jaws of a Rivertooth, every Fleet-jumper that is killed by a Wildfang while slaking its thirst, every bird that is pulled beneath the surface by a stingliz-ard, each of them adds to Gantamunu's strength."

"Then why doesn't he strike now?" demanded Matunay.

"He is Gantamunu," answered Balator serenely. "He will know when to strike."

"Ah!" said Matunay. "You are saying that he will wait until the day that the Men actually try to stop the flow of the river, for then they will truly understand how powerful he is?"

"I am saying only that he grows stronger by the day, and that he will know when to strike," answered Balator.

"Then shall I order my warriors not to act against the Men?"

Balator rolled the bones and stones again.

"You are to do precisely as you have done. You will order no one to act against the Men, but those who wish must be allowed to. And you will mourn no warrior who is lost, for his soul will simply hasten the moment of Gantamunu's fierce and terrible retribution against these beings who think that they can destroy Gantamunu's abode."

"So it shall be," said Matunay.

Balator arose and returned to his dwelling, which had been hollowed out on the riverbank.

Matunay sat on his throne for another few minutes, considering what his shaman had said. Finally he arose and once again began walking along the river, an enormous burden lifted from his shoulders. He need no longer feel guilty for not preventing his unarmed warriors from risking capture or death at the hands of the hated aliens; every one of them who died brought the day of Gantamunu's revenge closer.

Now, too, he understood why Gantamunu had not acted yet. To destroy a handful of Men when they had only half-completed their project would not have been decisive, and from what he knew of Men, they would return. But to wait until they erected their seven-hundred-foot wall of concrete and then to blow it down with a single mighty breath . . . *that* would show them whose god was the most powerful.

Yes, he thought, nodding his head grimly. Soon Gantamunu would show them the true meaning of power.

Thirty-four

"How the hell did this happen?" demanded Emily Peterson, staring out the window of her temporary office overlooking the dam.

"I don't know," said her foreman with a helpless shrug. "We put the pilings in deep enough, we gauged the flow of the river right, we built the damned thing seventy feet thick. There's no reason for it."

"Don't tell me there's no reason for it. We spent four years building a dam, and now the entire wall has a crack in it from top to bottom! I want to know why!"

"I don't know!" he yelled back at her. "Fire me if you want, but I did my job right. We used nothing but first-quality materials, we didn't just match the specs, we exceeded them. That goddamned thing was built to last a thousand years!"

"Could it have been sabotage?"

"You think a bunch of illiterate fishermen could put a crack eight hundred feet long and seventy feet wide in a concrete dam?" he said sardonically. "You think *anyone* could, without our knowing about it?"

Emily glared at him. "Then what went wrong?"

He shrugged again. "I don't have an answer."

"Well, *I'm* going to have to have an answer when the government asks me—and you can be sure they're going to ask me."

"I've run all the specifications through the computer again and again, and it can't come up with a reason. In fact, it says it can't have happened."

"John Blake is not going to accept that as an answer," replied Emily. "That man has his eye on the governorship of Rockgarden, and this is *his* project. He's going to find a scapegoat before he'll let it sink his career."

"You can hand him my head on a platter if you think it'll help," said her foreman earnestly. "But I'm telling you that there is no logical reason why the wall should have cracked. We've even checked for seismic activity, and we came up blank. Not so much as a tremor."

"If I need your head, rest assured I'll come after it," said Emily. "For the time being, I'll handle the political damage control. What are you doing about controlling the damage to the dam?"

"We're reinforcing the wall, of course, and I've got the computer working on another location for a new wall, about a quarter of a mile downstream."

"Why there? All our studies showed us that this was the optimum location."

"Because until I know what caused *this* wall to crack, I don't see any sense building another one abutting it."

"Won't that make it fifty feet wider?"

"Fifty-seven feet four inches."

She stared at him. "You're sure that's where we want to build it?"

"Mrs. Peterson," said the foreman, "at this point I'm not sure of a damned thing. But that's where the computer says we should put it, so unless you tell me otherwise, that's where I'm putting it."

"What will we do with the damaged wall?"

"I suppose we can use a molecular imploder on it after we finish work on the new one."

She lowered her head in thought for a long moment, then looked up.

"All right," she said. "Do what you can to reinforce the cracked wall, and then start putting in pilings for the new one. And I want security tripled."

"Yes, Mrs. Peterson."

"And I want our best engineers to work overtime with their computers until someone can tell me exactly what went wrong."

"Yes, Mrs. Peterson," he said, backing away toward the door to her office.

"All right," she said. "Get out of here."

He made a grateful escape, while Emily stared out her window at the enormous crack in the dam's wall and wondered, for the hundredth time, how it had happened.

Matunay, king of the Polombi, stood on the opposite bank of the river, hands on hips, and looked with satisfaction at the enormous crack in the aliens' wall. He knew, of course, that this was the revenge of Gantamunu, and would have been more than happy to explain it to the Men, but nobody thought to ask him.

Thirty-five

"What has happened?" asked Matunay. "Why does Gantamunu not strike again?"

"Possibly it took all his strength to destroy the first wall," answered Balator. "I do not know."

"You must roll the bones and ask him, for the Men have told us that we must leave tomorrow morning, that when the sun is at its highest they will begin flooding the land."

"I will roll the bones," said Balator with a shrug, "but Gantamunu has been silent since the last rains."

"And during that time the Men have built an even larger, thicker wall than the one he destroyed," said Matunay, frowning. "Why? We must know his answer."

Balator pulled the bones and shining stones from the pouch about his neck and cast them onto the ground. Then he gathered them up, cast them again, and repeated the process a third time, after which he leaned forward and studied their configuration.

"Well?" demanded Matunay. "What does he say?"

"Nothing," replied Balator. "Gantamunu does not respond to the bones."

"He *must!*" exclaimed Matunay. "You are reading the signs wrong, shaman."

"I am reading what the signs say."

"Cast the bones again," ordered Matunay.

Balator sighed, gathered up his little collection of bones and stones, and threw them onto the dirt once more.

"There is no answer," he said at last.

"He knows you are casting the bones?" queried Matunay.

"Is he not the all-powerful Gantamunu?" replied Balator testily.

"Then even his silence must be an answer. What, precisely, did you ask him?"

"I asked him if we should leave our homes."

"And since he didn't say yes, the answer is obvious: we must remain."

"There is no point to it, my king. The Men will turn our land into a lake, and if we remain we will drown."

"Gantamunu will not allow us to drown," said Matunay with absolute conviction. "We are his children. He saved us the last time, and he will save us again. You have misinterpreted his silence, shaman."

"Gantamunu will surely take his revenge upon the Men, but it is blasphemy to tell him that he must do so at a certain time or place," answered Balator. "We should climb to the safety of the hills in the morning, and wait for him to act."

"He may not act if he thinks we have lost our faith in him," said Matunay. He paused. "*You* climb the hills if you wish, but Matunay, king of the Polombi, will stay here where Gantamunu can see him."

All through the night they argued, neither changing his position, and when the sun came up Balator and the remaining Polombi ascended the hills to the point at which the human engineers had told them they would be safe, and Matunay remained on the riverbank.

Even when the floodgates opened and billions upon billions of gallons of water headed directly toward him, Matunay's faith never wavered. He stood facing the flood, arms folded resolutely across his chest, and calmly awaited Gantamunu's miracle.

Thirty-six

L ake Zantu was created in less than three days. It was
   317 miles long and 82 wide, reached a depth of almost 4,500 feet, and was dotted with 73 islands, from which
the surviving wildlife was being rescued and transported to
the newly made lakeshore.

And a week later Lake Zantu was only 76 miles wide.

"Correct me if I'm wrong," said John Blake, who was on
an inspection tour with Emily Peterson, "but this shoreline
looks like it was recently underwater."

"It was."

"You can't lose three miles of shoreline through evapo-
ration," he said. "What's going on here?"

"Every action has an equal and opposite reaction. I
thought you learned that in school."

"They taught me lots of things in school. How does that
apply to this particular situation?"

"We added trillions of tons of water to a limited section
of land, and the end result was that we put a dent in the
surface of the planet."

"A *dent?*"

"Our figures took it into consideration. Starting tomorrow we'll raise the lake to its original level."

"Will this do any lasting damage to the planet?" asked Blake.

"Not a bit," she assured him. "We'll have the generators operational in another month, you'll have a huge new fishing industry inside of three years, and if you can avoid a war with the Republic, you might very well draw more tourists to the lake than to the wildlife parks."

"Well, that's comforting, anyway." He looked up to the top of one of the hills. "Who are those snakes up there? Why aren't they working on the generators or moving animals or something?"

"They're the Polombi," replied Emily.

"Well, in a couple of years, they can go back to fishing," said Blake.

"We took away more than their livelihood," said Emily. "We took away their entire way of life."

"It wasn't much of a way of life from what I could see," said Blake.

"No," agreed Emily. "But it was theirs."

"Maybe I'll pay their king a visit and explain the facts of life to him."

"He was drowned when we created the lake."

"I thought we moved everyone to safety," said Blake, frowning.

"Everyone who was *willing* to move. He insisted on staying. He thought Gantamunu would protect him."

"Their water god?" said Blake contemptuously. "Well, I guess they know whose god is stronger now." He turned to Emily. "Take my word for it: in another year, they'll be working side by side with the rest of your snakes."

She shook her head. "In another year they'll be begging for handouts and waiting for Gantamunu to become strong enough to destroy the dam."

"Nonsense," said Blake. "We landed on the planet, and the Tulabete adjusted. We built Athens, and the Fani adjusted. We unearthed Castle Karimon, and the Rakko adjusted. The Polombi will adjust too."

"You didn't deprive the Fani and Tulabete and Rakko of their homeland and their culture." She looked at the mournful figures up on the hill. "Those poor bastards have nothing left. We've taken away everything they had, and we've replaced it with nothing."

"In three years they'll all be fishermen again."

"In three years Men are going to be cruising Lake Zantu with huge boats and pulling in thousands of fish every few minutes in their nets. You don't really expect the Polombi to go out with their canoes and their fishing spears and compete, do you?"

"Then they'll do something else."

"They can't farm the hills," she answered. "First, they don't know how, and second, it's Fani land. By the same token, they can't become hunters: they've never hunted before, and they're living in a national park where they can be arrested for hunting. What do you think they're going to do?"

"We *had* to have the dam," said Blake irritably. "You know that."

"Yes," she agreed with a sigh. "I know that."

Blake looked at the Polombi one last time. "What do you suppose will become of them?"

"Seriously?" said Emily. "I think every last one of them will be dead within a quarter of a century."

She was wrong: Balator, the last Polombi, lived for twenty-seven more years.

VI

BLAKE'S MILLENNIUM

Thirty-seven

A nother day, another delegation.

John Blake sighed, then got to his feet to greet the three men and five women who entered his office. They exchanged formal greetings, sat down around the conference table that had been set up next to a window overlooking Gardener Square, and then the self-appointed leader of the delegation got down to business.

"Mr. Blake, I'll come straight to the point of our visit," he said, pouring himself a glass of water from the pitcher that had been provided for that purpose. "We have spent the past six days studying the economic and political condition of the native populace of Rockgarden, and frankly, we find it appalling."

"The wheels of change grind slowly," answered Blake, lighting up one of his smokeless Denebian cigars. "But rest assured, Mr. Heinrich, they *are* grinding."

"I'm afraid that answer is unacceptable to us," said Heinrich. "You are running for the office of Governor of Rockgarden. It is incumbent upon both you and your opponents to address the problem confronting this planet, and none of you seems willing to do so."

Blake stared at him for a long moment. "As I see it, the major problem confronting me at the moment is that outsiders who have no stake in the future of Rockgarden are trying to influence our planetary election. You may tell the Republic that Rockgarden is fully capable of determining its own future without your interference."

"We are not here to exchange threats, sir, but merely to apprise you of the gravity of the situation," said Heinrich. "If you choose to become a pariah among human worlds, you must be aware of the consequences."

"That certainly sounds like a threat to *me*," said Blake. He paused, looking at each of his visitors in turn. "Who are you to tell us how to run our world? Did you clear the trees and the scrub and turn a wilderness into the most productive farmland in the Spiral Arm? Did you pull precious ores, ores that the Republic desperately needs, out of our land? Did you change the entire topography of this world by creating Lake Zantu?" He glared at them again. "No, you sat in your glass towers on Deluros VIII and let us tame a world and pacify its natives in a savage war, and now you're telling us to turn the planet over to the race that tried to hinder us at every step."

"It is *their* planet," one of the women pointed out.

"Rubbish," said Blake. "If we left Rockgarden, they'd be back to living in burrows and eating bugs for a living inside two weeks."

"I rather doubt it," said Heinrich, finishing his water and pouring himself a second glass. "More than two thousand of them have attended schools within the Republic. A number of them have even written books." He paused, then added accusingly: "The most brilliant of them is currently incarcerated, without charge or bail, in an Athens jail."

"Have you *read* Thomas Paka's book?" demanded Blake. "It's an outline for revolution."

"It is a cry for social justice," interjected another of the women.

"You tell me what disrupting communications and destroying the generators at Lake Zantu have to do with social justice!" said Blake heatedly.

"You have kept his people in servitude since colonizing Rockgarden," said Heinrich. "Surely he has a right to oppose your policies."

"If I were him, I might have written the same book," agreed Blake. "But I'm not. I'm a Man, and like every other Man on this planet, I'm outnumbered almost two hundred to one by the snakes. We've achieved a very uneasy equilibrium here, and we don't need members of the Republic coming in and threatening to upset it. If you want to walk away from Lodin XI and Peponi and five thousand other worlds that you opened up and tamed through human sweat and sacrifice, that's your business—but Rockgarden isn't bound by the Republic's rules, and we're not about to turn this world over to a race that is demonstrably not capable of running it."

"We are your last best hope, Mr. Blake," said Heinrich. "You are sitting on a powder keg here. If social justice is not achieved, and quickly, the inhabitants will not have to read Thomas Paka's book to know that they have no choice but to join in an armed rebellion."

"They tried it once before, and we put it down," said Blake. "If it happens again, we'll defeat them again."

"I am afraid we are making no more progress with you than with your rivals for office," said Heinrich sadly. "I think we shall have to return to Deluros VIII and recommend that all trade with Rockgarden be cut off until major changes are made in the fabric of your society."

"Last month it was Admiral McAffee of the Second Fleet, and three weeks ago it was the Assistant Comptroller of the Treasury," said Blake contemptuously. "And earlier this week it was the Commerce Division of the Department of Alien Affairs."

"I don't quite understand you, Mr. Blake."

"What I'm saying is that we've been threatened by experts, Mr. Heinrich."

"You are making a serious mistake."

"The Republic made a serious mistake when it tried to tell an independent world how to run its internal affairs. We know we have problems, but we'll address them in our own way and in our own good time. We will not be coerced, threatened, frightened, or bribed into doing the Republic's bidding."

"What you are doing to these natives is patently, blatantly *wrong*," said Heinrich severely.

"What we are doing," answered Blake, "is precisely what the Republic did all over the galaxy for close to two thousand years, until you were so overextended that you lost a couple of wars and found out that you couldn't afford fifty thousand colony worlds. You didn't grant Peponi and the others their independence for noble motives; it was economics, plain and simple." He glared at Heinrich. "So don't give us your smug, superior attitude. This is Rockgarden, Mr. Heinrich; we know better."

"I see no sense continuing this discussion any further," said Heinrich. "Our minimum demand is universal suffrage: one being, one vote. If you will not address the problem, our business here is done."

"I have never said I wouldn't address that problem," replied Blake. "Only that our timetables are likely to differ."

"By how much?"

"I'm giving a speech tonight," said Blake. "If you're still on Rockgarden, you might try to catch the broadcast."

"You didn't answer my question, Mr. Blake."

"I'll answer it in my speech."

They got up from the conference table and filed out of

his office, and Blake looked out the window, past Gardener Square, at the clean, broad avenues of Athens, and tried not to think about how quickly they would turn into slums under snake rule. Rockgarden was no paradise, despite all the brochures the government sent out to prospective colonists—how could it be, when Men were outnumbered hundreds to one by an increasingly hostile native population?—but he was damned well not going to let it become the raging inferno that Thomas Paka and his followers sought to make it. At least, he thought with satisfaction, all the candidates agreed on the major issue; the election for the governorship of Rockgarden would be decided on minor points, and if he lost he could live with that.

After a few minutes he sat down at his desk, activated his computer, pulled up the speech that his staff had written for this evening's rally, and began making notes and minor changes. This word was too difficult to pronounce and would break the flow of the speech, that concept had to be made less complex or it would be lost on his audience, this joke had been used too often and was due to be retired, that position would play better in Mastaboni than Athens and needn't be covered tonight.

Finally, by lunchtime, he had whipped the speech into its final shape, and he spent the rest of the afternoon out in the streets, pressing flesh, posing for pictures, soliciting votes, and providing sound bites for the evening news.

Then, at seven o'clock, amidst thunderous applause, he stepped onto the stage of the Athens Playhouse and addressed his select thousand-credit-a-seat audience.

The speech touched on all the partisan economic and political issues that his audience wanted to hear, poked gentle fun at his opponents, and carefully delineated the minimal differences between himself and the other candidates. Finally, when it was through, he raised his hands for silence and stared intently into the holo cameras that were transmitting his image throughout the continent.

"There is one final subject that I have promised to address," he said, "and that is the matter of universal suffrage."

The members of the press sat up alertly, as this was not in the prepared text that had been handed out.

"I have said throughout my political career that when the snakes have proven that they are ready to share power, we Men will have no compunction at welcoming them into the government, and passing laws that guarantee one being, one vote."

This was not what his audience had expected to hear, and suddenly the theater was completely silent.

"In my considered opinion," concluded Blake, "that day will not arrive for a thousand years."

If he had more to say, it couldn't be heard amid the impassioned cheering.

The next morning, the *Athens Times* enthusiastically endorsed "Blake's Millennium," and the *Mastaboni News* followed suit a day later.

And two weeks later, John Blake became governor of Rockgarden in the greatest electoral landslide in the planet's brief history.

Thirty-eight

I t began neither with a bang nor a whimper, but with a boycott. The Republic responded to Blake's election by cutting off all trade with Rockgarden. Of all the human-controlled planets in the galaxy, only Goldstone refused to honor the boycott and continued to supply John Blake's world.

Blake turned the boycott into both a political and an economic asset: political, because the citizenry was outraged that an off-world body was trying to involve itself in their internal affairs, and economic, because it forced Rockgarden to diversify its industries in order to become self-sufficient. Within six months there were factories lining the outskirts of Athens and Mastaboni producing everything from soap to groundcars, and within a year Rockgarden, while it was still undergoing some hardships, was able to supply all of its own most vital necessities.

The Republic summoned Blake's government to come to Deluros VIII and discuss the situation. Blake ignored the first two invitations and responded to the third with a curt negative.

Unrest continued to grow almost daily among the

snakes, and soon the jails couldn't hold all the dissenters, so Blake's government created large prison camps surrounded by lethally charged electric fences out in the bush.

Then, early one morning, while most of the human population was still in bed, a group of some three hundred Tulabete, under the leadership of a schoolteacher named Moses Selabali, attacked and destroyed the entire human town of New Oxford, which was on the road halfway between Mastaboni and Athens. Fourteen Men were killed and sixty-seven were taken prisoner, to be released in exchange for the freedom of Thomas Paka, the jailed author.

"My government does not deal with outlaws and criminals," answered Blake, when the proposal was made public.

Selabali executed ten hostages the next day, and ten every day thereafter, until all sixty-seven were dead.

The government responded by marching into Selabali's village—he himself wasn't there—and slaughtering all four hundred snakes that they found there.

A month later the Fani, demanding freedom for Paka, blew up a train that was traveling from Athens to Mastaboni. Seventeen Men were killed and more than one hundred hospitalized.

The government, not knowing which Fani village was responsible, took a scattershot approach, destroying ten Fani villages at random.

The next morning a bomb went off in the Athens Art Museum, destroying most of the collection that Violet Gardner had willed to Rockgarden.

Blake ordered his troops to burn down the most sacred shrine the Fani possessed.

All was quiet for another month. Then ten human farms were burned just outside Mastaboni.

Blake again ordered instant retaliation, and waited for news from his army.

And waited.

And waited.

When the officer in charge finally reported back, it was to inform him that they had met fierce, well-armed resistance. The Tulabete were supplied with both sonic and laser weapons, none of them made on Rockgarden.

And when the Fani took credit for attacking the outpost town of Fuentes, the troops who had been directed to quell the disturbance reported the same thing: they were up against a large, well-organized force armed with off-world weaponry.

Blake called a meeting of his cabinet, to lay out the situation to them.

"Well," said his Minister of Defense, "it's obvious that someone has been arming them. I just wish I knew *who.*"

"It's got to be the Republic," said another minister.

Blake shook his head. "No. The Republic has never armed an alien race and turned them loose on Men before."

"Then who could it be?"

"There's five thousand bleeding-heart organizations out there, each of them prepared to take the aliens' side in any dispute they have with Men. Most of these groups are well financed, and they have excellent intelligence capabilities. I'm sure that half a dozen of them have been supplying arms to the snakes."

"How?"

"We can't patrol the whole damned planet," answered Blake. "They could be using almost anyone as a contact: a Republic reporter, anyone who represents himself as a trader from Goldstone, an alien tourist, anyone."

"So do we close up the whole planet and not allow anyone in or out?" asked the Minister of Trade. "I suppose we could make do, though losing our commerce with Goldstone will be quite a hardship."

"We can't deny the whole galaxy access to Rockgarden," said Blake. "The Republic is temporarily content to give moral support to the snakes, but if we shut them out completely, and don't let them know what's going on here, the day will come when they decide to take us over by force." He paused. "Besides, our own citizens come and go every day. I can't very well imprison them on their own planet." He shook his head again. "No, we'll just have to tighten our security and try to pinpoint and then stop the flow of weapons."

"My reports say that the snakes have stockpiled an awful lot of weaponry already," remarked the Minister of Defense. "Evidently they've been planning this for years, perhaps ever since Paka and Selabali visited the Republic. This is no spur of the moment uprising; it's just the tip of the iceberg. I think we'd better prepare ourselves for a long, hard military campaign."

"Well, we have one thing in our favor," said Blake.

"What is that?"

"The Tulabete and the Fani hate each other a hell of a lot more than they hate us. If they get their hands on enough guns, they're going to forget all about their recent enemies and go after their traditional ones. I can see them spending the next half century trying to wipe each other out." He paused, and allowed himself the luxury of a smile. "I, for one, wish them each the best of luck."

Thirty-nine

B ut the Fani and the Tulabete *didn't* forget their most recent enemy. The attacks grew bolder and more frequent, the requests became demands, and unlike their disastrous defeat against Fuentes some decades earlier, this time they used the terrain to their advantage and fought a hit-and-run guerrilla war. They knew they outnumbered the enemy hundreds to one, but they also knew that Men possessed better weapons and a trained, disciplined military force that they were not prepared to meet head-on in battle.

The pattern was repeated over and over again. A human outpost or farm would be destroyed. When the army showed up, there were no snakes around. When they questioned the local snake villages, no one had seen or heard anything. But if a Man lingered too long behind his fellows in one of those villages, or on a forest trail, or in the foothills of the Tenya Mountains, as often as not he would simply disappear, never to be seen again.

The retributions were swift and terrible. Entire villages were razed to the ground, crops were burned, herds of Tallgrazers were confiscated or, more often, killed.

Finally Blake gave his permission to the army to hire human mercenaries from other worlds, mercenaries who had had experience fighting guerrilla wars. Within a month three hundred of them were under contract. Known informally as the Bush Brigade, they combed the forests and savannahs and engaged in a number of pitched battles with the snakes. For the most part they killed the enemy; but they also needed information, and they were not above using both drugs and torture to obtain it.

The snakes responded in kind. They needed no information, but they also began torturing their victims.

Then one day Thomas Paka, who had spent the past two years languishing in the Athens jail, sent a message that he would like to meet with John Blake.

Blake agreed, and had him brought to one of the interrogation rooms on the main floor of the jail. He waited until Paka's handcuffs were secured to the metal chair on which he was seated, then entered the room and ordered the guards to leave. Paka was just starting to shed his skin, and it was loose and starting to peel in half a hundred places; Blake thought it gave him the appearance of a revived corpse, but he had seen the condition thousands of time and made no mention of it.

"Good afternoon, Mr. Blake," said Paka in excellent Terran. "I thank you for agreeing to meet with me." He paused. "I have not seen you in some time."

"Good afternoon, Mr. Paka," replied Blake coldly. "I am not inclined to visit traitors in their cells."

"Whether one is a traitor or a patriot depends entirely upon one's point of view," said Paka. "And upon who is holding the weapon."

"It depends upon a simple reading of the law," answered Blake. "You have tried to overthrow the legally elected government of Rockgarden."

"From a prison cell?" replied Paka sardonically. "I was

imprisoned without being charged of any crime more than a year before the revolution began."

"A bunch of savages chopping up isolated farmers and settlers can hardly be called a revolution," answered Blake.

"I have never advocated such methods," said Paka. "Though I have been given to understand that your own army has been equally brutal."

"I thought you asked for this meeting because you wanted to deal," said Blake. "If you just wanted to talk about which side is more brutal, I have better things to do with my time."

"No," said Paka. "I have a personal favor to ask of you."

"A favor?" repeated Blake suspiciously.

Paka nodded. "Word has reached me that my wife is dying. I wish to go to her side."

"Just like that?"

"I give you my pledge that if you will release me, I will return as soon as she has died."

"I can't do that. You're much too dangerous to be released." Blake paused. "Besides, if you're like the rest of the snakes, you've probably got three or four more wives stashed away."

"I have only one wife, and I love her deeply."

"Snakes are incapable of love," said Blake.

"Snakes are capable of every emotion that Men feel," replied Paka. "Except, perhaps, contempt for other species."

"I doubt it," said Blake. "But even if that were true, I still can't let you go."

"I am not a military threat, Mr. Blake," said Paka. "I am a theorist and a writer. I have never led an army or participated in a battle in my life. I have never raised a hand against any Man or snake." He looked directly into Blake's eyes. "I give you my solemn word that I will not do so now."

"It doesn't matter," said Blake. "All over the planet, Men are being gutted like fish, frequently in your name. I don't care whether you know military tactics or not—the Fani aren't using them anyway. This isn't a war or a revolution; it's a legal government fighting a bunch of terrorists—and you and this Tulabete, Moses Selabali, are their leaders."

"How can I be a leader when I have been in jail for more than two years?" demanded Paka in frustration.

"You're not their *leader;* you're their *hero.* That makes you even *more* dangerous."

"Mr. Blake, I have never asked a favor of a Man before," said Paka. "But I am asking you—I am *begging* you—to let me visit my wife before she dies."

Blake shook his head. "I'm not without sympathy for you, Mr. Paka," he said, "but I can't take the chance. I've got three million Men depending on me to defend their lives and their property, and I can do that a lot more efficiently if you're in jail than if you're not."

"Your Christ would disapprove of you," said Paka bitterly.

"What does a snake know about Christ?" replied Blake contemptuously.

"I am a Christian," said Paka. "And Christians do not do this to one another."

"*You?*" snorted Blake. "Don't make me laugh."

"It is true."

"You think Jesus died for *your* sins?"

"I do not accept his divinity, only his wisdom," answered Paka.

"Then you're *not* a Christian."

"I am a believer in the doctrine of Jesus Christ, not that of his disciples."

"Did Jesus tell his followers to torture and mutilate innocent men and women?"

"No," said Paka. "And neither did I."

"This blasphemy has gone far enough," said Blake irritably.

"It is not blasphemy, but the simple truth."

"All right—you want to prove you're a Christian?" said Blake suddenly. "Then renounce the violence your people have committed. Make a speech telling them to lay down their weapons and surrender. I can have cameras in here in five minutes."

Paka shook his head. "Jesus lived in a world populated by Men. They crucified him. I will not have you crucify my people."

"I'll grant a general amnesty."

"I do not trust you, Mr. Blake."

"And I do not trust you, Mr. Paka," said Blake. "Therefore, I think we have nothing further to say."

"I have one thing," said Paka.

"Oh?"

"I want you to remember that I volunteered to return to prison if you allowed me to visit my wife, and you refused."

"That sounds suspiciously like a threat, Mr. Paka," said Blake.

"It is merely a statement." Paka paused. "I will make another one. Prior to this moment, I have fought for social justice, but I have never hated you or any Man. That is no longer true."

"I think I've wasted enough time with you," said Blake, walking to the door and summoning the guards. Three burly men entered the room, released Paka from his chair, cuffed his hands behind his back, and hurried him back to his cell.

Blake returned to the executive mansion and spent the rest of the afternoon reviewing some legislation that was awaiting his signature. Then he stopped by his private club for a workout, ate dinner in the club's restaurant, and spent a pleasant evening playing cards and talking politics. He returned to the mansion at about midnight, pleasantly tired and ready for bed, only to find an urgent message waiting for him.

A team of twenty Fani, under cover of night, had broken into the jail, killed the warden and seven guards, and had released more than two hundred prisoners.

Included among the escapees was Thomas Paka.

Forty

W ithin a month Blake realized that he wasn't going to be able to stop the flow of arms. A Republic ship, loaded with laser rifles, crashed on the Desert Continent, and once he knew that the Republic itself was supplying the snakes he knew there was no way to stop it.

Within two months, he realized that he should have allowed Thomas Paka to visit his wife; for if Paka was a writer and a theorist up to that fateful day, he was now a hate-filled leader capable of arousing enormous passions among his followers.

Within three months he realized that the Fani and the Tulabete were not going to fight each other until they had settled their business with the colonists. Paka and Moses Selabali had been seen together on five separate occasions, and the attacks from the Fani and Tulabete armies had become much better coordinated.

Within six months he realized that this was going to be a long, brutal war of attrition. Though more snakes joined Paka's and Selabali's armies every day, though they now outnumbered the human soldiers five-to-one, though the Republic kept opening up new channels through which to supply them with arms, they continued to fight a guerrilla war. The attacking parties were a little larger than before, and a lot better armed, but never did they congregate in large enough numbers for Blake's generals to join anything remotely resembling a definitive battle.

Within a year the Fani had actually secured the northern quarter of Faniland—mostly hills and mountains—to the point that Paka could address huge rallies there in relative safety.

Within eighteen months, Selabali was able to do the same in southern Tulabete Country. Athens and Mastaboni were still totally secure, as were the mines and most of the prime farmland, but Blake's forces were spread as thinly as he dared along the perimeters of what now became Human Territory.

Within two years sixteen thousand Men had been killed, and while it was true that more than one hundred thousand snakes had been killed, there were a lot more snakes left than Men.

Within four years Paka and Selabali had felt secure enough to leave their generals in charge and go off to nearby Flowergarden for a covert meeting with various politicians from the Republic. When they returned, it was to announce the creation of the Karimon government-in-exile, of which Paka and Selabali were co-chairmen.

The Republic immediately recognized the Karimon government, and at Paka's request, put a military blockade around the planet, thus halting the already-decreasing flow of goods from Goldstone. The Republic still wouldn't openly participate in the war, but it was doing everything within its power to support the natives against the colonists.

Two nights later John Blake spent the entire evening huddled with his advisors. The war was not going well, and it was certain to get worse in the coming months and years. The economy was still healthy, but it could only sustain an all-out war for so long before it began crumbling, especially given the naval blockade. Paka and Selabali were heroes in the Republic, visionary leaders who dared to stand firm against human oppression, and funds were pouring into the accounts they had set up on friendly worlds.

It was time, announced Blake, for action, for the kind of bold political stroke that would stymie the Republic, neutralize the ferocious Paka and the wily Selabali, and turn the tide of events in favor of Man once more.

It was time to turn Rockgarden over to the snakes.

Forty-one

J ohn Blake sat in the lounge of the presidential suite of
the Grand Athens Hotel, smoking a Denebian cigar and
sipping an Antarrean brandy. He had entered the building
through the kitchen entrance, ascended to the penthouse
via the service elevator, and had his security guards cordon
off the entire floor. It was essential to his plans that no
one—and especially no snakes—know that the Governor of
Rockgarden was holding a secret meeting here. As far as
the rest of the world knew, he was spending a quiet evening
at the executive mansion.

Tomorrow they would have some inkling that he had
spent the night doing more than reading and sleeping, but
if this meeting went as he hoped it would, tomorrow would
be too late for his enemies to do anything but adjust to the
new reality he planned to impose on the situation.

He had been sitting there in a high-backed chair long
enough to smoke his cigar halfway down when the door to
the suite slid open and two of his most trusted assistants
ushered his guest into the room.

"Will there be anything else, Governor?" asked one of
them.

Blake shook his head. "Just wait outside. I'll let you know when we're through."

The men nodded and left, and the visitor who had accompanied them stood where he was, staring at Blake.

"I'm sorry for the manner in which you were brought here," said Blake, "but the need for secrecy was absolute. Won't you please sit down?"

The visitor, a snake in late middle age, walked cautiously into the middle of the lounge and looked around.

"Anywhere will do," said Blake, gesturing to a number of chairs and couches. "Wherever you'll be most comfortable."

The snake sat down on a leather chair and stared at Blake.

"Can I offer you some brandy?"

"I do not drink," replied the snake.

"A cigar, perhaps?"

"No, thank you."

"Pity," said Blake. He picked up his brandy snifter, took a sip, and stared at his guest.

"Why am I here, Governor?" asked the snake at last.

"We have some business to discuss, Father Janna," said Blake. "I'm an enormous admirer of yours, you know."

The snake named Father Janna stared at him with distrustful orange cat's-eyes.

"It's true," continued Blake. "You are the first ordained Christian minister of your race. I think that's quite an accomplishment." He paused. "You're not Catholic. I would have thought you would be called Reverend Janna rather than Father."

"You brought me all the way here just to ask why I am called Father Janna?"

Blake chuckled. "No, of course not. But I *am* curious."

"It's no mystery. I prefer the term Father, and so I gave it to myself."

"Why not?" replied Blake. "I'm told on the Inner Frontier men change names as often as you and I change clothes. I think every man should have a name that satisfies him."

"It satisfies me," answered Father Janna. "And I should point out that I am not a Man."

"Every *being*, then," amended Blake. He noted that his cigar had gone out, and he relit it. "And you are quite an accomplished being, Father Janna. I have followed your career with great interest."

"I wasn't aware of that."

"Oh, but I have," said Blake. "You have led an exemplary life. You have fed the hungry and cared for the sick, you have converted huge numbers of your own people to Christianity, and, above all, you have been a voice of moderation in this damnable conflict that seems to just go on and on."

"I do not believe that killing ever solved anything, Governor Blake," said Father Janna.

"Nor do I." Blake sighed. "I wish Moses Selabali and that maniac Paka felt as you did."

"Please do not misunderstand me, Governor Blake," said Father Janna. "I disapprove of Thomas Paka's methods, not his goals. This is our planet, and I think one day even you will see that denying my race the right to govern itself is immoral."

"What would you say if I told you that day had arrived?" asked Blake, staring intently at the snake and trying to read his reaction.

"I would praise God and thank Him for bringing you to your senses."

"What if I further told you that I was prepared, as of this moment, to allow your people to share equally in the governing of Rockgarden?"

"I would tell you that my prayers had been answered."

"What I am *not* prepared to do," continued Blake, "is share power with either Thomas Paka or Moses Selabali.

They have committed too many atrocities against my people."

"They have not acted, but reacted," answered Father Janna. "They have responded to almost a century of repression, and whatever you think of their methods, you will have to involve them in the new government for it to have any legitimacy."

"They are unacceptable to my race," answered Blake. "The moment calls for moderation, not extremism. The transition must proceed by slow, careful steps. We are willing to *share* power, not *relinquish* it."

"That is an acceptable first step," said Father Janna, "but eventually you must relinquish it. Three million Men cannot govern half a billion snakes."

"Once we have secured our rights and our safety, once we know there will be no retribution against us and that we have created a society that is fair to both the majority and the minority races, then we will happily step aside. But I cannot put a timetable on it. To be perfectly frank, we will have to train an entire generation of snakes to take over the reins of government and to replace the human bureaucracy that now administers Rockgarden."

"That is a reasonable position," said Father Janna. "I feel certain that both sides can reach an accommodation on those grounds."

"The key to it," said Blake, "is turning over power to the right snake. It must be one who is willing to let the over-zealous actions of both sides be forgotten, who understands that his people must be trained and prepared for self-government before my people turn over the reins of power, and one who disdains all violent solutions to the disagreements that will always occur when different sentient species share the same planet."

"I think you underestimate Thomas Paka," replied Father Janna. "He—"

"He would execute every Man who had ever opposed

him, and probably their families as well. He is bitter and hate-filled, and totally unacceptable to my people." Blake paused. "And in truth, Selabali isn't much better. If it came down to a choice between the two, we'd take him ahead of Paka . . . but there are almost a billion snakes on Rockgarden, so there is no reason to choose between those two evils."

"Then who did you have in mind, Governor Blake?" Blake smiled. "I'm looking at him."

"You must be joking!" exclaimed Father Janna. "I have no political experience whatsoever!"

"You have something more important than experience, Father," said Blake. "You have intelligence and you have compassion, and that is what is required in the dangerous days ahead."

"But—"

"As for the rest of it, I'll teach you everything you have to know about running a government. We're going to be working together very closely, virtually side by side. If there's anything you don't understand, I'll always be there to explain it."

"This is insane!" replied Father Janna.

"Actually, it is a stroke of genius," replied Blake. "You haven't an enemy in the world, and there aren't too many on either side who can say that today. You are just the co-leader we need to pull this planet together."

"Are you quite sure you've given this sufficient thought?" asked Father Janna.

"There is no question in my mind that you are the perfect candidate for the job, the one member of your race best able to unify Rockgarden after this terrible ordeal we've all been through." He paused. "I would like to be able to announce this to the press tomorrow morning."

"May I have tonight to think about it?" asked Father Janna, getting to his feet.

"Certainly. I've arranged a room for you at a hotel in

Talimi"—the Grand Athens would not accept snakes—
"and I'll contact you just after sunrise."

"I pray that I will make the proper decision," said Father
Janna.

"I'm sure you will," replied Blake, standing up and es-
corting him to the door. "Especially when you consider
that the alternative is the continuation of a war that has
already left too many dead on both sides."

The door slid open, the security men escorted Father
Janna back to the street, and Blake contacted his waiting
staff via vidphone.

"How did it go?" asked his senior advisor anxiously.

"He'll sign up," answered Blake confidently.

"You're sure?"

"Relax," said Blake. "Tomorrow morning we announce
the end of the war, the sharing of political power with the
snakes, a desire to reestablish trade with the Republic, and,
most importantly, the appointment of Father Janna to the
highest office on the planet."

"And then?"

"Then we pull our puppet's strings and go back to running Rockgarden just as we always have," he said, "albeit
with a somewhat lower profile."

Forty-two

At noon the next day John Blake called a press conference, and with holo cameras sending his image to all points of the Rockgarden compass, he announced that Men had reached an accommodation with snakes, and that henceforth he would be sharing his position as Governor with Father Janna.

He then stepped aside and watched respectfully as Father Janna walked up to the microphone and faced the press and the cameras.

"I am quite overwhelmed by the speed with which this has taken place," said Father Janna, "but I will do everything within my power to govern fairly and impartially. Movement toward majority rule will be slow and occasionally painful, and we will undoubtedly take some wrong steps, but the government of John Blake has shown its willingness to redress our grievances after years of war, and I think I speak on behalf of all my people when I thank Mr. Blake for taking this enormous first step."

He paused, and consulted some notes he carried with him. "To those of you who are still in the field, I say: lay down your arms. The day of peace is at hand, and the day of full participation in our government is not far off. Mr. Blake has agreed to grant amnesty to all snakes who have taken up arms against his government; *I* hereby agree to grant amnesty to all Men who followed the dictates of their elected government and fought to curb the uprising. A new day has dawned on Rockgarden, a new era of understanding, and I urge every member of both races to move forward into the sunshine together."

Blake then stepped forward and shook Father Janna's hand, posed for an appropriate number of holographs, and then dismissed the press.

"That was an excellent speech," he said when he and his advisors were alone with Father Janna.

"The reaction among the reporters seemed . . . well . . . *subdued,*" replied Father Janna unhappily.

"They'll get over it," replied Blake.

"I hope so." Father Janna paused. "What do I do now?"

Blake chuckled. "Now you go to your office, which is just down the hall from my own, and for the next two weeks my advisors will brief you on all the problems confronting Rockgarden. The war may be over, but we've got a lot of other problems. We've got a thirty-percent inflation rate, industrial productivity has fallen off, we've got to find a way to bring all the returning soldiers back into the economy. We will have to rebuild everything that the war has destroyed, we must decide what our response to the Republic's forthcoming overtures will be, we have farm policy to consider. . . . We'll keep you busy, Governor Janna, never fear."

"Please call me Father Janna; it's going to take time to get used to Governor Janna."

"Whatever you say, Father Janna," replied Blake. "And now, if you're ready to go to work . . ."

"Absolutely," replied Father Janna. "The one thing I don't want to be is a figurehead. The people must see that I am actually exercising power."

"They will," Blake assured him. "But you can't exercise it until you understand the issues. From this day forth, my advisors are your advisors."

"Shouldn't I also have advisors of my own species?"

"Of course," said Blake smoothly. "We'll begin assimilating them into the government almost immediately . . . but for the first few weeks, I think it makes more sense for you to be briefed by Men of unquestioned expertise in their various fields."

Father Janna nodded his head. "Yes, that seems reasonable. But I *will* be allowed to bring my own people in?"

"You're the Governor," said Blake. "You can do anything you want that isn't against the constitution."

Satisfied, Father Janna went off to his office.

"All right," said Blake when he was alone with his advisors. "You know the order in which you are to brief him. You are each to make our case as strongly as possible. You are never to show contempt or disdain for snakes. You are to lead him to the conclusions we want him to reach. You are, to the best of your abilities, to make him feel he has reached the conclusions on his own. You are never to overrule him. And if you feel there are certain areas where he will not mirror our views, you are to let me know immediately. Are there any questions?"

"Does he really have all the powers of the governorship?" asked the Minister of Defense.

"Absolutely," said Blake. Then he smiled. "Until he tries to exercise them."

He went to his office, poured himself an Antarrean brandy, even though it was a bit early in the day, leaned back on his chair, and looked out across Gardener Square.

It wasn't a bad gamble, he reflected. There was no doubt in his mind that he could control Father Janna; the snake was as much a bleeding heart as those idiots sitting in their glass offices on Deluros VIII. And it ought to satisfy the

Republic, too: he'd done everything they wanted, if not in the manner they wanted him to do it.

Of course, there was always a chance that Janna would start exercising his power, would issue some edicts that were not in the best interests of Men—but before that occurred, the snake armies would have disbanded and given up their arms, and no human military was going to enforce a snake's orders. No, as long as Men controlled the army, the treasury, the mines and the farms, they could live with a snake governor, especially one as powerless as Janna would be.

It was truly a bold solution, one that even Violet Gardener would have approved. When faced with an intolerable situation, you deal with your weakest enemy and you retain control of everything that will keep him weak. Textbook politics, actually.

He ordered his lunch in his office, then contacted the commander of his northern army. There had been no fighting since the announcement, but the snakes hadn't started coming in yet.

Well, that was to be expected. It had only been a couple of hours. Probably it would take a day or two for word to filter down from Thomas Paka and Moses Selabali and their generals.

The Bush Brigade reported the same thing: no contact, no action, no surrender.

He took a nap after lunch, stopped by Janna's office to give him encouragement, then spent the rest of the afternoon going over paperwork and signing a number of minor bills into law.

At dusk, accompanied by his bodyguards, he walked three blocks to his favorite restaurant and went directly to the table that was always reserved for him. He had toyed with inviting Janna to dinner, but the restaurant didn't allow snakes, and while he planned to give lip service to desegregation, it wasn't a policy he was in a hurry to implement, and so he sat alone, waving to some of the diners he knew at other tables, smiling at an editor from the local newstape.

He had been there for perhaps twenty minutes when one of his aides entered the restaurant and walked straight to his table.

"Yes? What is it?" he asked between mouthfuls.

"Problems."

"Paka?"

"And Selabali," said the aide, nodding.

"Let's have it."

"At five o'clock tonight, Paka's snakes launched a major offensive in the north, attacking the town of Tentamp. Early reports list more than eighty Men dead and four hundred wounded."

"And Selabali?"

"His Tulabete attacked a factory on the outskirts of Mastaboni and burned it to the ground. At least fifty Men were killed."

"Shit!" muttered Blake. "I *knew* things were going too smoothly." He looked at the aide. "Have we had any communication with them?"

"I wouldn't call it *communication,*" said the aide wryly. "Paka radioed a message to General Tomlinson less than a minute before the attack. All it said was: *Death to Man Janna.* Selabali sent the same thing to the mayor of Mastaboni."

Blake sighed. "Well, they're smarter than *he* is, I'll give them that," he said grimly.

Forty-three

The attacks became more frequent.

A farm here, an outpost there, a safari bus in the Baski Plains—and just when it seemed that they were merely sporadic acts of small groups of terrorists, Paka's army, some thirty thousand strong, would meet a column of Blake's army head-on, or Selabali's forces would attack and destroy an entire town, leaving nothing—man or animal—alive.

Blake put Father Janna on video every night and had him plead with his people to lay down their arms and trust him to make a lasting peace. After a month, the snake army started jamming the signals, and within three months they were able to broadcast Paka's calls to arms on any channel they chose.

It was on a peaceful spring evening, just after the long rains had ended, that Blake turned on the news and found himself staring first at a blank holographic screen and then at Thomas Paka's image.

"This message is addressed to the government of John Blake and the traitor, Man Janna," he announced. "You think you can win a war of attrition; I tell you that you cannot. You think you can stop the flow of arms to my troops; I tell you that you cannot. You think you can keep my race in a state of perpetual servitude, even as the traitor Janna does your bidding; I tell you that you cannot."

Paka paused for a moment, glaring into the camera from his hidden location.

"In a meeting of historic importance this morning, Moses Selabali, Robert Pelinori, James Laki, Wilson Grebna, and myself have formed the United Karimon Front. From this day forth, we will be acting in concert, under a central command. All of our actions will be coordinated, and they will not cease until John Blake—not the false man, Janna—publicly agrees to the principle of one being, one vote."

He paused again for the full magnitude of his statement to hit his audience, and then continued:

"No longer are you fighting against Rakko and Fani and Tulabete and Pangi and Meskitan. From this moment, you are fighting Karimonis, united in our desire to take back control of the planet of our birth."

"And where the hell do you think *I* was born, you goddamned snake?" Blake muttered at Paka's image.

"We will not lay down our arms until we have attained our goal," concluded Paka. "And I promise you this, John Blake: what has gone before will seem like a mild breeze compared to the storm that is coming."

The screen went blank again, and Blake, checking all the other channels, found that they, too, were jammed.

The next morning three hundred farms were destroyed and four mines exploded, killing hundreds of human and snake workers.

The emigration started that afternoon. Men who had fought the elements, fought the weeds and rocks, fought the droughts, and fought the snakes, decided that there was simply no sense to continue fighting. More than fifty who owned their own ships left by the end of the day, and some eight hundred more applied for exit visas before the government offices closed that night.

By week's end, close to twenty thousand Men had decided to leave the planet, and Blake realized for the first time that he was on the losing end of the battle. He'd fought the snakes to a standstill thus far, but if their numbers increased every day while the number of Men left to fight decreased, it was only a matter of time before Athens itself would be overrun by Paka's and Selabali's armies.

Still, he hadn't been elected to preside over the loss of Man's primacy on Rockgarden, and he was the kind of man who fought best and most creatively when cornered. He spent the week in the executive mansion, coming up with hundreds of political, economic, and military plans, discarding each in turn as he was able to find flaws in it, then proceeding to the next. Finally, when he was down to just a handful of vague notions and ideas, he decided to pay a visit to Father Janna.

"Good evening, Mr. Blake," said Janna as he walked into the snake's office.

"Good evening, Father Janna," he said. "Do you mind if I sit down?"

"Please do."

Blake looked around, disdained the furniture that had been created for Men, and sat in a chair that was made for snakes. It was uncomfortable, but he wanted to put Janna at his ease.

"How's it going?" he asked.

"Not well, Mr. Blake," replied Janna. "I'm told I have received more than two hundred death threats since Paka's speech, all from members of my own tribe."

"From the Fani?" said Blake. "That's curious. I'd have thought the Tulabete would be the ones to threaten you, since you *are* a Fani."

"If Moses Selabali calls for my death, they'll respond,"

answered Janna. "But they're not about to take orders from Thomas Paka."

"I thought all that tribalism went out with the creation of this utopian Karimon Front."

Janna shook his head. "It will be many generations before tribalism ceases to be a major fact of life—if indeed it ever does."

Blake filed the fact away for future use. "Other than the threats, how are you progressing?"

"I feel totally useless," admitted Janna. "I am doing my best to understand the intricacies of our economic policy, but to what purpose? We've gone to a wartime economy, our farms have become battlegrounds, and even Goldstone has been prevented from trading with us. What is the good of knowing these things?"

"The war can't go on forever," said Blake. "Eventually we'll win, and those are precisely the things a good administrator has to know."

"Do you really foresee an end to the war?" asked Janna.

"Don't you?"

Janna sighed and shook his head. "They are *fanatics*, Mr. Blake."

"You want the same thing they do, and I'd hardly call *you* a fanatic," said Blake, lighting a cigar.

"I think it is a sin to kill any sentient being, no matter how much I may disapprove of his actions. Thomas Paka would say that a snake who is not willing to fight for his freedom after a century of subjugation is not a snake at all. You have heard and read his statements, Mr. Blake. From the moment I took the oath of office, he has called me Man Janna."

"A politician learns to turn a deaf ear to insults," said Blake.

"I don't think you understand the depth of this particular insult," replied Janna. "My understanding is that one of the worst things a Man can be called is a bastard. This is infinitely more hateful in the eyes of my people."

"I'm sorry I got you into this," said Blake, who found, to his surprise, that he *was* mildly sorry that he had used this being of such obvious naïveté and good will, and that he had every intention of using him again.

"It was a gesture of trust on your part," said Father Janna. "You could not have foreseen the consequences. Though," he added bitterly, "*I* should have."

"Well, we can't worry about that now," said Blake. "We're losing thousands of Men every day, and Paka and Selabali are slaughtering those that are left, while the Republic cordons off the whole damned world and keeps supplying the rebels with more weapons and ammunition. We *must* come up with some kind of gesture before they destroy everything we've built."

"I have a question, Mr. Blake," said Janna.

"Oh? What is it?"

"I don't know if you can answer it, but it has been troubling me for quite some time." Janna paused, frowning, as if trying to figure out how to word what came next. "I have known Thomas Paka most of my life. We were students together both here and on Lodin XI, and I spoke to him many times after he returned from Deluros and began writing his books."

"What's the question?" asked Blake.

"This Paka I see and hear now is not the same one I knew. Something must have happened to radicalize him. My guess is that it happened in prison." He looked at Blake. "I was thinking, if perhaps he was subjected to torture, if he was physically abused, possibly the public punishment of the guilty parties might . . ." He searched for the words, and then shrugged. "I don't know. He will never share my views, but he might hate your race a little less. Can it be done?"

"He was never tortured," said Blake. "I gave orders that

he was to be treated with all the dignity befitting a leader of his people."

"Many jailors feel that a leader of *my* people has no dignity."

"He wasn't mistreated," said Blake firmly.

"Then I cannot imagine what radicalized him."

There was an uncomfortable pause.

"*I* did," said Blake at last.

"You?" repeated Janna. "How?"

"That is a matter between Paka and myself. I made the right decision. He disagrees."

"Is there any way you can change it?"

"Not at this point."

"Then I see no way out. Eventually the United Karimon Front will overthrow the government, and you and I will hang side by side."

"I'm not ready to give up just yet," said Blake.

They spoke for another hour without resolving anything, and then Blake returned to his mansion, to find that Paka had wiped out another small town on the northern border of Faniland.

Every morning Blake would meet with his cabinet and his advisors and state his resolve not to yield to Paka's demands—and every morning another five thousand Men had left Rockgarden or another snake attack had killed those Men who were least expecting to be attacked.

It was on the seventy-fourth day after the creation of the United Karimon Front that Blake walked into his cabinet room and found letters of resignation from two advisors and a cabinet member awaiting him.

"If the situation doesn't change, I'll be leaving next month," added his Minister of Transportation when Blake had finished reading the letters. "Face it, John—we did our best, but the battle is lost. Whether we lose the war to them or make an accommodation with them, the end result is going to be the same: in two or three years' time the snakes are going to be running this planet. If I were you, I'd stop fighting a losing battle for our primacy, and start fighting to keep such money and land as we've managed to accumulate."

"I agree," added one of his advisors. "The war is lost. Some of us were born here, John; we've got every bit as much right to call ourselves citizens of Karimon as the snakes do. I think the battle now must be to keep what we've got."

"Is that the sense of this meeting?" asked Blake.

Every head nodded an affirmative.

"How about you?" he asked of his Defense Minister. "We've always acted on the assumption that the war can be won. Now I am asking you for your honest assessment of the situation: *can* we win?"

"We can hold them off for a few months or possibly even a few years," was the answer. "But they're gaining thousands of recruits every day, and of course the Republic is constantly resupplying them with weapons." He shook his head. "No, I can prolong the war, but under the current circumstances, there's no way we can win it."

"I'll take your opinions under advisement," said Blake. He turned on his heel and walked out of the meeting.

And, because he was a realist, a week later he decided to sue for peace and make the best deal he could get for those Men who remained on Rockgarden.

Forty-four

I t took the United Karimon Front, which Blake decided
was a little less united than its name implied, almost a
month to agree to peace talks.

Paka insisted that the talks be held on some other world;
he had no intention of showing up in Athens to talk and
being arrested.

Blake insisted that representatives of the Republic be
present. He was absolutely certain that Deluros VIII, having finally gotten what it wanted, wasn't about to leave two
million Men to the mercy of the snakes once the reins of
power changed hands.

Then Paka and Selabali issued a joint statement that they
would not attend the meeting if Father Janna was present.

Blake balked at that. He had no loyalty to Janna at all,
but having made him the co-governor, he felt that ordering
him to stay behind would be a public admission of what
everyone except Janna privately knew: that Janna was simply a figurehead who had been brought in so that Blake's
government could continue to rule the planet.

It was Janna himself who provided the solution: with
Blake and his advisors gone, *someone* had to be in charge of

Rockgarden; after all, there were still millions of troops out there. Therefore, he would stay behind in case this was not the display of good faith that he hoped it was.

Blake suggested half a dozen planets, all of them inhabited solely by Men. The United Karimon Front rejected them all.

Paka suggested three planets that Blake turned down simply because he felt it was required of him, having had his own suggested venues rejected.

At last Selabali suggested that the meeting take place on their sister world of Flowergarden, and Blake agreed. So, to his surprise, did Paka.

Then came the debate over the participants. The United Karimon Front submitted a list of thirty-four freedom fighters. Blake knew that this was just for show, that all the decisions would be made by Paka and Selabali, the leaders of the two major tribes. He accepted Paka, Selabali, Robert Pelinori and three other Tulabete, and turned down twenty-eight names. Selabali agreed, Paka didn't, and the conference was held up another week before Selabali finally convinced Paka to accept Blake's list.

Blake, aware that the conference would be covered by hundreds of members of the Republic's press, elected to attend it alone. Let the trillions of Men throughout the galaxy dwell upon the image of a lone, beleaguered Man standing against a table full of snakes. (He hoped a few of them would be shedding their skins during the conference; the more hideous they appeared, the more public sympathy he could stockpile.)

The last point to be settled was which members of the huge Republic bureaucracy would act as go-betweens and moderators. Paka wanted the Chairman of the Bureau of Alien Affairs, but Blake found that branch of the Republic too sympathetic to his enemy's cause. He responded by suggesting first the Department of Cartography, which he knew was anathema to the snakes, and once they had turned it down, he followed with the Division of Constitutional Law, a branch of the Department of Justice that had drawn up constitutions for more than a thousand planets that had been incorporated into the Republic. Since it showed a willingness to scrap the current Rockgarden constitution, the United Karimon Front finally agreed to it.

Blake agreed to any seating arrangement that the snakes wanted, and finally, after almost ten weeks of preparation and maneuvering, the peace talks took place.

Blake, well aware of the dozens of cameras trained on him, sat across a broad table from the snakes and made his opening statement:

"There has been too much killing, too much violence, too much misunderstanding between the races on Rockgarden. I have come here, of my own volition, representing the race of Men who inhabit Rockgarden, to seek an accommodation with our former enemies and to reach an agreement that is fair to both sides. I acknowledge that there have been injustices in the past, that innocent members of _both_ species have suffered, but I have not come here to trade accusations. I am here to help build a future in which my race and yours can live in harmony, in which one side is not made to suffer for the gain or benefit of the other. As far as I am concerned, everything, every point of dispute, is negotiable."

"You could have saved many lives by saying these words five, or even two years ago," said Moses Selabali in his sibilant voice.

"Everything is negotiable," replied Blake. "I do not regard acts of wanton terrorism as legitimate negotiating."

Selabali seemed about to reply, when Herbert Willis, the Director of the Division of Constitutional Law, intervened.

"Excuse me," he said, "but before we begin with a series of recriminations, perhaps I can be of some use here in sorting out the issues."

"I have no objections," said Blake promptly.

Selabali said nothing, but nodded his acquiescence.

"Mr. Blake, for some years now both the natives of the planet and the Republic have been pressing for the government to accept the principle of one being, one vote. It seems to me that that principle is basic to any cessation of hostilities and any constitution that may come out of this conference. Is your government prepared to accept it?"

"First," said Blake, "I must point out that I, and well over ninety percent of the Men of Rockgarden, are also natives of the planet. We were born there, we grew up there, we have worked to develop it into a modern, functioning world, and I resent the implication that we are any less Rockgardeners than the gentlemen sitting across the table from me." He paused. "In answer to your question, on the day that I asked Father Janna to share power with me, the government of Rockgarden has been totally committed to the principle of one being, one vote."

Paka uttered a snort of derision, but made no comment.

"Have any members of the—you call yourselves Karimonis, do you?—have any members of the Karimonis exercised that franchise?"

"No," said Paka.

"Mr. Blake?" said Willis.

"It's not that simple," replied Blake. "You make it sound like everyone could simply go out and vote tomorrow."

"You claim to support that very principle. Therefore, I feel I must ask why they cannot?"

"First," said Blake, "there happens to be a war going on. Second, we must take a planetary census to establish a voter roll. Third, since we are dealing with a population that has a literacy rate of about fourteen percent, we must agree upon a form of balloting that will not instantly disenfranchise five out of every six Karimonis. Fourth, we must call a general election, and we have been unable to do so when the very people who will benefit from such an election are

out in the bush shooting any human that wanders into
their line of fire."

"Your first and fourth reservations will vanish with the
cessation of the war," said Willis. "Let us see if we can
address the other two. Mr. Paka, what suggestions have you
for a ballot that will be comprehensible to your people?"

"Let them vote by voice," answered Paka, "in front of
members of all competing parties who will then tabulate
that vote."

"Mr. Blake?"

"That's not a very good idea," answered Blake. "It un-
dermines the concept of the secret ballot."

"Why must a ballot be secret?" asked Paka.

"So that the voter cannot be intimidated," replied Blake.

"Men may intimidate other men," said Paka. "Karimonis do not intimidate Karimonis."

"The Fani and the Tulabete have been butchering each
other for thousands of years," shot back Blake. "Why
should they stop now?"

"Please, Mr. Blake," said Willis. He turned to Moses
Selabali. "Would this be acceptable as a temporary measure that could be replaced by written ballot at such time
as your race achieves a literacy rate of, shall we say, fifty
percent?"

"Yes," said Selabali.

"You're making a big mistake," said Blake, staring directly at Selabali. "The Tulabete took huge losses in the last
war, and you're bearing the brunt of the fighting in this
one. The Fani have got you outnumbered, three to one."

"Do not listen to him, Moses," said Paka. "He is trying
to divide us. The alternative is not to vote at all until we
have raised our literacy rate to *his* standard."

"I will accept balloting by voice," said Selabali after a
moment's consideration.

"Fine," said Willis. "We are making excellent progress.
Now, what about a planetary census?"

"That is impossible," replied Paka. "Many of our people live in isolated areas under very primitive conditions. It is entirely conceivable that ten percent of my race has never even seen a Man."

"What has that got to do with anything?" asked Blake.

"It would take years to complete such a census, and those who would take the longest to find and count are those with the least interest in voting."

"What about a census of the more populated areas?" continued Willis. "How quickly could it be done?"

"Within a year," said Paka.

"If the Republic's Departments of Census and Cartography were to help, it could be done within four months," offered Selabali.

"An excellent suggestion, Mr. Selabali," said Willis. "I shall certainly suggest it to them, and I see no reason why they should refuse." He paused and smiled. "We are truly making excellent progress, gentlemen. I had no idea we would solve the major questions so quickly."

"You have not come to the major questions yet," said Paka, staring fiercely at Blake.

"Oh? I am afraid I don't understand."

"He gives us the vote because he knows we will win it in battle, and because in his heart he knows it is ours to begin with," said Paka. "Soon we must come to those things that he does *not* believe are ours, and then we shall see how earnest he is to live in peace and harmony with the enemies of his blood."

"What do you mean, Mr. Paka?" asked Willis.

"Let us begin with the land," said Paka. "Two million human farmers own ninety percent of the farmland on Karimon, while almost a billion Karimonis must scrape at their meager two- and three-acre plots for their subsistence. Tell me, Mr. Blake, are Men willing to turn over their farms to us?"

Blake looked into the video cameras and spoke.

"You must understand," he said, "that less than two percent of the land on Rockgarden was under cultivation when Violet Gardener received the Republic's permission to open the planet up to human habitation and development. Neither Mr. Paka nor Mr. Selabali can point to any instance where a cultivated farm was appropriated by a human being. This is an industry that Men developed— and we developed it to the point, in less than half a century, where we not only are able to feed a billion Karimonis, but our greatest source of hard currency comes from the export of food to neighboring worlds. We bring in more from food production than from our mining industries." He paused. "That land was cleared by Men, cultivated by Men, worked by Men—and now Mr. Paka, who has already received the thing he says he has been fighting for, the vote, wants two million Men to walk away from the land their families have farmed for generations. I say that this is unfair. If the Karimonis have suddenly developed a desire to take up farming, let them pay a fair market price to those Men who are willing to sell them their farms, and let them leave the rest of us alone."

"How can we pay for farms or anything else when you have spent the last century exploiting us?" demanded Paka.

"Are you implying that you had a stockpile of money when we arrived on your planet, and that we appropriated it?" asked Blake with a smile.

"We had a *planet* and you appropriated it!"

"Please, gentlemen," said Willis. "This is obviously an extremely sensitive point. We are not going to solve it today, and there is no sense arguing about who is most at fault. We are here to negotiate a peace and a constitution; this is one of the points that will require long and serious negotiation."

"There is another point that goes hand in glove with it," said Blake.

"And what is that?"

"Proportional representation," replied Blake. "We can't allow it."

"You see?" said Paka angrily. "I told you this meeting was a farce."

"Let me finish," said Blake. "Men currently control ninety-five percent of the wealth on Rockgarden. We own all the mines and, as Mr. Paka pointed out, most of the farmland. These were industries that didn't even exist until we landed on the planet, and they have benefited both races. The mines have offered employment for Karimonis since the day they were opened, and no Karimoni has ever had to go hungry since our farming industry was created." He paused. "Yet there are a billion Karimoni and less than three million Men on Rockgarden—and the total will probably be under two million Men before this current situation has been resolved. If they are given proportional representation, no man will ever again hold elective office, and we will have no recourse against any abuses perpetrated by a Karimoni government. Mr. Paka could rule that a single credit constituted fair market value for a ten-thousand-acre farm, and we would have no way to protest or to fight against that ruling."

"So you give us one being, one vote with one hand, and with the other you wish to sign into law a constitution that gives you ninety percent of the power of our government?" demanded Paka.

"I'm not demanding any particular percent," replied Blake. "I am simply saying that proportional representation is unfair and unacceptable. Like many other Men, I consider Rockgarden my home, and I have no intention of leaving it. Therefore, I wish to secure my rights now, rather than have to fight for them later."

"No matter what arguments you use," said Paka, "what you are really saying is one Man, one vote, and one Karimoni, one one-millionth of a vote."

"Are you proposing that?" asked Blake.

Paka stood up, glared at Blake, and left the conference room without another word.

"Oh dear, oh dear," muttered Willis. He turned to an aide. "Somebody must stop him."

"He'll be back," said Blake.

"What makes you think so?" asked Selabali.

"Because any minute now he'll realize that you're still here, and he doesn't want a government run by the Tulabete any more than he wants one run by Men."

"You are mistaken, John Blake," said Selabali. "We are Tulabete and Fani and Rakko no longer. Now we are all just Karimoni."

"We'll see," said Blake confidently.

Five minutes later word reached the conference room that Thomas Paka had returned to his quarters at the hotel, and would join the afternoon session.

Forty-five

T he first peace conference didn't settle much of anything, except to prove that John Blake was truly willing to negotiate and that the United Karimon Front was
willing not to pursue the war until the last Man was dead.

But there was a second conference five weeks later, one
that was *not* broadcast back to the Republic. It was attended
by Paka, Selabali, Blake, Willis, and some two dozen legal
scholars from the Division of Constitutional Law, and from
that conference came a permanent ceasefire and a new
constitution.

The constitution rambled on for some forty-seven written pages, but the gist of it was this:

The name of the world was once again officially Karimon.

Every sentient being now residing on Karimon was automatically a citizen and possessed the right to vote.

The government would have a single legislative body,
composed of two hundred fifty members. For a period of
twelve years, thirty of those seats were reserved for Men,
and they could veto any legislation they felt was inimical to
their race; after the twelve years had elapsed, proportional

representation would be the rule. (As much as Paka hated that provision, Blake hated it even more, but it was the best deal he could get, and at least it bought his people another dozen years.)

There would be a judiciary, all members to be appointed by the Governor.

And there would be a single Governor for the entire planet.

The day the constitution was ratified, three citizens of Karimon announced their candidacies for Governor: Moses Selabali, Thomas Paka, and John Blake.

Forty-six

"Mr. Blake?"

Blake looked up from his desk and saw Father Janna standing in the doorway.

"Come on in," he said, deactivating his computer and leaning back on his chair.

"Thank you," said Father Janna. "Are you sure I'm not disturbing you?"

"Not at all," said Blake. "Hell, I'm just going through the motions anyway. Another three months and I'm out of here."

"Yes," said Janna. "I have seen the polls."

"Well, there's nothing I can do about it. I may have a secure seat in the Parliament, but there's no way a Man is going to beat a snake in a general election for Governor."

"That is what I came to speak to you about."

"About my running for Governor?"

"About *my* running," said Janna.

"You?"

Janna nodded. "I do not trust Thomas Paka, Mr. Blake," he said. "Each time I hear him speak, he is less and less recognizable as the Paka I used to know." He paused. "He is a Fani, and as such he must be favored to win, since there are more Fani than Tulabete. I do not want this to happen. Thomas Paka is a dangerous demagogue, and he must be defeated."

"And you think *you* can beat him?" asked Blake, unable to keep the amusement out of his voice.

"No, I am not that far removed from reality," replied Janna. "But I, too, am a Fani. If I announce my candidacy, perhaps I can take enough votes away from him so that Moses Selabali can win."

"I don't want to hurt your feelings, Father Janna," said Blake bluntly, "but you couldn't draw two percent of the Fani vote. Paka's their hero; they still think you're a traitor."

"I know I am unpopular," admitted Janna with no display of defensiveness. "But if there is even a chance of defeating him, I am willing to undergo the public abuse and humiliation that will certainly pour down upon me."

"It's a noble thought, and I appreciate it, but that's not the way to beat him," said Blake.

"*Is* there a way?"

"Possibly."

"How?" asked Janna.

"We are dealing with a basically illiterate society here," said Blake. "Forget about the war and the fine ideals. I don't expect ten percent of any tribe to vote. With one exception."

"Which is that?"

"*My* tribe," answered Blake. "We'll turn out one hundred percent of our people at the polls."

"Surely you don't expect to win?"

Blake smiled. "I'm no more out of touch with reality than you are, Father Janna. No, I don't expect to win." He paused and lit one of his ever-present cigars. "But if I throw my support to Selabali, it just might be enough for *him* to win."

"Have you mentioned this to him?"

"Not yet," said Blake. "I've set up a meeting with him next month. That will be plenty of time to work out a deal. He's going to need a cabinet and advisors and judges; I think I can recommend some very good people, in exchange for my support." He chuckled. "He'll never figure out that I'd give it to him anyway, just to keep Paka from destroying this planet."

Forty-seven

The meeting between John Blake and Moses Selabali was held in secret, promises and assurances were given, agreements were made, and two days later John Blake publicly withdrew from the race and urged all his supporters to give their votes to Moses Selabali. There wasn't a Man on the planet who didn't understand exactly what had happened.

The next poll, a week later, showed that Selabali had edged almost two points ahead of Thomas Paka, and Karimon's human population breathed a collective sigh of relief.

Then Paka announced that he was carrying his campaign to Mastaboni, the heart of Tulabete Country, and that he would be giving a major address that would be carried by all the video networks.

Nice try, you clever snake, thought Blake. *But you're still a Fani. They might forget they're supposed to be civilized and tear you to pieces before you get ten words out.*

At eight o'clock that evening, Blake turned on the holo. Instantly there was an image of a huge sporting stadium, filled with Tulabete and a handful of Men. If there was a Fani anywhere in the crowd, Blake couldn't spot him.

There were a few brief speeches by minor candidates for minor offices, and then Thomas Paka walked onto the stage to polite but unenthusiastic applause.

Dumb, thought Blake. *You don't want your own people to see you get booed off a stage.* Unless, he thought suddenly, *you want them to humiliate you so badly that your own people are inspired to go to the polls in even greater numbers to make sure you win. Maybe you're not as dumb as I thought.*

"Fellow Karimonis!" said Paka, raising his hands. "Five months ago I went to the planet of Flowergarden to battle for your rights against John Blake, the Man who represents everything we have fought against during this long and bitter conflict. Now I address you not as Fani to Tulabete, but as Karimoni to Karimoni, and I bring you glad tidings."

He paused and waited for silence, then pointed into the darkness to a spot some three miles distant, a spot he himself had never seen.

"Jalanopi's tree still stands!" he shouted.

The cheer from the crowd was so loud that it shorted out the sound system. They screamed, they laughed, they began dancing in the aisles, and Paka finally had to leave before they could fix the microphones. But it made no difference: nothing he could have said would have made a difference after that. Blake could even hear cries of *"Jalanopi's tree still stands!"* coming through the closed windows of his executive mansion.

Damn! thought Blake. *It's all over. You're going to take Rockgarden straight to hell, just because you came up with a slogan the Tulabete love.*

Two months later, Thomas Paka won the governorship of Karimon with eighty-one percent of the vote.

John Blake's thousand years had lasted less than a decade.

VII

PAKA'S
TIGHTROPE

Forty-eight

I t was Thomas Paka's fourth day in office, and he was starting to wonder if he was ever going to get any work done. So far he had attended two inaugural celebrations, held a press conference, and played host to a seemingly endless stream of diplomats, human and alien alike, who had come to congratulate him or wish him good luck.

He glanced at his computer, and saw, thankfully, that he only had one more appointment for the day, this one with Mordecai Kiichana, the President of Alpha Bednares II. He walked over to the wetbar in the corner of his office, a leftover from Blake's days as Governor, poured himself a glass of water, and returned to his desk. He stared out at Independence Park—the new official name for Gardener Square—for a few minutes, watching the Karimonis and Men walking through it as if they were all in a hurry to get to important meetings, and then, finally, he drank his water and informed his receptionist that he was ready to see his visitor.

The door slid back and Mordecai Kiichana stepped into the office. He was tall, taller even than Paka, humanoid in shape, though his purple eyes were very wideset on his head and his nostrils were mere slits in his face. His ears were pointed and mobile, constantly twitching. His body was covered with a tawny fur, over which he wore what seemed to pass for a military uniform. His weaponry was abundant, but so polished and shining that Paka was sure none had ever been drawn in anger or fired anywhere, even on a practice range, and he wore so many medals that a smaller frame might have been weighted down with them.

"Good afternoon, Mordecai," said Paka, getting to his feet and greeting Kiichana warmly. "I am so glad you could come."

"It is my pleasure to be here," replied Kiichana.

"I have met too many strangers this week; it is very nice to see an old friend once again," said Paka. "Not only a friend," he amended, "but one of my heroes."

"Please, Thomas," said Kiichana. "You embarrass me."

"Won't you sit down?"

"Thank you, but I prefer to stand," said Kiichana. "I have never become used to human furniture."

"I haven't had a chance to refurnish the office since I became Governor," said Paka apologetically. "Things will be different on your next visit."

"I am sure they will." Kiichana cleared his throat. "I have come here to wish you success as Karimon embarks upon its bold new course as an independent world."

"For which I thank you," said Paka.

"And I have also come to tell you how to assure that success."

"I reject no one's counsel," said Paka, "and certainly not the hero of Alpha Bednares II. I will be happy to listen to you."

"I hope so," said Kiichana, "for they did not listen to me on Greenvalley or Laginappe II or Scheinwald V, and they have all suffered for it."

"May I offer you something to drink before we speak?" asked Paka.

"Just water," said Kiichana. "My metabolism rebels at both your drinks and those of Men."

"So be it," said Paka. He considered getting up and pouring the water himself, decided that such an act was too servile for a newly elected planetary leader, and summoned his receptionist to do it for him. After Kiichana had been given his water and the receptionist had returned to the outer office, Paka looked at him expectantly.

"How much do you know of the history of my world, Thomas?" asked Kiichana.

"I know what I've read and what you have told me over the years: that you fought the Republic for eight long years and finally obtained your independence, and that you yourself were a great warrior who was proclaimed President for Life."

"Not unlike yourself," noted Kiichana.

"I'm no warrior," replied Paka, shaking his head. "I'm a simple scholar and schoolteacher who got caught up in momentous events. Until an incident occurred a few years ago that changed my outlook, I even leaned toward pacifism."

"Be that as it may," replied Kiichana, "our careers parallel each other, much as the history of our worlds parallel each other. Alpha Bednares II had been under the yoke of human tyranny for almost two centuries, and our slogan was identical to yours: *One being, one vote.*"

"And eventually you got it."

"Eventually." Kiichana paused. "And, as you noted, I was elected President for Life. I had wonderful plans, Thomas. I was going to turn my world into a paradise for my people. There would be farmland for everyone, jobs for everyone, equality for everyone. Never again would we be under the thumb of Man. I planned to redress all our grievances and give us a fresh new start. I could see Utopia just around the corner, just as I am certain you yourself can see it." He smiled sadly. "I was very idealistic, but I was a fool. I am here to advise you not to become a fool as well."

"But I know that you instituted your reforms," said Paka, confused.

"Certainly I did. I fulfilled every promise I made."

"Well, then?"

"Alpha Bednares II has been independent for seventeen years," said Kiichana. "During that time we have changed from an exporter to an importer of food and raw materials, our per capita income has dropped by almost eighty percent, most of our factories have fallen into disrepair, and we are now on the Republic's list of the one hundred most impoverished worlds. Even as I speak to you, my military forces are bracing themselves for a fifth attempt at a coup."

"What went wrong?" asked Paka.

"I made one foolish, emotional decision," answered Kiichana, "and I set my world back more than a century because of it." He paused. "It is a decision I hope to prevent you from making as well."

"I'm listening," said Paka.

"I banished all Men from my world," said Kiichana. "I repossessed their farms and divided them up among my people. My government took over ownership of their factories. We set up segregated townships where Men could live, as they had done to us for two centuries. It was very satisfying—but it spelled disaster for my world." He leaned forward and stared into Paka's eyes. "I urge you, Thomas, no matter how much you hate them, no matter how badly you wish to redress your grievances, no matter what moral imperatives you think apply to the situation, think of Karimon first and vengeance second. You may hate the sight of Men, but I've toured your world this week, and it cannot function without them any more than mine can. You need their technical expertise, their ability to produce high yields from their farms, their ability to attract human investment."

"And what of the suffering they have caused, of the

injustices they have perpetrated since they day they arrived?"

"You live with it, and you never give them an opportunity to dominate you again—but you don't kick them off your planet," answered Kiichana. "You need only compare my world with Peponi, a planet whose president literally begged its human population to remain after independence. They have a thriving economy, they still manage to feed themselves, their factories still function." He paused. "My people are deserting the cities and going back to subsistence farming. There is no employment for them, no safety net of social programs, not even any food for sale. I made a mistake, and I will live with it—but I have traveled to other newly independent worlds urging them not to make the same mistake, as I am now urging you."

"My people expect me to take some action against the Men who remain," said Paka. "We were coerced into accepting a constitution that gives them a disproportionate amount of political power."

"Use it to your advantage," said Kiichana promptly.

"To my advantage?" said Paka, startled. "How?"

"Your people will be land-hungry," said Kiichana. "You can leave the productive farms in the hands of the Men who developed them, and blame the constitution for your inability to repossess the land. Give them a few minor victories, but leave the economic power in the hands of the Men who remain until you can train a generation of your own people to take over and run the planet as efficiently. You're an accomplished politician or you wouldn't be sitting in this office. Use that political skill to walk a tightrope between what your people want and what is best for Karimon."

There was another, longer silence, as Paka considered what his visitor had said.

"This has been a most unusual conversation, Mordecai," he said. "I will think long and hard upon it."

"When you do, you will see that I'm right," replied Kii-chana. "I *hate* them," he added passionately, "but I'd give half my planet to have them back."

"Have you considered asking them back?" suggested Paka. "Surely there are ways to entice them."

Kiichana shook his head. "Don't you think I've tried? There are a million worlds out there. Once you've kicked them off your planet, you've proven that it can be done—and what has been done once can be done again. Once they leave, they don't come back—and they make sure that you suffer the full consequences of your decision." He paused. "They are no more forgiving than I would be if the circumstances were reversed."

"No," agreed Paka. "Compassion for others was never one of their virtues."

"Nor, in truth, is it mine," added Kiichana. "But practicality and pragmatism are essential virtues for a leader. As much as you may hate them, you need them even more. You have taken the weapons from their hands; settle for that until your people have the expertise to take everything else from them as well. If you move prematurely, what happened to my world will surely happen to yours."

"I thank you for your thoughts, my old friend," said Paka. "I shall consider my next actions very carefully."

"That is all I ask," said Kiichana, getting to his feet. "I will be sending a permanent ambassador next week, and I hope that Alpha Bednares II can obtain a favored trading status with Karimon." He smiled wryly. "Against the day that we once again have something to trade."

"I would welcome a close relationship with your world," answered Paka, "as I cherish my close relationship with its President." He paused. "I would like to consult with you on a regular basis during the weeks to come."

"I am at your disposal," said Kiichana. "I will have one of my aides give you the code that will route your messages through to me."

"Before you leave, I wonder if you would do me the honor of joining me for dinner?"

"It would be my pleasure," replied Kiichana.

"I plan to invite some of my most trusted associates as well," said Paka. "I would like them to hear what you have to say."

Forty-nine

P aka, sitting in his office, activated his holo screen and watched Moses Selabali rise from his seat in the Parliament to address the assembled members.

"It is time," said Selabali in his deep, stentorian voice, "for this august body to address the issue that has been facing us since independence—the equitable redistribution of land. There can be no greater injustice than for two hundred thousand Men to control ninety percent of Karimon's arable farmland, while more than a billion Karimonis must eke out a meager living on their pitiful one- and two-acre tracts of overused land. I have here"—he held up a thick document—"a report from the Ministry of Agriculture suggesting three different methods of land apportionment, any of which the government will support. No Man currently owning farmland will be deprived of it in its entirety, but the current situation is intolerable, and I say that the time for action is now."

John Blake raised his hand for recognition.

"Speaking on behalf of my constituents," he said, "I say to Mr. Selabali that we have absolutely no objection to any reapportioning of farmland anywhere on the planet." He paused. "Providing, of course, that fair market value is paid for the land, and that no farm owner is forced to sell against his will."

"That is ridiculous!" snapped Selabali.

"Is it?" replied Blake. "Is it ridiculous to point out that once you turn the land over to a billion snakes, it will *still* be apportioned in two-acre sections, but that with no large, efficient farms left, you will have destroyed our ability to feed our cities, you will have left us without our primary source of foreign exchange, and you will have condemned Karimon to an aeon of subsistence farming? Once the land is divided, every family will own two or three acres—but families grow, while the land doesn't. Within two generations, those two-acre plots will become quarter-acre plots, and even the owners will not be able to live on what they produce. We have a system that works now; it would be catastrophic to change it."

"We have a system under which less than one percent of Karimon's population controls ninety percent of the planet's farmland," retorted Selabali. "Simple justice cries out for land reform."

"Does simple justice tell you how you're going to feed three billion Karimonis twenty years from now when the biggest farm in existence is three acres?" shot back Blake.

He's right, thought Paka, watching the debate in the comfort of his office. *I hate to admit it, but he's right. Mordecai Kiichana knew whereof he spoke.*

The debate continued for three days, with neither Blake nor Selabali yielding an inch.

Finally Paka announced that he himself would address the legislature, and the next morning, right after it was called into session, he walked over from the executive mansion and stood before the members.

"I have listened to the arguments in this chamber for the past three days," he began. "I do not doubt the sincerity of either side. One argues for justice, one for pragmatism."

He paused and looked into the holo cameras that were focused upon him. "We have had a century of pragmatism, and it has spawned nothing but hatred, mistrust, and revolution. It is time for justice!"

The snakes rose to their feet and applauded, and Paka left the podium and returned to his office.

That afternoon the vote was taken. Each of the three reapportionment plans received the votes of an overwhelming majority of the snakes. Each was vetoed by John Blake's party, and no action was taken.

"And to think," mused Paka in the privacy of his office as he watched the vote on his holo screen, "that I fought tooth and nail against this constitution."

That night there were riots in Athens, Mastaboni, Tentamp, and half a dozen smaller cities. Paka waited until noon the next day, then addressed his people and explained that while he was as outraged as they were, Karimon was a world of laws and that the laws must be obeyed.

"We have not given up," he told them. "As long as I am the Governor of Karimon, we will never cease our effort to make land available to all our people. We have lost only one battle; the war goes on."

He then went back to his private quarters at the executive mansion, sat down on a customized chair with a satisfied smile on his face, and thanked the god of his ancestors for the enemy of his blood, John Blake.

Fifty

During the next seven years, Paka's government was a whirlwind of activity.

Many of the changes were symbolic: Athens was renamed Talami, for the native village that had existed there before Violet Gardener built her city. Peterson Dam became Paka Dam, Fuentes National Park was rechristened Baski National Park, the Gardener Spaceport outside Mastaboni became the Moses Selabali Spaceport.

Some of the changes were cosmetic: the shantytowns that existed on the outskirts of every formerly human settlement were razed to the ground, all hotels and restaurants and public meeting places were required by law to have furniture fitted for snakes as well as men, and the major newstapes now issued editions in the Fani and Tulabete dialects as well as Terran.

A few of the changes were meaningful: Paka decreed mandatory free schooling for every Karimoni, upgraded the roads to the more remote villages in Faniland and promised to do the same in Tulabete Country as soon as the budget could accommodate it, and mandated free hospitals for any citizen who could not afford medical care.

The changes he *didn't* make were perhaps the most meaningful of all: Men continued to control most of the farmland, all of the mines, the tourist and travel industries, and constituted almost ninety percent of the merchant class. And while the people complained—and none complained more vociferously and publicly than Paka himself—Karimon was a world that worked. He had inherited a world that had been forced to become totally self-sufficient during the war and the embargo, and as long as he didn't dismantle the apparatus, it continued to function.

Still, there were problems. As the calendar edged toward the twelve-year deadline for the current constitution, more and more Men began emigrating to Goldstone and other nearby worlds. With very few exceptions the land was sold from one Man to another . . . and on those few occasions that the government was able to purchase one of the large farms, Paka made enormous political capital by turning it over to hundreds of land-starved snakes from the locality.

Finding enough teachers and doctors to run his schools and hospitals proved another problem. Men were uninterested in teaching or curing Karimonis, and there were not enough qualified Karimonis to supply even a fiftieth of Karimon's needs. So Paka depleted his tiny treasury still further by financing the education of the best and the brightest of his race on the worlds of the Republic. The return on his investment was less than he had anticipated, as fully half of them elected to remain off-planet, where they found greater economic opportunities.

The biggest problem of all, strangely enough, came not from Men, but from Moses Selabali. The Tulabete leader had taken to criticizing Paka at every opportunity for dragging his feet on the true reforms that were needed: land distribution and government ownership of the mining and manufacturing sectors.

Paka ignored him for as long as he could, and when even some Fani began calling for more action, he called an executive session of the legislature, created the office of Associate Governor, and offered it to Selabali, who accepted.

If he thought that becoming a member of the executive branch would put an end to Selabali's sniping, he was mistaken, for now Selabali stated his case not only publicly but in every cabinet meeting, every state dinner, every function at which he served as Paka's stand-in.

When the polls showed that Selabali was picking up support, Paka took to the airwaves and publicly accused Selabali of trying to undermine the government. Stopping just short of accusing him of treason, he removed him from office and then, by a bare majority of two votes—Blake and the rest of the Men abstained, since this was strictly a Karimoni affair, and Blake had long since figured out who his real ally was—he abolished the office of Associate Governor a mere seven months after creating it.

Selabali, who now held no government position, having resigned from the legislature when he joined the executive branch, went back home to Tulabete Country, where, in Mastaboni and elsewhere, he continued condemning Paka for refusing to take action and began calling for his removal from office.

Paka responded by issuing an order for Selabali's arrest and marched his army into Mastaboni to search for him. The Tulabete refused to give him up, and an overeager officer ordered his men to fire into the crowd.

The result was seventy-three dead Tulabete and riots in every city in Tulabete Country. Paka sent in more soldiers to quell the riots, and ordered them to fire only in self-defense. They defended themselves 3,241 times in the first week, and suddenly guns that had been secreted away after the war were brought out, oiled, polished, and used against the Karimon army.

When the dust had cleared some two months later, more than sixty thousand Tulabete were dead, three villages had been razed to the ground, and rumors abounded that Moses Selabali had fled the planet. Some reports had him hiding on Flowergarden, others on Goldstone, a few had him arguing for Paka's removal in the highest chambers of Deluros VIII.

Shortly thereafter, Blake requested a meeting with Paka, who granted it.

"Things have changed," noted Blake upon being ushered into Paka's office.

"This office is no longer occupied by a Man," replied Paka. "Therefore it no longer requires human furnishings. I can send for a human chair if you wish."

"No, I'll make do on one of these things," said Blake, sitting on the edge of a chair that had been created expressly for Karimonis.

"Well, Mr. Blake?" said Paka.

"I'll get right to the point," said Blake. "You've made a bloody mess of things, and if you're not careful, you're going to have a civil war on your hands."

"My government will not allow armed disturbances by Men *or* Karimonis," said Paka firmly. "The Tulabete must be—" he searched for the proper word "—*pacified.*"

"If that's your official story, fine," said Blake. "But you know and I know and most of Selabali's followers know that the Tulabete weren't armed until after your army started using them for target practice."

"They are armed now, and that is all that matters."

"And if you wipe out another fifty thousand Selabali voters before they are disarmed, you won't weep bitter tears over it, will you?" said Blake with a grin.

"You may not say such things to the Governor of Karimon!" exploded Paka.

"Even if they're true?"

"I could have you thrown into jail for your conduct!"

"True," agreed Blake. "But then you'd still be facing a civil war. I'm here to give you a way out, but if I can't speak frankly, I might as well leave and let your government go straight to hell."

He made as if to stand up, and Paka held up a hand. "Speak," he said.

"That's more like it," said Blake. He lit a cigar and leaned forward on his chair. "You need two things, Mr. Paka," he continued. "You need support from someone other than the Fani, and you need a meaningful gesture of conciliation for the Tulabete. I am prepared to supply you with both."

"Just like that?"

"Just like that."

"There is a price, I assume."

Blake smiled. "There is always a price, Mr. Paka."

"Let me hear your proposal and your fee, and I will give you my decision," said Paka.

"Fair enough," agreed Blake. He took a long puff on his cigar and was delighted to see Paka's nostrils wrinkle in distaste. "As I said, you need support from someone other than your own tribe. My party will support your actions against the Tulabete and will endorse your candidacy for reelection next year." Blake paused to see Paka's reaction, but the Fani's face was an emotionless mask. "You also need to make a major gesture to the Tulabete. We will cede the government ten square miles of farmland south of Mastaboni at fifty percent of market price, which you can then turn over to however many million Tulabete want it as a gesture of good will."

"And the price?" asked Paka.

"As I said, fifty percent of market value."

"Do not be obtuse, Mr. Blake," said Paka. "The price?"

"The current constitution has only five years to go before it's replaced by one of your own devising," replied Blake. "At that time, I expect that not a single Man will ever again sit in your legislature." He stared into Paka's orange cat's-eyes. "You must promise me never to enforce a program of land redistribution for as long as you hold office. That's my price."

"And if I refuse?"

"You won't refuse, because you know that it's in the best interests of Karimon."

Paka lowered his head in thought, his long tongue flicking out absently. Finally he looked up at his visitor.

"I agree to your proposition," he said. "But I must add a condition of my own."

"What is it?"

"News of this agreement could come back to haunt me politically," said Paka. "It must remain secret. If I find out that you have told anyone else, I will feel free to disregard it."

"How can I enforce it if only you and I know about it?"

"Because, as you say, I know that land redistribution is not in the best interests of Karimon," replied Paka.

It was Blake's turn to consider the offer. Finally he nodded his head.

"Governor Paka," he said, "you've got yourself a deal."

He extended his hand. Paka stared at it for a moment, then forced himself to reach out and take it.

Fifty-one

T homas Paka won reelection easily, though not by the overwhelming majority he achieved in the first election. The Tulabete supported Moses Selabali, whose name appeared on the ballot although he himself was still in exile deep within the Republic, but the election went peacefully.

A good politician rewards his supporters, and Paka, over the years, had become an excellent politician. As the damage from the war had been repaired and the manufacturing and mining sectors had regained their former strength, more money poured into the treasury. It was never quite enough, but Paka spent what there was on the Fani. Those hospitals and schools that could be staffed were placed in Faniland, the newly paved roads led to Fani villages, the government was staffed by Fani appointees. Men could take care of themselves, and Paka took care of the rest of his followers.

Within a year Tulabete Country was once again seething with unrest. A series of dams on the Punda River had cut their water supply, their requests for public works were denied, their schools were inadequate, their medical facilities almost nonexistent. The Moses Selabali Spaceport was not upgraded, and the newer, heavier ships that were now in operation landed at the Paka Spaceport in Talami, which meant that their passengers tended to spend their money in Faniland rather than Tulabete Country.

Still, Paka knew just how far he could push the Tulabete before they required another gesture, and when the time came he declared amnesty for Moses Selabali and publicly invited him to rejoin the government, offering him any position he wanted short of Minister of Defense or the Governorship itself. Selabali, who felt he could do more for his people by making peace with Paka and working within the government than by continuing to oppose it from light-years away, agreed, and accepted the post of Minister of Public Works, and Paka allowed him to siphon just enough public monies away from Faniland to keep the Tulabete, if not satisfied, then at least hopeful.

As for the Men, they continued to emigrate, though at a lesser rate, as John Blake constantly stated his faith in the fairness of Paka's government and his willingness to live out his life on Karimon. And, since he was every bit as skilled a politician as Paka, and he was fighting a holding action, he urged his fellow Men to begin placing qualified Karimonis in positions of authority in their various enterprises.

"If we don't do it ourselves," he explained to various associates, "sooner or later Tom Paka is going to be forced to make us do it. He's walking a narrow enough tightrope as it is, and if he gives in to one demand, they're going to figure out that eventually he'll have to give in to all of them."

Within a year Karimonis had been assimilated into middle-management positions in the mining industry, the manufacturing sector, the huge farms, even the tourist and safari industries. More schools were built, and for the first time there was widespread optimism that Thomas Paka's government might well turn Karimon into the planet its populace hoped it might become.

It was one of the very few times John Blake had misread the political climate on his world, for with the problems of employment and education on the road to resolution, the inhabitants turned once again to their major grievance: the land itself.

Fifty-two

Thomas Paka sat, alone and isolated, in his huge office. He had ordered the computer to turn the windows opaque, for he had no desire to see the protesters and picketers marching across the street in Independence Park.

He had ordered the army to disperse them last week, but after six Fani were killed, he recanted and allowed the marchers to congregate as long as they didn't precipitate any violence.

Sitting on his broad chrome desk was a printout of the private poll he had commissioned. His approval rating was twelve percent in Tulabete Country, eighteen percent in Rakko Country, and only thirty percent in his own Faniland. There was no mechanism for a recall election, but Moses Selabali, who had resigned from his position ten months ago and had once again been elected to the legislature, was proposing a constitutional amendment that would make such a recall possible.

All because of that damned farmland.

The old constitution had expired last month, a vote to extend it had been overwhelmingly defeated—not a single Karimoni had voted for it—and now that John Blake and his fellow Men had lost their power, there was no legal reason why a land-reform bill should not pass unanimously.

How could he address his people and tell them that they would destroy the land, that once it was divided into a billion tiny plots it could never be put back again, that within two decades of such a redistribution famine would be the order of the day? He would be impeached before he was finished explaining his position.

He wished that there was somebody he could talk to. His wife, perhaps, or his old friend Mordecai Kiichana. But his wife had died during the war, and Kiichana had been deposed and killed some eight years ago.

John Blake? Blake would listen, might even sympathize, but could offer no advice. All he would do was remind Paka of the deal they had made so many years ago—and Paka didn't need reminding. He needed someone to tell him how to honor the agreement without losing his job.

He called up his library on the computer and began trying to find legal reasons to stall, to put off the one thing everyone wanted him to do and the one thing that he knew would bring his planet back to the primitive conditions that had existed in the days of the fabled Jalanopi. He could ask Cartography to survey the entire world and recommend the most practical way of subdividing it . . . but Karimon was an independent world, and Cartography had no legal rights there. And even if he invited them, he was postponing the reapportionment by no more than half a year.

He could announce that land reform would begin in Rakko Country. There were very few human farmers there, and the government could afford to buy them out at market value. But the Fani and the Tulabete would never be willing to wait in line for their land, and the debate over where to begin could take months.

Months. As opposed to centuries of famine and poverty.

He could put the planet under martial law, but he'd need some pretext, some exterior threat. If it was the Canphorites, the Republic would be there to protect their interests within a day. If it was the Republic, there would be a pogrom directed at the Men whose farms and expertise he was trying to save for Karimon. If he claimed that the enemy lay within, sooner or later he would have to produce it, and then he'd be back to where he was now.

It was getting very precarious, this tightrope of his. Finally he closed his eyes, leaned back on his chair, and found himself longing for the days of his youth, when he lived and fished beside the broad Karimona River, when he wanted nothing more than the feel of the sun on his back and soft grass beneath his feet, and when all problems seemed capable of solution.

Fifty-three

T homas Paka was still wrestling with his conscience, his doubts, and his devils three days later when word reached him that John Blake had suffered a massive stroke and died before he could be taken to a hospital.

Paka attended the funeral, the only Karimoni, other than his bodyguards, to do so.

As he was driven back to the executive mansion, he felt more alone than he ever had in his life. As long as Blake was alive, he had a personal as well as a moral reason not to allow a land-redistribution bill. With Blake gone, there was no one to release the details of their secret agreement should he break it.

The next week Moses Selabali introduced legislation to purchase eighty percent of the existing farmland for the purpose of breaking it up into three-acre tracts for "the dispossessed Karimonis who have waited patiently for their elected government to redress the imbalance and give them what is rightfully theirs."

A Fani politician suggested that the purchase be enlarged to ninety percent of the farmland under cultivation. The remaining ten percent, not surprisingly, was owned by

Fani and Tulabete politicians. The amendment passed overwhelmingly.

Paka sent word from the executive mansion that he could not sign the bill into law when the treasury was unable to pay for the land, that passing a bill the government could not possibly enforce would cause a constitutional crisis.

Selabali took the floor and proposed that the government set the price for the land—that whatever they chose to pay would perforce constitute fair market value.

Paka waited another day, and then sent the question to the legislature: what if a human farmer was offered more money by someone else—for example, an off-world conglomerate? How could the government refuse to allow a landowner to accept the highest offer?

The legislature wrestled with the problem for another day and concluded that they would condemn all the land in question, thereby taking it off the market, and then pay whatever price they chose.

Fools, thought Paka, when he had received their answer. *Have they never looked at Alpha Bednares II, or any of the other worlds that followed this course of action? I hate Men as much as any of them, and with more cause—but can't anyone but me see that we* need *them?*

He activated his holoscreen and watched the various newstapes. Tulabete and Fani, Rakko and Pangi were shown dancing in the streets of their cities and villages at the news that the land they so hungered for would finally be theirs.

The scene changed to a statue of Paka himself, not a quarter mile distant in the center of Independence Park. Some fifteen or twenty Fani were camped out in front of it. When asked why, their leader responded that they planned to tear it down should Thomas Paka reject the land-reform bill.

"Ah, Karimon, Karimon," whispered Paka in the silence

of his office. "I have done so much for you, and I can do so much more, if you would just let me. Is that so much to ask—that you let me continue doing what I do best, rather than turn the planet over to Selabali and his group of Tulabete incompetents? They're going to send this world straight to hell whether I remain Governor or not; at least as Governor I can slow its descent."

The next morning he walked into his office and signed the bill into law.

Epilogue

T homas Paka was elected to a third term.
Within five years only four hundred Men remained on Karimon; more than three hundred of them were missionaries.

Within seven years the Baski and Pundi Pools National Parks were subdivided into two-acre farm plots to satisfy the land-starved populace, and the tourist and safari businesses sought out other worlds.

Within eight years Karimon was importing more than half its food.

Within ten years Karimon's per capita income had decreased by forty percent.

Within twelve years most of the mines had been shut down due to obsolete and malfunctioning equipment.

Within thirteen years, famine had decimated the Rakko.

The government did what little it could, and promised that better times were coming.

Fifteen years after Paka signed the Land Reform Act, the generators that supplied power to Mastaboni broke down. No one on the planet was capable of repairing them.

That winter they chopped down Jalanopi's tree for firewood.

SF
Resnick

4/93